MAMA GRACE

MAMA GRACE

BY
DANA BAGSHAW

Based on an original novel by Letha Crossman

(Cover: Grace Yourt at 18 circa 1894, before she was married.)

For Katie, Casey, and Liam

Table of Contents

Foreword

The author, Dana Bagshaw, came to Waynoka in search of information about her great-grandmother, Mama Grace. Grace had brought her five children to Waynoka a century ago to stay with her father until her brick-layer husband could support the family. From the 1906 Atlas of Woods County, Oklahoma we easily located the family farm.

Within weeks, I was privileged to read the amazing story of Mama Grace. What a story! She was a courageous woman, a true pioneer who braved the unknown, driving a covered wagon from Blackwell across northern Oklahoma to Waynoka. With Dana Bagshaw's vivid descriptions of the long, hard journey, I felt that I made the trip with them. When the wagon finally pulls into town, it is the turn-of-the-century Waynoka that we, the readers, see: the town square, the 2S Hotel, the hardware store where Grace gets directions to the farm, the railroad crossing, and the horse-watering tank into which Grace's hot and thirsty children plunge.

Their arrival in Waynoka brings great relief, and marks the end of the trying trip and the beginning of life on the farm with her father. I continued to be fascinated. Grace became an entrepreneur, peddling milk to the folks in town, finding ways to make extra money while helping with the farm work and rearing her family. And she was a wife who longingly watched the road for her husband's promised coming.

In early Western Oklahoma, the seasons and the weather were the backdrop for much of rural life, but life was by no means simple. Through the life of Mama Grace, we see how one woman coped, and 'played the hand that was dealt her.' We are blessed because her daughter, Letha, penned her story, and that Dana Bagshaw brought it to life. I am eagerly waiting for the publishing of *Mama Grace*!

Sandie Olson
Waynoka Historical Society

Preface

This novel is based on a book that my grandmother Letha wrote in the 1960s. When she died my mother gave me her manuscript saying she hoped that someday I could make it publishable. I began rewriting it in 2001, taking it through several drafts.

Three people were instrumental in helping me get the revised novel off the ground. My brother, Rick, read the first draft, and had valuable suggestions and corrections particularly pertaining to the natural history of the region. He drove me through Oklahoma on a research tour retracing Grace's journey from Blackwell to Waynoka, and talking to many people along the way.

Sandra Olson, whom we met at the Waynoka Historical Museum, offered her enthusiastic encouragement, and also read a draft, contributing her local and historical knowledge of the area.

Meanwhile, back in England, my friend Duska Trkulja, contributed her literary expertise. Believing the novel contained a good story, she painstakingly edited the chapters, ruthlessly rooting out any clichés and overdone sentimentality.

In addition, my Aunt Helen, wife of my grandmother's youngest brother, Victor, and their daughter, Nina, read the novel and gave me permission to supplement it with material from Victor's memoirs. Their son Bob accompanied me on my second research trip to Oklahoma and discovered some interesting facts about the family.

Through it all, my husband, Clive, contributed to my well-being and sanity.

The work that lies ahead is to turn my uncle Victor's remaining memoirs into a second novel. Running from Grace, will take up where Mama Grace leaves off, but with quite a different slant. Seen through the eyes of her youngest son, Grace is demoted from heroine to villainess. The story resumes with a move to the oil boom town of Ponca City, Oklahoma, with Victor balancing odd jobs and a would-be boxing career, winding up in the offices of Conoco Oil, charming the ladies, and trying to escape the clutches of his mother.

Dana Bagshaw
April 2006
Oadby, Leicester
England

Mama Grace
Part One
Summer 1907

Chapter 1

Refugees

Mama sat bent forward, concentrating on driving the wagon across the prairie, baby Victor feeding at her breast.

Letha lay swaying in a double-decker bunk bed, strung parallel to Mama's broad back. It was too much effort to sit up. Mama blocked the view, and besides that, there was nothing to see. Miles and miles of nothing. So Letha lay there looking up at the clouds—cotton balls tossed across the sky.

Though Mama's back shaded her from direct sun, the afternoon was becoming increasingly warm and Letha felt herself getting drowsy. She reached down and tickled her little sister in the bunk below, but May, sound asleep, didn't respond.

Letha refused to fall asleep herself, because whenever she did, the nightmare of the flood came back. To keep awake she tickled her own arms, then rubbed them with her knuckles. She pinched her cheeks, pulled down on her earlobes, tugged one braid and then the other, forcing her eyes to stay open.

The flood had sneaked up on them while Letha and her big brother Arthur were at school. When they left the house early that morning everything was fine. But just before noon a sudden rainstorm beat down so loudly on the schoolhouse their class could hardly do their lessons. When school was out, they walked home together. By the time they reached the bank overlooking their home, the Chikaskia was swollen an angry red, but starting to recede. They looked upstream toward where their house should have been and were startled by an awful sight: Mama's Majestic cookstove stood alone, surrounded by a rubble-heap of bricks.

Now whenever Letha closed her eyes, that stark image came back. Along with Mama's harsh words when Letha broke into tears once the significance of her lost home hit her.

"We'll have no cry babies here, Letha Faye. We Barnets

3

don't feel sorry for ourselves. We just pull ourselves up by our bootstraps and move on."

Mama's cookstove now stood in the middle of the wagon. Mama had insisted on bringing this, her most prized possession.

"You can't take that," Papa told her. "It's too heavy. It will wreck you before you get half-way there."

"Over my dead body will I leave my Majestic behind," she said.

Mama, as usual, won the argument. Papa tied the cookstove in the center of the wagon to form a partition between Letha and May's swinging bunk bed in the front and a second swinging bed strung along back of the wagon for their brothers, Arthur and Lester.

After loading the wagon with the few belongings they had managed to salvage from the flood, Papa hitched the two horses, Old Roany and Old Sam, on either side of the wagon's tongue. Then he turned to the children and called, "All aboard!"

As they left Blackwell, Papa rode alongside the wagon on his horse, holding the reins gingerly in his burned and bandaged hands. Papa had tried to save his brick kilns when the flood first hit.

The sky looked bright and innocent as the family headed south, passed through Tonkawa, crossed the Salt Fork of the Arkansas and then faced west, squinting against the sun.

"Pay no attention to meandering roads or trails when you get out on the wide-open prairie, Grace," were Papa's parting instructions.

"Go due west by the sun, and you'll at least get in the vicinity of your father's farm. You've got to steer a course south of the Salt Fork to avoid the Salt Plains and keep north of the Cimarron and the Glass Mountains." He pulled a Big Ben alarm clock from a coat pocket and started explaining how she could use the face of it to find her direction.

"Never mind, Professor. Just because you have a degree does not mean you can lecture me. Any fool knows to go west you just keep the shadows in front of you in the morning, and behind you in the afternoon. But I'll take the clock, thank you." She grabbed it.

4

"And what will you do at midday?"

"Stop for dinner," Mama said.

Papa laughed. Mama found a spot on his cheek that wasn't bandaged and gave him a peck. She clucked to the horses and they headed westward to Grandpa's homestead, a quarter section near the town of Waynoka, the only shelter now available to them.

As they rode away, Letha heard Papa singing at the top of his lungs.

"Amazing Grace, how great thou art . . ."

Letha could still hear the sound of his singing in her head, and she smiled to herself. Papa was always looking for a way to goad Mama into action. He had a way of making a joke of things. It was awful now without him. Mama was entirely too bossy when Papa wasn't around.

It was the third day they had been driving on their own. The summer sun bore down on them relentlessly, the familiar tall grasses of home increasingly giving way to monotonous barren ground and clumps of sagebrush.

A wind was stirring and Letha watched the clouds change from cotton balls to looking like Mama's drop biscuits[1], puffy on the top, but flat across the bottom. Suddenly she realized how hungry she was.

"Mama is it time for supper?"

No reply.

She raised her voice. "Mama, is it time to stop for supper yet?"

"No!" Mama yelled back at her.

Letha could almost taste Mama's wonderful biscuits, dripping with butter and jam. Mama was right to insist on bringing the cookstove. When they got to Grandpa's they could have those steaming hot biscuits again, and cakes, and pies . . .

Well, then, if she couldn't let herself sleep and Mama wouldn't let her eat, what she needed was <u>action</u>!

"Hey, y'all," she called to her brothers in the back of the wagon. They peeked over the cookstove. "Let's play Hide the Thimble? Wake up, May. You can be the thimble," she suggested cheerfully as she pulled May out from the bunk below.

5

"Arthur and Lester, you stay behind the oven, and close your eyes. No peeking." The boys' heads obligingly disappeared again.

In spite of Mama's instructions to stay clear of the stove, Letha hid her groggy little sister in the oven and returned to her swing-bed giggling. "Okay! Find the thimble," she called to her brothers—just as the horses started climbing a sharp grade. A gust of wind snapped the rope holding the canvas taut across the hoops of the wagon.

"MA-MA!" Lester screamed.

"Whoa," Mama cried, tugging on the lines. Her timing was off! The horses stopped short, and the front wheels of the wagon banged down inside a steel ribbon pair of railroad tracks.

Letha screamed then jerked around in her bunk and peered up at Mama. A second glance down to Mama's hand, gripping the back of the seat, told her that Mama was scared too—even if she was wearing her don't-let-fear-show face. Letha kept quiet, waiting for developments.

The wind, and the howl of baby Victor, all but drowned out Mama's demand. "Where in heaven's name are the others?"

Arthur and Lester's small faces reappeared over the rim of the cookstove. They climbed up onto the Majestic and clawed at the flapping canvas hiding them from Mama's view, hopping around on the lids of the stove in their bare feet as if a fire roared beneath them.

"Where is May?" thundered Mama's iron voice.

No one ever evaded THAT voice! Somehow Letha found the courage to break through the frozen silence.

"She's in the oven."

"In the OVEN?" Mama screamed. "She'll smother!"

Mama dropped Victor down in the bunk beside Letha and threw a skirted leg over the side of the wagon, stepping onto the rim of the wheel. As she heaved her two-hundred pounds out of the tilting wagon, it started to rear back on its hind wheels. She threw herself back into the seat, but she was too late. Added to the double strain of the steep grade and the strong wind, her absent weight had tipped the balance. The stove broke its rope moorings and slid backwards. The boys jumped off the cook-

6

stove, just as the oven door smacked against trunks and other stowage, crushing them against the endgate. May screamed like a bobcat. The wagon's tongue had flown up between the horses, cracking the neck-yoke against their lower jaws. The horses reared up and let out piercing whinnies that did nothing to calm the "thimble" in the oven.

Victor, separated from Mama's breast, wailed louder than ever. Arthur and Lester began a droning whimper, and Letha, knowing she was the guilty one, let out a bellow like a calf separated from its mother.

Old Tudy, the sloe-eyed greyhound,[2] sat on his haunches and offered a bayed prayer heavenward. Bessie, the milk cow tied to the back of the wagon, tugged at her rope and mooed mournfully. The chickens in a coop fastened beneath the wagon, added to the crescendo by squawking and cackling.

Once Mama got the horses under control she turned to the children and shouted, "This must be the railroad built along the Chisholm Trail.[3] We've got to move quickly."

"Arthur, get hold of anything in the back of the wagon you can lift and hand it up here to me."

"Letha Faye"—when Mama used her full name she meant business—"you climb out of the wagon and take the baby over there—beside that clump of brush."

"Lester, you crawl down beside the oven and play a game with May."

These commands were obeyed in the same rapid-fire order Mama barked them. Letha stood holding Victor, watching her mother. One thing about Mama—you could count on her in an emergency. When Arthur had loaded enough weight into and under the seat to overcome the leverage of the cookstove, Mama gingerly lifted herself out of the wagon, ready at the slightest hint of movement to hop back in. All the time she was dismounting she spoke soothingly "Whoa, boys, whoa" to the horses. She sent Arthur to grab the rein of Old Sam, the more frightened of the two. Seeing her efforts rewarded for the moment she untied the ax from beneath the wagon and looked about. "Not a tree in sight," she groaned.

With no further hesitation, she proceeded to chop the ends off

7

two railroad ties. Splitting them into wedges, she pounded them beneath the hind wheels to keep them from rolling backwards even if the front wheels should try to slip back over the rail. Next she used the rope that was meant to hold the stove in place, to tie the wagon tongue down to the west rail of the track.

Having conquered the wagon tongue and chocked the wheels, Mama threw her weight into the front of the wagon, grasped the cookstove by its front corners and by some superhuman force born of desperation managed to inch the heavy stove towards her. Then she worked her way toward the back pushing and pivoting the stove forward on one side until Lester could open the oven door far enough for May to crawl out.

Not one to show affection, Mama now clutched May to her bosom as if she were her only child. May clung to Mama soundlessly. Mama sat her on the wagon tongue, kissed her, and told Lester to sit beside his sister. Then she got up, told Arthur to untie the rope from the tongue and help retie the cookstove firmly in the back where it landed, lashing the wagon contents against it so it wouldn't slide forward when they went across and back down the bank of the tracks.

"Stand back everybody," Mama yelled as she stood in front of the horses and coaxed them and the wagon across the rails and down the slope.

That done, she tied the horses to the clump of brush where Letha was standing. Then, without a word, she ripped four choice switches from the brush, stripped them of their leaves. Then she took Victor from Letha, laid him down behind the brush, and jerked Letha, then Arthur, then Lester and May over to the wagon, lining them up along the side of the wagon, and proceeded to soundly thrash each of them, even little May. When Mama meted out punishment to one of them, she usually meted it out to all of them—under the usually correct premise that they all were equally guilty.

Having thus demonstrated her control of the situation again, Letha saw Mama go behind the brush to which the horses were tied. There she knelt in the sand beside the wailing Victor who was still clawing and kicking. Momentarily she closed her eyes and bowed her head. Letha reckoned she was praying, thanking

8

God for their lives.

But Arthur was confused. "What was that whipping for?" he wailed bitterly. "It wasn't our fault the wagon got stuck."

Letha knew. "It was for hiding May in the oven."

Swooping baby Victor up in one arm Mama returned to where Letha and her three siblings stood in a row against the wagon, faces nestled in the crooks of their arms, putting the finishing touches on their sobs.

Like a pianist running a thumb down the keyboard in a glissando, Mama gathered them up with her unoccupied arm. Letha felt her mother's strong arms around her, squeezing them all together. Then she thought she felt something fall on her forehead and looked up to see her mother's tear-streaked face. The other thing about Mama was that following an emergency, she often went to pieces.

Mama gave one swift glance back to the railroad that had nearly been their undoing and gave instructions anew to each of them.

"Letha, you get into the wagon in front of the seat. Here, take May." She boosted May up with one hand, still clinging to the kicking baby with the other. Then she climbed wearily into the seat.

"Letha, you and May make yourself a bunk here beneath my feet with the featherbed.

"Arthur, you may sit here in the seat to my right and Lester you are to sit beside me to the left."

Her detailed instructions completed, she nestled baby Victor in her lap where he continued his interrupted dinner as they again set off across the uncharted prairie to find a campsite for the night.

A Majestic cookstove built in 1904 and still working.
Photo courtesy Red Rock Retreat in Jasper, Arkansas.

Model of a wagon like the one Grace drove across the prairie. *Photo taken by author at the Top of Oklahoma Museum near Blackwell.*

The Chikaskia River at Blackwell looks harmless, but regular flooding still occurs there. *Photo by author.*

Grace's trip began in the "tall grass" now nearly extinct, but still seen in Oklahoma Tall Grass Prairie Preserve, east of Blackwell. *Photo by author.*

The sage prairie approaching Waynoka. *Photo by author.*

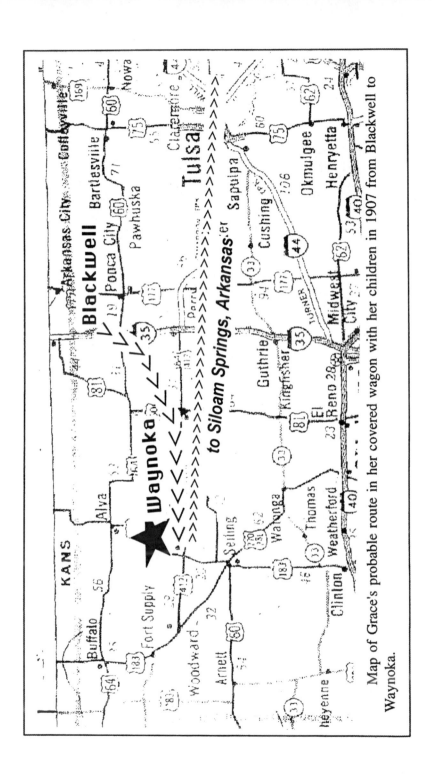

Map of Grace's probable route in her covered wagon with her children in 1907 from Blackwell to Waynoka.

The foundation of Grandpa Yourt's house is all that remains on the quarter section he homesteaded outside Waynoka. *Photo by author.*

The road up Sandhill, explored by Victor's son, Bob, in 2005. *Photo by author.*

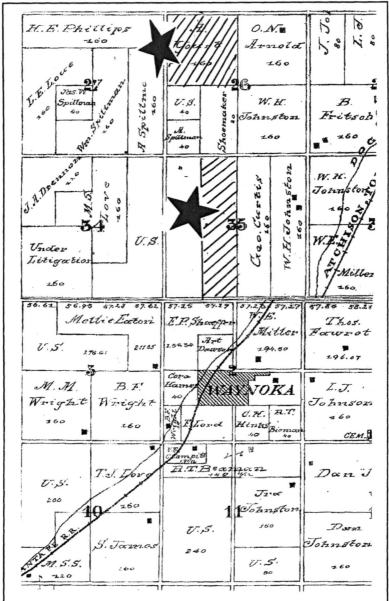

Map showing A. Yourt's homestead in 1906 (in NW quarter of Section 26) as well as the probable location of the claim filed by his daughter, Grace (the middle strip of W Section 33). *Map courtesy Waynoka Historical Museum.*

The "2S" Hotel in Waynoka in the early 1900s—the likely inspiration of Mrs. Swan's hotel in the novel. *Photo courtesy of Waynoka Historical Society.*

Housing built in Oklahoma at the turn of the century for migrant railroad workers from Mexico. *Original photo available courtesy of Waynoka Historical Society.*

The only sign of life remaining today on Sandhill is this gas pumping station.

Photo by author.

Waynoka's beloved Dr. Clapper, upon whom the character Dr. McGinnis was based, in the office he opened in 1901. *Photo courtesy of Waynoka Historical Society.*

Imported to control jackrabbits, greyhounds were a common sight on Oklahoma homesteads. *Photo courtesy of Charles Cook.*

Left: Letha at 18, circa 1918. Above:Letha's first teaching job in Oklahoma. She is the second tallest, the taller woman probably her sister. Her contract, signed in 1919, for "Teacher of Public School District No. 109 Woods County" states a salary of $70 per month.

The author and her brother Rick on a research trip in 2004. *Photo by Sandra Olson.*

Chapter 2

Why? Oh Why?

As the journey resumed, the only sounds Letha heard were the creaking of the wagon and the constant shifting and shuffling of the load adjusting itself to the ups and downs of the roadless stretch of prairie.

Mama had braced herself, feet spread apart on the dashboard[1] in front of her to support the boys leaning against her, determinedly facing the unknown ahead.

With the sound of the wheels and the steady drone of the wind, Letha snuggled up to May on a pallet beneath Mama's feet. "I'm sorry," Letha whispered to her little sister.

Arthur was stretched out in the swinging bunk that had been Letha's before his bunk behind the cookstove had been wrecked. Young Lester, snuggled his head beneath Mama's left arm with his nose against her breast. In her lap lay baby Victor, filled with his long-delayed meal, sound asleep.

Letha stared up at the sky, trying to stay awake, watching it slowly change color with a glowing sunset.

"Why must I face these things alone?" she heard Mama groan to herself.

"Look at the sky, Mama," Letha offered.

"You still awake, Letha?" Mama looked up. "Yes, the sky is beautiful. And to think no one has ever seen a sunset like that before, and no one will ever see one like that again."

"Where are we going to camp, Mama?"

"We'll find a place. Now go to sleep."

Mama began to sing softly—the old religious songs—the only ones Mama knew. From them Mama seemed to draw strength when all else failed. She sang slowly and thoughtfully. Like chewing and savoring the goodness of an apple while eyeing it over to see where to take the next bite, she took it one line at a time, singing with a pause to think about the words.[2]

11

"Have you ever tried to bear your burdens all alone?" Pause. "Don't you know there's One who waits to help you, who will make your burden His own?" Pause.

"When I have crosses to bear, my Savior is there." Pause. "He always takes the heavy end, and gives the light to me."

Mama laughed. "He must have a terrible backache now."

In better spirits now she continued in full voice, "I know not what lieth before me, what shadows may fall on my way . . ."

Letha was almost falling asleep, when the timbre of her mother's singing abruptly changed.

"Praise the Lord, there's something ahead. There's a house-top there among the treetops," she chanted into the song, turning the horses sharply.

Letha poked her face up between Mama's legs still braced against the wagon bed. May joined her in peering into the semi-darkness.

At the sight of a possible safe campsite, they let out a "Whoopee!" Their screams awakening their sleeping brothers.

Mama guided the team near the neat but unpainted house, flanked by a storm-weathered soddie—half-house, half-dugout. The house nestled, door agape, in a cluster of old cottonwoods caught in the bend of a meandering creek. The giant trees bent over the creek bank and bathed their bared roots in the cooling waters. Before Mama could halt the team, Arthur and Lester leapt from the wagon, joining the roots in the waters.

When the wagon stopped, Letha and May spilled over its side like milk from a tilted bucket and, heedless of Mama's shouted orders, began splashing beside the boys. Next to their own small feet, the gnarled roots of the trees looked like the toes of giants.

When Mama stopped yelling at them, Letha looked over her shoulder and saw a smiling woman rushing from the house to the covered wagon. She spread her arms wide in a gesture of invitation to the family.

Wearily Mama lifted the once again howling Victor and passed him to the outstretched arms. The woman snuggled him to her bosom, swayed and rocked him back and forth to stop his cries. Victor looked strangely bigger in this thin woman's arms.

12

"Oh, what a darling baby," she cooed. "Takes me back to when my two boys were babies." She turned and carried him toward the house.

Mama slid nimbly to the ground. She bounced up and down like a sprinter loosening up for a few moments before she followed the woman into the house, Letha and the others timidly forming a train behind her. There they found baby Victor kicking and bawling full bellows from the middle of a huge homemade bed where the woman had laid him while she went to the kitchen to get him a drink.

"I only need a safe camping place to nest my family for the night and perhaps some wood for a campfire," Mama was saying to the woman just as a tall, gaunt man and two half-grown boys came into the house.

"Hello," said Mama nodding to the man. "Hello," she said to the boys. "And what are your names?"

"I'm Jerry," the oldest proudly declared. "And that's my little brother Jack."

Letha thought they were the ugliest boys she had seen in her life.

"I hope we're not intruding," Mama offered.

"Any of God's children are welcome at our house and table," the man said. "I heard your singing a mile away." He grinned and added, "I hope I can be God's instrument in answering your prayers."

Mama was not the kind to accept charity. Instead, she started giving out her inevitable instructions right in front of the strangers. "Arthur, you go with the man and help take care of the horses. May, you go stay beside the bed where Victor is and see that he does not fall off. Letha, you go to the kitchen and do as the good woman tells you in helping get supper ready.

"Lester, go to the wagon, get the ax and take it to the wood pile while I get some food from the wagon to help out with the supper." Then hastily she added, "Mind you now to lay the ax down when you get it to the woodpile. I don't have time for any cut feet!"

Over the protest of the man and his wife, Mama went to her storehouse in the wagon and brought bread, jelly, pickles and

13

chow-chow. "These are just some of the things left over from last year's canning," she said.

"As for bread—well, I hate to brag, but it was generally agreed for blocks around back in Blackwell that I was the best breadmaker in the neighborhood!" She confidently brought some flour and "everlasting" yeast from the wagon, saying she would set it and bake bread before leaving the next morning.

"Lord knows I'm glad to see that yeast," the woman replied. "I had some but it froze last winter and we've had no good bread since."

Mama fairly beamed that she had something so worthwhile to share. She handed the yeast and flour to her hostess and went back out into the yard, telling Lester to tether the cow in a good grazing spot until Arthur could milk her. Then she hustled to the woodpile.

Letha turned from the door and addressed the friendly woman, whom she had liked instantly.

"What can I do to help you, ma'am?"

"Why don't you set the table?" She pulled out a drawer. "Here's the silverware. Well, not silver really. Guess I should call it tableware. Hope there's enough."

"Oh, we can share," Letha replied. "I usually cut May's food and she still likes to eat it with her fingers."

She carefully laid the table remembering to put the knife and spoon on the right, and the fork on the left.

"How old are you, Letha?" asked the woman.

"Six."

"My. You certainly are grown up for six. I wish I had a little girl as nice as you."

Letha rarely received a compliment and didn't know what to say, so she just smiled.

As she laid the last setting, she heard Mama's voice raised in song again, this time accompanied by the whack of the ax. She looked out the back door to see the man come running from the barn to try and stop Mama from chopping. He waved his arm at his two sons and Arthur as well, who looked eagerly on and seemed to grow an inch with the sweep of the man's arm.

Mama set the ax on the ground, but clung to the handle. No

doubt she made a very direct statement to him for he stepped back as if she had thrown a bucket of cold water in his face. He attempted to make further objections, then he began to laugh.

As he reached out a hand to her, Mama pulled the ax from behind her skirt, sliced it safely into a log, and shook his hand firmly.

Then, without another word she picked up the ax and the log, splitting it in one blow. Letha heard the man whistle a salute, then he led his troops back to their chores at the barn.

The woman came out of the kitchen with some glasses, and hearing the sound of the ax above Mama's lusty singing, joined Letha at the doorway.

"Say," she shouted out to Mama. "There are menfolk on this place, so stop that! Come on back to the house and let's talk!"

Mama either didn't hear her or paid no attention, but carried on chopping.

When Mama returned to the kitchen with a stack of wood, the woman scolded her as she took the wood from her two sticks at a time. "You don't have to do anything around here—let alone chop wood—just be my guest. Now get in here and sit yourself down. Don't you know, you've been good for my soul already? As a matter of fact, it's been months since I've seen a person other than my own family and maybe a year since I've seen another woman. Let's have some conversation!"

At last Mama smiled, but she didn't sit down in the indicated chair. Instead she shouted from the doorway at Arthur as he returned from feeding the team with his new friend Jerry. "You had better go now and milk Old Bessie. Bring the milk to the house as soon as you can."

"We've got plenty cold milk in the house for supper. We keep our milk and butter in the dugout, as well as our meat supply," the woman said. "Take the milk to the dugout, son," she called out to Arthur, "and Jerry will help you take care of it."

Mama went back out to put the ax in its place under the wagon and returned to the house, Lester and Jack following.

"Is your baby brother still in the bedroom?" Mama asked Letha.

Letha pointed the way and peeked in behind her.

15

Victor lay contentedly, gurgling for anyone who would pay the slightest attention. May stood close by the side of the bed silently guarding Victor from Jack, who was hovering over Victor, twittering about for the baby's amusement. Lester stood quietly by, watching the boy's strange antics.

"This is just about his first happy moment since we began this trip," Mama said with a funny sound to her voice. Seemingly satisfied that all was well with her two smallest ones, she returned to the kitchen and began chattering with her new friend about raising babies in this God-forsaken place, where doctors were nearly non-existent, and the hardship of clothing a growing family.

"It's all I can do to keep Jack and Jerry in clothes, and they're boys!" the woman said. "I don't see how you ever clothe five, especially when two of them are girls." She went to ring the supper bell for her husband and the older boys.

Amid the prattle of children and the yapping of dogs, the two families gathered around the supper table. Since she had contributed to the meal, Mama ate heartily and the children followed suit, helping themselves to seconds.

Chapter 3

The Raging Chikaskia

Letha was helping clear the table.

"Mama, Mama, may we go back to the creek?" Arthur asked. "It's still light." He was standing on tiptoe, his hands clasped below his chin in prayerful supplication, his eyes beaming.

"Please, please Mama," little Lester added as he bounced up and down.

May shot out of her chair straight into Mama's ample rear end, nearly knocking her off balance. "Me too! Me want to go too," she said yanking at Mama's skirt. Obviously May had forgotten her assignment to tend baby Victor while Mama helped clear up the supper dishes.

Mama turned to May in front of everyone and automatically corrected her.

"I want to go too, May."

May looked quizzically at Mama a moment and then began to giggle.

"You'd look awful funny, Mama, with your feet in the creek." she said.

"I mean . . . Oh, never mind, never mind. . ."

"There isn't anything down there that can hurt them," the man said, "and my boys can go along to sort of look after them Mrs.—Uh, what did you say your name is?"

"I don't believe we ever did introduce ourselves," Mama said. "Our name is Barnet. I'm Grace."

"Pleased to meet you, Ma'am," the man said rising and extending his hand. "We shook hands out by the woodpile, but didn't exchange names. Our name is Comfort."

Mama seemed surprised at the formality, but she shook hands with her host. Then hesitating, she finally extended her hand to Mrs. Comfort.

17

"Comfort, is the right name, all right," said Mama, "for that's exactly how you made us feel." To Letha's surprise, Mama began giggling with the other woman, and they threw their arms around each other in a big hug.

Her brothers, stunned at such goings on, became silent, their mouths agape.

Mama turned to them and said, "You remember three days ago you all swore you never wanted to see any water again that wasn't in a cup? Well, I guess that creek's waiting for you. Now scat."

The whooping children stampeded out the door like a cloudburst straight into the creek. All but Letha. She wanted to hear the "conversation" Mrs. Comfort had proposed earlier.

"Can I stay? I feel tired," she feigned.

"That is because you did not take a nap," Mama said.

The rest of the children screamed as they ran pell-mell for the creek, but May's cry could be heard above all the others. Mama bounded to the door. "May, do you want me to send for Miss Gubbins?"

May's shriek ceased at once. Laughing, Mama turned back into the kitchen. "My little May has a scream worse than a treed mountain lion," she said.

"But who is Miss Gubbins?"

"An old maid who lived next door to us in Blackwell. We tried to be nice to her, but my children's screams must have been more than her poor nerves could take. One evening, after May let out her wild yell near Miss Gubbins' door, she called her over and said: 'The next time I hear you scream like that I'm going to grease your head and swallow it!'

"Little May's eyes grew big as saucers as she took stock of Miss Gubbins' wide grin. The way May backed away, you could tell she thought Miss Gubbins' mouth completely capable of carrying out the threat!"

Amid their laughter the women started clearing the supper dishes while Mr. Comfort tilted back in his chair and lit up his cob pipe, just the way Papa used to.

Mama must have noticed it too, for with that simple gesture of male contentment she stopped picking up dishes and closed

18

her eyes tightly. As the smell of the pipe smoke wafted towards her, tears ran down her cheeks.

"What's the matter?" Mr. Comfort asked.

"I miss my husband," Mama replied.

"We were wondering about him."

"He went back up to Blackwell. He'll join us later when we get to Waynoka."

"Heard there was a lot of rain over in Blackwell last week."

"Rain! I would never call it rain. I would say the old devil himself tipped over God's water bucket and then skedaddled without bothering to set it back up!"

Mama sounded very intense. This was the first time Letha had heard her talk about the flood. She was glad she stayed inside to listen. Maybe it could help her get rid of the nightmare.

"You don't say," Mr. Comfort said urging her on.

"We had already had ten inches in less than a week," Mama said. "Then last Friday, we got over five inches, which was the straw that broke the camel's back."

"We had a little here, but not more than we needed," Mr. Comfort said. "The creek scarcely rose. Funny thing about weather out here on these plains. It can rain one day and blow dust the next. Prairie grass can almost catch fire during a rain. A day or two later you'd never know'd it had rained from the way we've got to watch out for fires."

"Well, it will be some time before Blackwell ever catches fire," Mama said, shaking her head sadly. "The river nearly swamped the whole eastside, what with no time to dump one drencher downstream before we got another."

She sat down as if the last bit of strength had gone out of her. But she continued her story. "Most of the time the Chikaskia River is no more than a creek wiggling its way past town like a snake, never knowing when it might bite."

"I was over to Blackwell once," Mr. Comfort said, "and I remember that crooked riverbed well. Not much in the way of banks to it as I recall."

"That is right," Mama said. "We thought we were safe on the third bottom."

"Third bottom?"

"It's like this: The first bottom is the normal stream bed, the second bottom the normal flood plain. At Blackwell the third bottom was eight to ten feet above the second. No one had ever known floodwater to get that high. It had an outcrop of fine red clay and was near enough to the river for us to get water for making slop-brick." She paused, then added. "You see, my husband John is a brick maker."[1] She sat silent for a few moments.

"Was your house washed away?" Mrs. Comfort gently asked.

Mama tried to smile, "It would be more like it to say our house washed <u>down</u>. Our house was made of the ill-fired brick John refused to sell to others. Sort of an adobe affair, so when the flood waters got up about midway, the walls just crumpled and went down like a child's playhouse made of mud."[2] She placed her head in her hands. "All that was left standing was my Majestic."

There it was again. That haunting image. Letha shuddered.

Fortunately, Mama continued, "When that big downpour came last Friday the river couldn't decide whether it was a sidewinder snake or a giant inchworm. First it swung from side to side sloshing things onto one side of the river and then the other. Then when the water passed through the steeper banks and narrower channel, it humped into great silt-laden waves.

"It lashed at the treetops, and some poor souls who had sought safety in the trees were washed out into the surging waters. You wouldn't believe the death and destruction caused by that river!"

Letha shivered. She was glad she hadn't seen any of the dead bodies being washed away. Things were only sounding worse.

Resolutely Mama got up and Mrs. Comfort followed suit. They began doing the dishes again. Mama kept shaking her head and running her hand over her brow and hair while she dried the dishes, as if trying to wipe the whole thing from her memory.

Mr. Comfort sat and smoked his pipe. Before long he was able to get Mama back to the flood again.

"So your husband was in the brick-making business?"

20

"With his father and two brothers," she said, sitting down despondently at the table.

"Sorry, if I keep bringing up a sore subject.   On the other hand, you might as well talk out your troubles."

With a deep sigh Mama said, "They had a thriving brick-yard right across the river from my father's house. That's where we were living when the flood came." She paused and smiled. "John sort of joked about living in little Venice.   We had two rowboats and we tried to keep one on each side of the river so they could get to or from work without going to one of the bridges."

"Sounds right cute," said Mrs. Comfort.

"Well, it surely didn't turn out so cute," Mama replied. "But when the flash flood did come, having the boats there saved our belongings. John saw danger coming as he was working by the river.   He jumped into his boat, rowed across, yelling at me to get the babies to high ground and managed to get most of the things out of the house just in the lick of time.

"Later we took our things up to a new building that he was delivering bricks to." She sighed. "We were more or less comfortable there, until half of the other unfortunate ones from the riverside decided to join us."

Mr. Comfort straightened up and looked puzzled. "What kind of brick did you say they made?" he asked.

"Slop-brick," she smiled affectionately.   "Most folks call them sand-roll bricks because they are made from a mixture of sand, clay, and water. But to us it looked like the slop you would feed hogs!"

Letha squirmed because she remembered seeing dead hogs floating in the river.

Mr. Comfort kept Mama talking. "How did he make the mixture?"

"John had his own recipe, so to speak. He dumped the sand, clay, and water in the right proportions into a big hopper—something like your feed grinder. He hitched his horse to the pole, and as he drove it round and round, the materials became thoroughly mixed."

"Like mixing a big cake!" Letha contributed.

21

"Well, it *is* sort of like mixing cake batter," Mama laughed, "It's poured into wooden moulds like loaf pans, and left to set for a few hours while some of the water soaks into the wood and some evaporates. Then the loaves are rolled out onto the sand spur where heat from the sun dries them more before they are fired."

Mama's hands lay relaxed on the table. Mr. Comfort saw that the making of brick was a safe topic—and he seemed interested. He leaned forward thoughtfully and said, "But what do you mean by fired?"

"The mud loaves are baked just like bread, except the oven is built of the very bricks that are to be fired. After letting them dry in the sun for a day or so, the men would lay a long fire, then build a row of arched brick domes over it, each dome with air holes in it so that the fire would burn and the bricks would dry.

"Others could do the slop work but only a trained brick setter could arch those domes right. And John is one of the best. It is a beautiful thing to watch him build them." Mama's eyes moistened.

Mrs. Comfort got up quickly and began to work with the dishes. "You don't have to tell us any more if you'd rather let it alone," she said.

Mama pushed her chair back to join her. "I've been churning it over and over in my mind these past three days as we traveled along. Maybe you're right, and telling about it will get it off my mind, or at least dim the horror of it."

"Then you just stay put, and go right ahead," the woman replied.

"What did you use to make the fire with?" the man asked.

"Driftwood from the river bed and some green wood we cut from the trees along the river. The driftwood gets the green wood to burn. After the fire is lit in the middle of these long ovens, the ends are bricked up leaving only man-high peepholes at each end. The men can look in and tell when the bricks are fired enough or if more wood is needed. Of course, they try to get enough wood in at the beginning so they won't need to open the ends again to stoke in more."

Papa was usually the one to do such explaining, but Mama

22

seemed to relish taking his place for this talk-hungry couple.

"Sounds like an art to me," Mr. Comfort said.

"That it is, but it's a slave-driving job, too. And to make matters worse, or better—whichever way you want to look at it—about two years ago the city decreed that for the sake of fire safety, all business buildings must be built of brick or stone. John's business boomed so much he sent back to Missouri for his father and brother who had a small brickyard. They came to Blackwell and the three went into business together.

"Things got pretty lively after that. You see, John and I lived with my father, who had been a Confederate soldier during the war, and John's father had been a Union soldier, so you can imagine what happened when we all got together.

"Practically every evening for over a year I heard the Civil War being fought over again, battle-by-battle. We'd sit outside on our brick patio and didn't know whether to laugh or cry at those two old men rattling their sabers and shouting at each other about their victories, or their excuses for losses, whichever the case might be.

"One night my Pa had to defend one too many Confederate losses against his Union antagonists. He lay down his arms, packed up, and moved out. Went west and filed on a claim. As it turns out, it was a good thing he did, because that's where I'm headed now: the western part of the Strip."[3]

"What town?"

"Waynoka."

Mama sat still a long time, then said, "They had five kilns being fired when the bottom dropped out of the sky. What's left of them is just five heaps of mud in the river bed. It was in defending those kilns that John's father was drowned—while John was rescuing our belongings."

Giving in to denied tears at last, she dropped her head on the table.

Mrs. Comfort tried to console her, while Mr. Comfort poked about in his pipe of tobacco embers. Letha fiddled with the hem on her skirt. Mama finally raised her head and said, "I can still see John standing there at our ruined home holding his dead father in his arms, whose face was scalded and cut from the hot

23

bricks that fell on him as he lay in the water. He had tried to the last to save what they had worked so hard to build." [4]

Letha suddenly realized that her own image of the Majestic oven was nothing compared to what Mama had seen.

Mr. Comfort stood. "It's getting downright dark. I'd better call the children in from the creek."

Mama wiped her apron across her face and joined in getting the kitchen cleaned up. All seemed normal again. But after a few moments, Mama suddenly leaned on the table and started laughing hysterically. She continued to laugh as May and the boys came frolicking into the house. At the sound of her strange laughter, they stopped in their tracks and stared at her, Mr. Comfort stopping behind them.

"Don't worry," Mama said. "I'm not going crazy! Really I'm not, although I'm probably not far from it. I just happened to think of the funniest thing I ever saw in my life." Finally she got control of herself enough to say, "When the rains first began, an old umbrella salesman came to town to peddle his wares. And he wasn't the only one to take advantage of the situation.

"On the day of the flash flood the bank was robbed. The robbers put the money in their saddlebags, then tried to cross the swollen river, but they lost the saddlebags in the rushing waters." She stood, giggling some more before going on with the story.

"When this old umbrella salesman saw that, he tossed aside his umbrellas and plunged waist-deep into the water and mud to go after the saddlebags. People had picked up all his umbrellas that were floating down the river! Then he was really empty-handed!

"Some said it was his empty head that kept him on top of the water and saved him from drowning." Among peals of laughter Grace dried her hands. Then she signaled to Letha and the others it was time for bed. They stood up in response, little May first, then Lester, Letha, and finally Arthur.

"You know," she said, "My husband and I have never been separated even one night until this happened." Her eyes bounced meaningfully down their stair-stepped row of heads and back again. Mama continued.

"It was hard to leave John with the task of taking his father

24

back to Missouri. You see, his father always wanted to be buried beside his wife."

"Now I see why your husband isn't with you." Mrs. Comfort said.

"That, and the fact that he feels he cannot move in on my Pa until he finds some way to make a living again," Mama added in his defense. "He still has his pride."

"Oh, goody," Letha said. "I'm glad we left Papa something. I felt so awful when we drove away with all our things and left him without anything at all."

The burst of laughter startled Letha. "What was so funny about that, Mama?"

Without waiting for an answer Mrs. Comfort said, "Well, my dear, pride is for dessert."[5]

"Dessert!" exclaimed Lester. "Do we get another dessert?"

"No, you do not. What you get now is bed!" Mama said and she began to hustle the children out to the wagon for the night.

Mr. Comfort jumped to his feet. "Here, here," he said. "You and the girls and the baby can sleep in the boys' room. You and the baby can sleep on the boys' bed and I'll get your featherbed from the wagon to make a pallet for the girls." Mama tried to protest, but Mr. Comfort insisted.

"Yesterday I got some sweet hay and put it in the upstairs part of the milk house. The boys will have a real picnic sleeping out there on that hay tonight."

"That's very kind of you, Mr. Comfort."

Once the bedroom was arranged to their satisfaction, the Comforts left Mama with her children. Letha snuggled into the wonderful featherbed, hugging her little sister. Mama tucked them in and sang a hymn to them. Letha fought against the heavy darkness fogging her head. When she heard Mama slip back into the kitchen, she strained to listen.

Chapter 4

The Opened Floodgates

Letha heard Mrs. Comfort talking to Mama in a changed voice, like she had a secret to share. She climbed out of bed and walked softly to the open door.

"Just look at this beautiful piece of challis I ordered to make me a dress to wear when I go home this fall," Mrs. Comfort was saying.

"Is the table clean? Let's spread it out and take a look at it, if you don't mind these rough hands of mine touching it," Mama said.

"Go right ahead."

"It is beautiful indeed. And where's home?"

"Kansas. I haven't been home since we came down to the Strip in the Run, and I do want to look nice when I go back for a visit. But I haven't the nerve to cut into this pretty piece."

"Oh my. Don't cut into it without first cutting a pattern. Give me some newspapers and scissors, tell me what you have in mind, and I'll cut you a pattern in no time," Mama said.

"The only paper I have are some pages from the mail order catalog," Mrs. Comfort said. "We can't get newspapers here except when we go to a town to get supplies."

"H-m-m. No newspapers. I suppose that's something you do without on the prairie. Let me see . . . do you have some flour sacks? You could sew them up after we've used them for a pattern and have a good corset cover."

Mrs. Comfort laughed as she dug out some flour sacks. "A person as resourceful as you will do fine in the prairie."

"Kansas makes the best of flour," Mama admitted examining the sacks, "but I do wish I knew some way of fading out the 'Sunflour' brand name on their sacks."

27

"Oh, don't bother about that," Mrs. Comfort replied. "Nobody but us is here to see them anyway."

"Before we get started," Mama said, "my children were wet to the skin from the creek when I undressed them before bed. If you don't care, I believe I will hang their clothes up in here so they will be dry in the morning."

Letha leapt for the bed again, just in the nick of time.

"Mama, I want to come out where you and the woman are and talk, too," Letha said. "I'm not sleepy—really I'm not."

"No," Mama said firmly. "You just lie there and get sleepy. I don't want you cross as a bear tomorrow. We've got traveling to do, and you know what always happens when you get that way." Letha knew all right. Her hands went almost automatically to the usual seat of correction and she shrank down in the bed. But as the two women were hanging the wet garments about the kitchen, using every chair or nail available, Letha slipped out of the bedroom and under the kitchen table. She crouched down, gathering her nightgown around her and sticking it under her feet so they wouldn't get too cold on the wooden floor.

She heard Mama come back to the table and begin ripping the flour sacks open.

"What style of dress did you have in mind?" she asked Mrs. Comfort.

"Oh, something simple. Long sleeves, fitted bodice, a little collar around the neck, buttons down the front, a softly gathered skirt."

"Well, the skirt is no problem, but I'll fit the sacks to you for the bodice. I'll need some pins and a good pair of scissors."

Letha heard Mrs. Comfort walk to a cupboard, come back, and lay the objects on the table. Soon Mama was humming with the task of pinning the sacks to Mrs. Comfort.

"Come to think of it—water—especially too much of it —has had something to do with nearly every major turn in my life," Mama mused through a mouthful of pins.

"What do you mean?"

"When I was just a kid . . . across the river from me, there was John . . ."

28

"Yes?" asked Mrs. Comfort in a tone that indicated she was sniffing romance.

". . . a dashing, cocky, hard-working young fellow, who had put in his brickyard on the east bank of the Chikaskia exactly opposite the acreage Pa had taken for truck farming." She paused again.

"Is that how you met him?"

"Well, not exactly," Mama said smiling. "I met him at the Kansas border the day of the Run in a very odd way, over a cup of spilled water that Pa had just paid a dime for and John knocked over. I met him again when he came across the river in a canoe to try to buy one of Pa's horses to use in running his mud mixer."

"Got you along with the horse did he?" joked Mrs. Comfort.

"Not then. But it wasn't for the wishing of it," Mama admitted. "I had fallen head over heels in love with him at the Kansas border. I was just a kid of fifteen then. Since he was a grown man of twenty-five I reckoned he couldn't see a fat kid like me.

"And as a matter of fact, he began dating the school teacher at Blackwell. They kept company for two years, but she wouldn't give him an answer until the end of her second term of school. Then she went back East and married her former beau. John only heard about it through the men about town."

"That must have been a blow to his pride," Mrs. Comfort said. "Then I suppose he could notice you."

"It wasn't as simple as that," Mama replied. "It took some more water to turn the trick. One day I fell in the river. I couldn't swim so I started screaming for Pa. But he couldn't swim either and started screaming helplessly from where he stood waist deep in the river.

"John heard us from his side of the river, jumped in shoes and all, swam to my side and saved me from drowning, delivering me dripping like a hundred fifty pound dunked cat to my frightened father."

"How romantic," squealed Mrs. Comfort in delight. "Are you sure you didn't fall in accidentally-on-purpose?"

"Cross my heart. I'm deathly afraid of water. Pa was so

29

grateful that he pulled his most prized material possession from his pocket, a gold watch and gave it to John. After we were married Pa had an engraving put inside of the lid of the case saying John had saved me from drowning."

Mama cut away some of the extra sack material and it fell to the floor near Letha. "I don't know why he paid any attention to me in that bedraggled condition. He never seemed to notice me in my best moments before. But after that he crossed the river in his canoe nearly every evening and sat on our doorstep with Pa and me."

"You mean he didn't ever offer to take you any place?" asked Mrs. Comfort.

"He asked, but Pa wouldn't let me go. He insisted I was far too young to go out with a man ten years older than I was. Besides, the teacher had come back to Blackwell to teach again. Of course, her husband came along and he got a job in the bank. But I think Pa wanted to see if John was really ready to forget her." The sound of the scissors cutting stopped.

"Funny, how fathers seem to think their daughters too young to get married, but we're never too young to take on the work of a grown woman around the house. I was seventeen and had been doing a woman's work since the death of my mother three years before. I thought I was a woman, but Pa still looked upon me as a kid."

After another silence Mrs. Comfort asked, "Well, did you run away and marry him anyway?"

"No—and yes. Several months later a girlfriend of mine was going to marry one of the men who worked at John's brickyard. Pa consented to my accompanying the couple to Newkirk for their marriage license. It was not until they drove up in our yard to get me that either of us knew John was going.

"There he sat, grandly perched in the driver's seat of a surrey he had rented at the livery stable—complete with wrought iron trimmings pulled by a pair of prancing bays—the young couple innocently sitting in the back seat.

"When Pa began to object again, John said 'It's only sixteen miles to Newkirk. We can go there easily and back today with this team.' Pa let me go, but I knew he wasn't too happy about it."

"My goodness, but I'll bet that was fun," Mrs. Comfort said, urging her on.

"It was thrilling riding across country in that grand carriage with such a dashing escort—the pick of bachelors in town. I forgot all about my fear of water when he urged the team to ford several creeks on the way.

"The couple got to Newkirk and got their license. And while we were hunting a preacher to marry them, the skies suddenly opened and rain—such as we hadn't seen since we came to the Strip—fell for an hour or more.

"Finally the couple got married in their soaking wet finery and we started for home. When we came to Stick'em Creek, about five miles or so out of Newkirk, we were faced by a boiling torrent, which the horses refused to enter.

"John declared that a horse has more sense than a man and that something was really wrong if they would not ford the same creek as they had crossed coming over.

"He unhitched and unharnessed one of the horses, mounted it and after much forcing got the horse to start into the surging current. He wouldn't go far, though, and John came back saying it was quicksand. We just couldn't make it across.

"The banks were too steep at any other place and so there we were."

"What did you do?" Mrs. Comfort asked.

"There was only one thing we could do," Mama said. "We drove back to Newkirk. Then John gave me the strangest proposal I ever hope to hear if I live to be a hundred. 'I don't want your Pa to skin us both alive or shoot me on sight in the morning,' he said, 'so I guess we'd better get married too.'

"My girlfriend and her brand-new husband broke into shrieks of laughter. I was dismayed and a little bit frightened. It wasn't exactly my idea of a proper proposal, but I didn't see any way out even if I had wanted to. Besides, I'd been trying for several years to get him to that point of view. So, we got married."

Letha could stand it no longer.

31

"She married him to get that watch back," she shouted from beneath the table.

Both women jumped as if they had heard a gunshot. Pins spilled on the floor.

"What do you mean by that?" Mama demanded as she poked her head under the table. "I did no such thing."

"You did so. You know you did. I heard Papa say so himself."

Mrs. Comfort laughed. But Mama stayed Mama.

"You may pick up the pins while you are down there and then you may go to bed."

Letha looked at the scads of pins on the floor and happily realized she would be staying up much longer.

"So how did it end? I wouldn't want to have been in your shoes when you got back to your Pa's house."

"Well, in the end, John had to telephone the livery stable to say that we couldn't get the horses back that night. And he got the man there to carry the message to Pa that we had got married so there would be no scandal. And you are so right. Pa was beside himself the next day."

Letha collected a handful of pins. "Do you have a pin cushion I could put them in so they won't spill again?"

"No, I wish I did. Put them in this box." She passed a little wooden box under the table. Letha dropped the pins inside and continued her task.

"Some of them are stuck in the cracks of the floor," she announced.

"Oh, I'll show you how to do that." Mrs. Comfort got down on the floor beside her. "You just pick them out with another pin."

"Oh. Just like playing pick-up-sticks!"

Soon Mama was on the floor too, her broad bottom sticking up in the air, just as Mr. Comfort came in from outside.

"Excuse me ladies, what is going on down there?"

Letha burst into giggles and the two women joined her. Once they had recovered the rest of the pins as well as their dignity, Mrs. Comfort let out a sigh.

32

"Mrs. Barnet just told us the most romantic story."

"Well, that is all well in the past," Mama said unpinning the pattern from her human model. "I can only look forward—and forward to bed is the next move I'd say. It's late and I must get an early start in the morning. I know that you have a full day ahead, too.

"Here now is the pattern for your new challis dress," she said as they folded up the flour sack material. "When you get the dress done it may not look like you had got it back East, but at least it is an original and no one will have one like it."

She turned to her daughter. "Letha Faye, you get right now!"

Letha scooted back to bed, snuggled up to May, and closed her eyes. This time, instead of seeing flood water, she saw pins scattered on the rough wooden floor. She giggled again, and fell asleep.

Grace lay tossing on the sweet-smelling cornhusk mattress. Funny, how you'd tell a perfect stranger something you wouldn't dare tell someone else and hadn't thought about in years. She listened to the sound of her breathing children. A stir here. A cough there. In spite of the kind welcome she had received in this house, she realized she felt most comforted when she was with her children. She had proven she could get along without John, but she knew she could not survive without her children. She heard Mr. Comfort knock his pipe against the stove and go off to bed with his wife. Suddenly, she felt utterly alone. All right, admit it, she did miss John. She fought against a yearning mixed with bitterness. Although she had tried to slam the gate on the past, it was as if she had slammed it too hard, and it had rebounded open.

Dammed up memories flooded her mind. She recalled her father's helpless anger when she returned as a bride at the end of two fateful days, married to a man her father thought too old and worldly for his "child."

In the quarrel with her father that followed, John had refused to take part even to defend his reason for marrying her without parental consent. Without a word he had climbed into his canoe and rowed across the river to his bachelor one-room house a half-dugout, half above ground affair made of broken brick, and stayed there. She was left alone to face the sad anger of her father, a pattern she was beginning to see repeated ever after in the face of any trouble that came along.

She rolled over in her bed as if to crush the memory, but it did no good. Other memories swam about her restless mind.

After three days of being separated from her new husband by the river between them and stubborn pride, she had in desperation moved across the river into the one-room dugout with him, leaving her father to live alone in his two-room house. No matter which side of the river she lived on, she felt miserable. For months she watched her father as he worked daily in his truck garden until finally he broke down and came across the river to bring her some vegetables he claimed he couldn't sell and he couldn't let go to waste. An excuse, but a welcome one.

She sat upright in bed and hugged her knees. It was no use trying to sleep. Fearful of waking the household, knowing full well that the floodgates to pent-up emotions were now impossible to close, she got up silently. She saw to it that Victor was secure so he could not fall off the bed, and then she tiptoed outdoors into the quiet, star-studded night.

Getting a quilt from the wagon she went down the path to the creek that had so fascinated her children. Old Tudy and the farm shepherd dogs followed, each as silent as the person they were following.

As she spread the quilt beside the creek, her mind continued to go over every minute detail of their crowded one-room abode on the east side of the river, especially after John's father came from Missouri to help with the increasing business.

John had finally been forced into action when she became pregnant. He built a room addition to the two-room house owned by her father, and they moved back in with him. In this room a few weeks later Arthur was born. Eleven months later Letha became the second of what was to be a long procession of children arriving to overcrowd even this arrangement.

Alone now for the first time in years, seated in the darkness

34

by the waters, she sunk into a rare moment of self-pity. With Old Tudy's warm muzzle resting across her left shoulder, and the farm dogs curled in the grass nearby, tears of pent-up emotion began to flow freely. She had admonished Letha to not be a cry baby. And she set the example by never crying in front of the children, but here there was no one to hear her, so surely she could indulge herself at last.

The fireflies flitting about in the grass and brush across the creek did nothing to alleviate her bittersweet memories. They resembled with strange exactness the blinking firelight coming from between the bricks she had once watched from across the river yearning for John.

She threw herself face down in the grass and sobbed. Old Tudy stretched himself across her heaving back doing his best to comfort her. He snapped menacingly at the other dogs as they extended their noses toward the movement of her feet in the dew-covered grass.

Her rage changed its focus. Never through the years had she allowed tears to relieve the tension brought about by her mounting jealousy of the teacher who had spurned John's offer of marriage. She felt John still carried a torch for that woman. Now the long-needed tears came in abundance.

Other faults of John came floating into view. She recalled his habit of hobnobbing and drinking with the oilfield roustabouts—"dirty in mind and body" she had declared to him with no avail. Even more hateful was his practice of raising and selling gamecocks and then instigating free-for-all cockfights backed by bets by the new owners. She now, in her unloosened emotional condition, vented her indignation at this hateful practice by pounding the grass with her feet and fists.

Whether she then dozed off in weariness or whether her mind had raced on for hours she did not know, but all at once she was laughing as uncontrollably as she had seemingly just seconds ago been crying.

One incident when John had stood up for her came to mind. Just before Lester had been born, one of the roustabouts had insulted her in front of John, remarking on her bulging appearance

35

and bovine bent toward procreation.

Without a word, John grabbed the man roughly by the neck, guided him down to the creek bed and repeatedly pushed his head into the water until the dirty-mouthed and half-drowned rat sputtered out an apology.

Even if this was not the Chikaskia and she was miles away from it, alone on an unfamiliar creek bank, and it had happened four years ago, the image of the two of them was so vivid she felt they were there in the water beside her.

She chuckled at the look of the half-drowned man when he apologized. Within the hour, he quit his job with the local oil well wildcatter who in turn was furious over losing what he considered an invaluable worker.

To fill the gap, John worked as an oilfield tool-dresser during the early night shift until another could be found. This left her a helpless bystander in the long evening hours with both of their fathers, now free to review and re-fight the Civil War without John as their witty and skillful conciliator.

She remembered when the two old men lunged at each other one evening in the gathering darkness, fell and grappled on the brick path. She had dashed to separate the antagonists and ended up being thrown into the waters.

The memory of that cold plunge brought her back to reality. For after that her father, to whom she was now going in need, had left for the western part of the Strip within a few weeks. He had found out that when he bought the rights to some land along the river from a half Cherokee, it had given him full homestead rights to the Cherokee Strip.

And now John's father was dead, a victim of the flood, and she didn't know where John was. As she realized that the moon was gone and morning light was beginning to dim the light of the stars, she felt her agony fade away. Suddenly the past seemed comforting compared with the uncertainty of the unknown. She realized that the undercurrent of the night-long vigil by the creek had been an apprehension of what lay ahead.

The prayer she had felt crossing the prairie the day before had left her during the long night. Where had her faith gone?

36

She shivered in the damp coolness of the early morning. Gathering her gown and quilt about herself, she started toward the house, the dogs following her back.

The glistening morning dewdrops caught her eye, reminding her in that moment that somehow God had been with her. Wiping a few straggling tears with the back of her hand, she slipped silently back into the house.

Thankfully, no one was stirring, and hopefully her absence had gone unnoticed. She replaced her damp gown with her flower sack petticoat and lay down comfortably in the corn husk bed. The words of the Psalms came to her, "Weeping may endure for a night, but joy cometh in the morning," and she fell asleep at last.

Chapter 5

Day of Respite

Arthur woke with a start. The sun, unobstructed by trees and hills, had popped up full blast in his face through the window by his bed. He squinted then remembered where he was. No creeping dawn here like along the riverbank at home.

Mama and the children were sound asleep, but he heard noises outside. He slipped out of bed, carried his shoes into the kitchen where he put them on and went outside to find Mr. Comfort with the boys examining his family's wagon.

"Hey, there, son. Your axles need some grease, and the rims are getting loose. I'm sorry I didn't notice that last night so I could have put the wheels in the creek," Mr. Comfort said.

"What with the reloading and greasing, most of the morning will be gone. Do you think we can talk your Mama into staying another day? I just wouldn't feel right about letting you start until I know the wagon is in good shape."

"I don't know, sir. When Mama makes up her mind to do something, there's no stopping her."

"So I noticed. Help us with the morning chores, and I'll work on her when we go in for breakfast."

When they got back inside, everyone else was at the breakfast table.

"Do you want me to set the table for you?" Letha was asking Mrs. Comfort hopefully. Arthur thought it disgusting the way his sister was always trying to please adults.

"We don't bother at breakfast. It's just help yourself."

"Say, Mrs. Barnet, I've been looking your wagon over and I think more needs to be done than fasten that cookstove down," Mr. Comfort said as they sat down.

Just as Arthur predicted, a sudden squaring of Mama's jaw gave out a warning that she might not accept a suggestion.

"You look tired and you've got a hard trip before you yet," he continued without giving her time to speak. "In my opinion, I think you should lay up here a day. Do some more talking with my wife—from what I overheard last night you two won't run down in another day." He winked at his wife.

"Do stay," Mrs. Comfort hugged Mama. "I didn't get talked out last night. In fact, you did most the talking."

Mama broke into embarrassed laughter. "I'm sorry."

"Don't be. My wife needs it as much as you do," Mr. Comfort said. "And my boys need your boys to frolic with."

Mama looked over at Arthur, and he grinned encouragingly back at her.

Seeing that his point was all but won, Mr. Comfort added, "Besides, I noticed there are some mighty big thunderclouds in the northwest, and that kind of cloud in that direction is almost a sure sign of rain."

At the word rain, Mama needed no more persuasion.

"Well, the Lord has his way of looking after people who don't have the sense to look after themselves," she conceded. "Besides, for some reason I forgot to set yeast last night, and I'd hate to go off today without bread."

Mrs. Comfort automatically chimed in, "The Lord looks out for fools and children." The surprised look on Mama's face prompted her to add hastily, "Mind you I'm not calling you the fool. As a matter of fact, I didn't get the washing done Monday. My men were far too busy to bring water up from the creek for me. Every dud we own is dirty. And now, thankfully, the Lord has sent someone to spell me a while at the washboard."

Breakfast became a noisy, merry meal–Arthur making himself at home squabbling over who should have which spoon from the big goblet in the center of the table.

"At home I had a spoon with my name on it," Letha bragged, eating her oatmeal. Then she looked up at Mama. "What happened to it?"

All eyes turned to Mama.

"I'm afraid it got lost in the flood," she replied grimly.

"Well," Mr. Comfort said as he pushed back from the table, "there's lots of work to do here today. Jerry, you build a fire

40

under the wash kettle, and maybe Arthur will help Jack pump water from the cistern to fill it. Then all of you can fill the tubs from the creek."

He turned to Lester. "Why don't you help Jerry by bringing wood from the woodpile." Lester bolted from the table for the door so fast that he knocked over his stool. Arthur started to follow the other boys out as well.

"I help too," cried May as she clambered down to set the stool up again. And with the expression of "Now I have done my part" she climbed up on the stool and began to suck her thumb.

Mr. Comfort watched Letha who had automatically started clearing up the breakfast table. "Such work-brittle people I've never seen in my life," he said to Arthur as he went out the door with him.

After Arthur and Jack had hauled the water to the women, they joined Mr. Comfort at the wagon.

"Look at these axles. Dry as a bone." He opened a big jar of grease. "Lay it on, boys. Don't be stingy with the stuff."

Arthur dipped his fingers in the jar and began smearing the axle with the slimy, smelly substance. The younger boys joined them and watched.

"Arthur, I noticed a pretty nice arsenal there in your wagon," Mr. Comfort said, meaning the Kentucky muzzleloader slung on the outside of the dashboard and the Sharp's repeater rifle fastened by clamps under the spring seat.

"The muzzleloader is my Grandpa's. Mama brought it along with my Pa's gun for protection."

"Is the muzzleloader the one you shoot?"

"Yes, sir," he lied, avoiding Lester's eyes. He was sure he would be shooting it soon. Made sense. Two guns, and he was the oldest, so Mama surely would have to teach him. "We keep it ready for use except for the nipple caps, since it hasn't got safety catch on it."

"And where do you keep the nipple caps?"

Arthur felt streaks of flame red beginning to creep up his face, for he knew Mama kept them tucked in her bosom.

"Oh, close by," he said to cover up his embarrassment, he

41

launched into a tale of why they had both guns along. "Mama brought both guns because she says you never know what you might come across out on the prairie. We had an outlaw scare at Blackwell just before we left. Some cowboy in town claimed he got cheated at cards and shot at two men. One was wounded and the other killed. The frightened cowboy grabbed one of our rowboats and fled across the river where he hid in our brickyard sand pit."

The axle grease rubbing stopped and Arthur felt all eyes upon him.

"A posse caught him there, but it turned out he was a hero. The men he shot were the outlaws who had robbed our bank and lost the loot in the river like Mama told about last night.

"The man he wounded was Dynamite Dick, sometimes known as Three-fingered Dick because he had only three fingers on one hand. He rode out of town, and so far as anyone knows he is out here on the prairie somewheres if he didn't die of the wound."

"If I were you, I wouldn't worry about an escaped outlaw too much," Mr. Comfort said. "Outlaws aren't after women and children. What they are after is money. Cowboys aren't likely to bother you either, although they are none too happy about settlers taking their grazing ground, and I don't think Indians will bother you."

At the thought of Indians, Arthur was the one to stop greasing. He looked over at Lester whose big eyes were fixed on Mr. Comfort.

"Honestly. Indians won't bother you if you don't show fear. They may ransack your wagon nosing into everything, maybe even taking whatever you have that they want. Just sit perfectly still. Look them straight in the eye every time they look you in the face. Don't flinch a muscle and you won't get hurt."

Their faces were as frozen as if the real thing was happening.

"That's it. You got it. You'd scare off anyone with that look."

Suddenly they heard a shriek of laughter from the women. In the distance Arthur saw they had strung shirts and trousers

42

together in pairs on every fence post and low hanging limbs of trees in sight, lined up like headless horsemen. Silly Letha was curtsying to one of them. It was at times like this he thanked God he was born a boy, even if it did mean getting his hands greasy.

As if reading his thoughts Mr. Comfort said, "Those women are like self-winding clocks that run down, merely to wind themselves up again."

Arthur grinned back at him. He was enjoying the man's company. He felt a lot more at ease with him than he'd ever been with Papa.

They wiped the grease off their hands in the grass.

"Now, look here, the spokes are getting loose on the hubs, to say nothing of the rims being loose. Could be dangerous, for you're bound to drop into a prairie dog hole on the plains. Let's get these wheels soaking in the creek and by morning they'll be as tight as drumheads again."

Arthur hitched up the horses, and they pulled the wagon to the middle of the creek where they left it while they went into dinner.

Inside, Arthur found Letha sitting at the table with pen and paper, copying recipes, not for meals it turned out, but for home remedies.

"My children are uncommonly healthy," Mama was bragging as she sat nursing Victor.

"Good thing. And I hope they stay that way," Mrs. Comfort said. "Doctors are scarce enough in this part of the Strip, but farther west where you're headed it's mostly range country and I've heard it is well nigh impossible to get a doctor."

"Colds are about all my children ever get. And I brought along several bottles of Ballard's horehound cough syrup and a big batch of horehound candy that's good for mild cases. And as a parting measure, John got me a couple of bottles of Mule Lightning cough syrup. That concoction will cure you for sure, if it doesn't kill you first!" Mama explained.

Mrs. Comfort joined her in laughter, then added. "But what every pioneer woman needs to know is how to make a good, sure-fire home remedy. That recipe for making chinaberry cough

43

syrup works wonders on my boys—though sometimes I think they stop coughing just so they won't have to take any more of the bitter brew."

She offered Mama a jar and a spoon. "Here, try some of it. And remember it is not only a sure-cure but safe. It hasn't killed any of us yet and it is about all the medicine we've had all these years."

Mama tasted it and choked. "I sympathize with your boys."

"Here's another recipe for making chest cold salve from a mixture of skunk grease, turpentine, coal oil and quinine, with hen grease as a substitute if you couldn't catch a skunk." She handed it to Letha.

"Sounds like a good way to keep colds from spreading—no one would dare go near someone wearing a skunk poultice," Mama laughed.

While show-off Letha was copying the remedies down, Mrs. Comfort told Mama ways to make poultices for stone bruise or to draw out splinters using salt side pork or the crushed warm body of some small animal.

"Sounds awful," Mama said.

"I've heard it's good for snake bite too," Mrs. Comfort replied. "Better write it down for I've heard there are lots of copperheads and maybe some rattlesnakes out in the hills where you are headed."

Mama responded by taking the pen and paper from Letha.

"Well, I'd better serve dinner, but I've got one more you may need." She began dictating as she started preparing the plates. "Good for bee sting and even poison ivy: a spoonful of sulphur in mud."

"Expect I would use this more than any of the others," Mama said, "but I don't have any sulphur."

Mrs. Comfort went to the cupboard, returning with a small box that she thrust beneath the sleeping Victor in Mama's lap.

"We always keep plenty of it on hand. You may even need it on this trip."

A flicker of fright crossed Mama's face, but before it could take hold, dinner appeared on the table, and Mr. Comfort began a report on what they had done to the wagon.

When the meal was nearly over Mr. Comfort looked at Lester who hadn't said a word or cracked a smile all morning.

"Say, fellow," he said tilting back in his chair, "you sure are stingy with words. Come on, give us a few. What you thinking about anyway? Cat got your tongue?" And he prodded Lester playfully in his ribs.

Without looking up, changing the expression on his sober face or missing a bite, Lester said, "Learn more when I listen."

After some laughter in which Lester did not join, Mama came to his defense. "He doesn't speak his mind for fear the rest of us will find out what is inside his head, and then we will be smarter than he is." She thumped him playfully on his head like a marble player shooting a taw. "He says nothing until he gets his idea fully clothed, and by that time the weather has changed so the idea needs a different outfit to go out in," she teased, but patted him sympathetically on the shoulder. As usual, it was plain to see that Lester was Mama's favorite.

"Say, Lester," Jerry badgered, no doubt hoping to get his share of the laughs, for after all, it was his house. "Did you ever stop to think what it would be like if everyone did nothing but listen so he could learn more?"

"We could hear ourselves think then," said the unruffled Lester. And he went right on eating, looking directly at his plate.

Jerry squirmed in his chair, looking like he was pretty sure Lester had turned the tables on him.

"Come on men," Mr. Comfort said as he gulped the last of the water in his cup, banged the legs of his chair down and got up. "Plenty of work to do in the Strip yet. Got to get those furrows plowed around the buildings before a fire comes along and leaves plenty of nothing."

Lester—slow on the talk but swift on action—was again the first one out the door. Arthur rose from the table, glad he could help Mr. Comfort in return for fixing the wagon.

"What do you mean about plowing around the buildings?" Mama asked before they could get out the door.

"In this open prairie there is always danger from fire by someone careless," Mr. Comfort explained. "Some of the neighboring families have narrowly escaped being burned to death

45

because they weren't careful, or didn't know about keeping a wide strip plowed around their buildings.

"This time of the year the big dry tumbleweeds, last year's crop, are really bad. The wind has uprooted them during the early spring and they tumble and blow about in the least breeze, and a high wind will carry them for miles. When they catch fire they burn as if they had been soaked in coal oil.

"The plowing is often all that has saved us. Our stock has learned to break for home whenever they smell smoke. Our shepherd dogs never have to be told to start rounding up the cattle. Smarter than many humans, animals are, if left to have their own heads."

They went back down by the creek and rotated the wheels half a turn.

"Papa," Jerry said, "Can't we have a little rest before we work again? I'm stuffed from dinner."

Mr. Comfort agreed and they stretched out in the grass beside the creek.

As Arthur studied the clouds up in the sky, he ran through all the dangers of the prairie in his head. Without Papa there, it would be up to him to keep on the lookout. Mama would be too busy with the children and driving the wagon.

Chapter 6

Across the Long Miles

The next morning the Comforts hovered close to the family as if their nearness would add strength to the coming journey. The women and children were crying. Arthur wished they could just get in the wagon and go. He was surprised to see even Mr. Comfort wipe a tear on his work shirt as he reached across the children to gather both women into the circle of his long arms.

Speaking to Mama he said, "I don't want to hurry you, but if you must go, you'd best make the most of the day, and get as much of the prairie as possible behind you before stopping to make camp for another night."

"Can't get to Waynoka too fast to suit me, but I sure hate to leave this warm and friendly campsite," she said with a wavering smile.

"Unfortunately, after you get west of the Chisholm Trail it's nearly all open range with few if any houses that you can camp near," he said quietly, but Arthur heard him.

"I figured as much," Mama said. "We didn't have too much help in the way of roads the day we stopped here. But don't worry, the Lord has been with us too long to think of forsaking us in the middle of the job. He'll see that we make it OK. I figure another three days." And she tried another smile.

"For one who acts so independently, I find your talk of dependence on the Lord hard to believe," Mr. Comfort said.

Mama met his questioning gaze.

"Well, if you pray for potatoes, you've got to pick up a hoe."

"I have no doubt in your ability to cope with whatever lies before you," he responded.

Mama gently released herself from the huddle. Turning to face the sun rising in the East, she quoted from the Bible in her holy voice, "This is the day that the Lord hath made. Let us rejoice and be glad in it."

Without another word she at last moved towards the wagon and climbed up into the front seat. The Comforts hoisted Victor and May up into her lap, while Arthur climbed up the spokes of the front wheels, and scurried into the canvas-covered wagon, Lester and Letha following.

Mama did not look back as she drove into the west. Arthur took turns with Letha and Lester, framing his face in the puckered peephole at the back of the canvas, waving good-bye to his new friends until the sight of them was lost behind the tips of the greening sage.

As they jiggled across the prairie he could tell by the way the wagon moved along that it was well packed and evenly loaded this time. Mr. Comfort knew what he was doing.

By mid-morning Arthur found his siblings annoying him with their restlessness and he began to bicker with them. Their clamor, growing louder and louder, began to irritate Mama. After shushing them twice without success, she tried something new.

"One, two, button my shoe." Mama bent over pretending to button her shoe. All but Arthur immediately did likewise.

"Three, four, shut the door." She pinched her lips closed. That didn't work so well, for the doors burst open with giggles.

Ignoring this as best she could, she continued the jingle. "Five, six, pick up sticks." And without any prompting they bounced about in their swinging beds pretending to pick up sticks. Arthur joined them in this one.

"Seven, eight, <u>shut the gate</u>," she said when their bouncing started getting out of hand. With this she signaled for them to lie down and close their eyes, trying to coax them into a nap. But the gates didn't stay shut. Up they bounced to begin the game all over again, their antics growing louder and louder.

As Letha stooped to "button a shoe" her upturned bottom swung toward Mama who gave it a playful swat saying, "Take that and button your trap!"

That was something new to add to the game. Letha promptly delivered the swat along the line until she got to Arthur, who returned it harder than he meant to. Letha fell crying across the back of the wagon seat. As Mama raised her hand to slap him,

48

her eyes met the coolly appraising ones of Lester whose look said, "Who started all this, anyway?" Nothing could have stayed her hand more quickly. For once, Arthur was grateful for his younger brother.

He decided enough of the silly stuff, and returned to his self-appointed lookout duties. Very soon he noticed they were passing through a town of burrowing prairie dogs. The creatures stood guard over a territory completely bare of grass. "Look! Prairie dogs!" he cried out. Suddenly, May, then Letha and even Lester, insisted they needed to "go out." Reluctantly, Mama stopped to let them out of the wagon.

The little creatures, who had been standing like chattering sticks in their holes before they stopped, now disappeared in the blink of an eye. As Arthur and the others ran each toward a different mound of earth to claim territory, nothing could be seen but vacant mounds of barren earth.

Arthur turned his back to relieve himself, when above his own sound effects he heard a shriek from Letha. He twisted his head around to see her leap from her squatting position, jump over her mound and bound across the prairie desperately trying to pull up her flour sack panties. A huge bumblebee flew out from her billowing dress. May obviously had seen or heard the bee as well, for she followed Letha in hot pursuit, also screaming at the top of her lungs.

Calling "Whoa, whoa, boys" to the horses, Mama wound the lines of the team around the dashboard stick with one hand as she plopped Victor down with the other. Then with lightning speed she spilled across the wagon sides, from seat to axle to ground, and started after the fleeing girls. She continued to call out "whoa, whoa" to the girls as they were easily outdistancing her best efforts.

Meanwhile, from the mound Lester was investigating, Arthur heard a quavering "Who, who" and saw a big-eyed burrowing owl poke his face into the wondering one poised above it. A startled Lester joined in the chase following Mama.

Arthur, finding no sign of life in the hole he had picked to pee into, grabbed up a stick and began to poke it into the hole trying to stir up an acquaintance of his own. He continued to dig and stir until Mama returned with a girl in tow in each hand, Lester hanging to the back of her skirt as if she were the team of horses he was steering back to the safety of the wagon.

"Come on, Arthur," she yelled in his direction. There was no need to repeat her request for at that moment a black snake stuck a full foot of its length out of the hole and began to flick its tongue in front of his own startled face. Automatically he gave a backward handspring and came running after them.

Back in the wagon, Mama's investigation of Letha's difficulty revealed a rapidly swelling welt on her buttocks from the sting. She found the box of sulphur Mrs. Comfort had insisted on giving her.

"Bless your dear heart," Mama breathed as she generously plastered Letha's backside with sulphured mud. Arthur thought it was funny but didn't dare laugh.

Barely had they started off again before the prairie dogs reappeared like magic, like a bunch of western rodeo cowboys, guffawing and shank-slapping at the sight of the invaders fleeing.

The whole family laughed, Mama summing up the experience by saying, "Only my tribe of Indians could manage to scare a whole town of prairie dogs and still make contact with a bumblebee, an owl, and a snake—all in the space of five minutes!" Saying the word Indians quieted them down—for a while.

At the next outburst, Mama tried a new tack.

"You barking prairie dogs get back in your holes," she said as she playfully pushed Arthur, then Lester to the back of the wagon. They laughed and scudded back, while May and Letha hunkered in the seat beside her. That game lasted for another short span, each finding a new hole several times until they ran out of new places to hide.

As the miles ticked on, Arthur surveyed the landscape. When they met the prairie dogs they had been driving across a flat plateau. Now they began to slope gently down into a strangely greening valley with distant hills appearing beyond.

There must be water there, he thought to himself. Strange how he wished for water with the same intensity he had wished it to go away back in Blackwell.

50

As they approached the lush green carpet, Old Tudy barked, leapt ahead, stretched himself out, and was rolling over again and again in delight.

Mama halted the team, but before the wheels had even stopped, Arthur bounded out, rolling with the dog in the grass. The others joined him.

When Mama unhitched the horses from the tongue of the wagon, they began grazing hungrily before she could even remove the harness. Mama called Arthur from his frolicking to drive stakes in the ground and tether the horses. Once done, he tried to return to the grass with the dog and his siblings.

"Be a man now and don't have to be told everything to do," Mama admonished him as she called him back to stake Old Bessie where she too could taste the wonderful grass. He did her bidding, but not happily. He resented what she said to him, and didn't think it was fair that just because he was the oldest he had to do things some of the others were perfectly capable of doing. But still, he knew he had to prove that she could rely on him.

"Let's look for water, now," she said to him. They left the joyful gathering in the grass for short trips in all directions looking about for water, but found none.

"Maybe it's underground," Mama suggested. She gave up and started spreading the lunch Mrs. Comfort had packed.

"That's what I call a good lunch," Arthur said.

Fastened to the tongue of the wagon near the dashboard, swaddled in two layers of gunnysack between which prairie hay had been packed, was one of Mr. Comfort's ten-gallon galvanized milk cans. He had filled it with water from the cistern, advising them, "Change this can at noon to the shelf I've fixed next to the cow's head at the tailgate. That way, the can will be in shade all day long."

His second piece of advice was to haunt them many times during the next few days. "Use this can of water, as well as your own, very sparingly. You may need it not only for your own use but for the animals as well."

Mama and Arthur left the others again after they had eaten and went further afield to search. But look as they would, no source of water was to be found.

51

Returning to the wagon Mama called all of them about her. "Children, you are getting to be big people now." She paused to let this sink in. Then she continued.

"So you are going to have to act like big people." Again she waited a moment. "From now on when you have milk to drink, you are not to ask for water, too."

They blinked back at her.

"The horses and Old Bessie can't drink milk—"

Nervous tittering stopped her briefly.

"I can't find any water on the prairie for them to drink, so it is only fair that they have what is in the cans while you have the milk."

She went immediately to the can tied to the wagon tongue, and poured out a small wash pan of water while they squabbled over who would be the one to offer it to the next animal.

Lester served a small portion of milk to the dog saying, "Now, Old Tudy, don't you whine for any water, 'cause you can drink milk like the rest of us."

They tied the can onto the tailgate shelf and then reluctantly piled into the wagon to leave. It was hard to drag themselves away from this little haven of cool grass.

After playing in the grass and eating a full meal, the younger ones promptly went to sleep. Arthur got in the seat beside Mama and drove the wagon while she nursed his baby brother.

For some time they rode silently, watching birds fly away from the oncoming wagon, while an occasional snake slithered its way between the clumps of grass. He was getting used to snakes now, and wouldn't be startled again if he came across one.

But he couldn't contain himself when it came to spotting some bounding jack rabbits—wily creatures they were, stopping at intervals to poke their ears above brushtops to find out what was going on.

"Mama, let me shoot a rabbit for supper," Arthur begged shaking her arm. When she hesitated he offered a clincher. "You said I was a man now and every man needs to know how to shoot doesn't he?"

"Well, I must admit there is truth in what you say, and it is sensible for you to learn how to load a gun now under less tense circumstances." Proud Mama had to make it clear that it was her line of reasoning and not his insistence that swayed her to let him try.

She took the musket from its place just outside the dashboard and handed it to him. Then she retrieved the cap box from the hiding place between her breasts, and placed one cap carefully on the musket nipple. Her hand was none too steady as she made these preparations for him to use the gun.

Then she began to school him in its use.

"Put the gun against your right shoulder. Keep it firmly there while you locate the target you want to shoot. Squint one eye and with the other look right down the top of the barrel. Squeeze the trigger on a muzzleloader—don't try to pull it—just squeeze."

She removed the cap and showed him what she meant.

"Now lift the gun and get the feel of it a few times, but don't shoot until you see some rabbit ears to shoot at. Move the gun to aim just below the ears. That's it. You'll do fine. Just remember what I have told you."

It seemed an eternity before an accommodating rabbit poked his ears above a clump of brush. Eagerly Arthur lifted the old rifle. It was heavy and so hard to hold steady in the moving wagon. Mama didn't stop the team possibly because she knew to do so would signal the rabbit, but more likely because she did not think he would hit the mark anyway. He pulled the trigger.

Mama jumped when the gun fired, and the team, not being prepared at all, bolted. To stop the frightened animals it took her full weight pulling back on the lines as she was dumped over the back of the seat, feet and legs stiff in mid-air above the dashboard.

Whether it was the kick of the gun against his shoulder, the flight of the horses, or his big leap of triumph, Arthur landed fully ten feet from the wagon and was running like mad by the time Mama collected herself.

"Whoa," she yelled, followed by a louder "Arthur!" The horses stopped, but Arthur did not. He leapt barefoot like Mexican jumping beans over clump after clump of tall grass to the right spot behind a clump of brush, and there it was. His first

53

kill! He ran back faster than he had gone, if such a thing were possible, holding the big rabbit high for all to see and shouting, "I got it! I got it!"

Mama hollered at him "Drop that rabbit, go back and get the gun from the grass where you dropped it, and get in the wagon so I can tell you how to reload it." Arthur stopped, hurt and confused.

"Indians on the top of that hill!" she yelled in desperation, waving wildly westward. "They'll surround us any minute!"

"Indians?" screamed the children.

Arthur swung around and looked in the direction she was waving. On the hilltop a mile or so to the west was silhouetted the motionless form of a horse whose rider was standing full height in the stirrups. Before Arthur's mind could take this in, a second pony and rider appeared. Before his startled eyes both ponies leapt high in the air and sped down the slope toward them. In his imagination a whole tribe of Indians on the warpath were about to follow.

At that point Arthur did exactly what Mama had told him to do—except drop the rabbit. Instead he heaved the warm, bleeding creature over the side of the wagon bed where it landed squarely in the crook at the back of Letha's legs as she knelt on her knees. She might as well have been attacked by a live panther, her screams could have been no more terrifying. As May joined in, Lester calmly climbed down atop the girls and retrieved the rabbit. Holding it up by the ears as he had seen Arthur do, he said to the girls, "Just an old rabbit, you sillies!"

Mama and Arthur ignored this small drama as well as the added wail from Victor behind the seat. They had one eye on reloading the musket and the other on the brush from which they expected a circle of war whoops to come at any moment.

"Put in a spoon of powder, now some wadding. Tap it down gently with the ramrod. Now a spoon of shot—wish we had some real buckshot instead of this birdshot—now another piece of wadding. Ramrod again." Taking neither of her hands from the rifle, she instructed Arthur to reach for the cap box in her bosom. He did as he was told.

"Now go to the peephole at the back of the wagon," Mama

ordered. "Take a cap out of the box and place it on the nipple of the gun, but don't pull the trigger until you see an Indian stick his head up like that rabbit—and DO remember what I told you: hold the gun tight against your shoulder, sight and squeeze the trigger."

"Yes, ma'am!" he replied. His moment of glory had come, but his hands were trembling.

The girls were now hiding beneath the seat trying to stifle the screams of Victor whom Mama had handed down to them.

Lester was holding the team, having found his station of duty without being told. Suddenly the two riders re-appeared some hundred yards in front of the team. When they spotted Mama's quickly raised gun, they separated—one bounding ahead and the other circling to the rear of the wagon. Her gun followed the rider ahead. When the other one appeared before the peep-hole in the rear, Arthur squeezed the trigger and the muzzle-loader spat out its load. The frightened horse leapt high and swerved in midair. This all but unseated the rider, but recovering his balance he let the horse follow its instincts and gallop off to the east. The rider Mama had been covering followed his partner.

"Indians!" sneered Arthur, noting the headlong flight. "Who's afraid of Indians!" At first no one answered. They just looked at him with terror in their eyes.

"They didn't look like Indians to me," Lester piped up.

"They didn't get close enough for us to tell. Indians don't wear war paint and feathers these days you know," Arthur replied. "They dress just like cowboys."

Mama didn't seem convinced. She took the reins from Lester and drove the tired team as hard as she could into the fading light of the west, increasing the distance between them and the fleeing horsemen, Arthur standing guard at the peephole in the rear.

When it was almost dark, and their hearts had stopped racing along with the team, they began looking for a place to make camp. Finding no safe shelter, Mama finally stopped the plodding beasts near an overlarge clump of brush.

"Ah, look at the canvas on the wagon—proudly white when we began the trip—but now, thankfully, it's soiled enough to blend in with the landscape," Mama stated.

"Like camouflage," Arthur agreed. It was a war term he'd learned from his grandpas.

Hastily the two of them unhitched the horses while Lester got the wash pan from the wagon. Arthur held the rope of each horse in turn so it could roll in the grass while Mama poured a pan of water. May and Letha washed in it, and then Mama offered it to Old Sam. He emptied it quickly, muzzling noisily in the pan.

She poured a second pan in which she washed Victor's hands and face. Lester washed in it and then Mama dabbed it on her face. This over-used pan of water she then offered to Old Roany who, instead of refusing the silt-laden brew as you might expect, met it with nostrils distended.

Old Bessie was given a pan of clean water to keep her milk supply pure. Then she was milked and the children's thirst satisfied.

Mama poured a scant pan of water for Arthur to wash his bloody face and hands. "Give it to Old Tudy when you are through washing. He won't mind the blood. He will just think he is having fresh meat."

That made her think of the rabbit under the seat. "Give Old Tudy the rabbit to go along with the blood he just drank."

"I won't!" he replied in dead earnest.

"We can't build a fire tonight, because of the Indians, Arthur, and the meat will spoil before morning." Seeing he was not convinced she added, "And besides Old Tudy needs to keep up his strength so he can help us if we need him."

With that Arthur finally gave in, and gave the rabbit to his dog, helping to tear it to pieces. Since no more water could be spared for a second washing, he mopped his hands on the grass. Then he wiped them on the seat of his pants.

While the horses and cow grazed in the gathering dusk, the family hunkered on their heels, or leaned against the wagon, eating their supper. Going without roast rabbit was not too difficult as Mama had untied the oven door of the stove Mr. Comfort had fastened shut against small fingers. There she had uncovered an extra supply of bacon, cured ham, side meat, cookies and

56

eggs—each egg wrapped separately.

As they ate their fill in silence, Mama wondered out loud what to do. Finally she decided to let the horses graze until dark, then hitch them to the wagon and tie Old Bessie behind so that if they needed to make a quick getaway, all would be set.

While she got the girls and Victor off to bed, she offered Arthur and Lester the first watch, saying she would take a nap and then relieve them for the night. She let Arthur take "his" gun, but kept the rifle with her.

Now Arthur could take even more satisfaction in his new-found man status. Still he was glad to have Lester to keep him company. Rather than listen to the little noises of the night, they talked softly about whether the men, who had appeared out of nowhere and had disappeared into nowhere in the opposite direction, were Indians or not. Lester noted their nut-brown skins and graceful riding. Arthur said that Indians would not have given up their quarry so easily. Nor were they cowboys, he reasoned. No cowboy would have tried that trick of splitting forces. Besides, they would not be looking for trouble. That left only outlaws! Only outlaws and gamblers were smart enough to co-ordinate their moves the way these men did. It was all well and good for Mr. Comfort to say an outlaw never hurt a woman or child, but they had no proof of it. They would have to stay on guard until Mama relieved them.

Fatigue was about to overtake him when Arthur definitely heard a sound. He nudged Lester and pointed in its direction and through the darkness they saw some movement. Arthur crawled as quietly but quickly as he could to his sleeping mother, Lester behind him, and woke her.

"See 'em? See 'em right over there behind that clump of brush?" Arthur asked.

This time they saw nothing, but they heard the sound of horse hooves stopping in one spot a little east of where the family was camped.

After clomping about for a few minutes the horsemen dashed off across the prairie making enough noise to wake the dead—but apparently the dead were not as tired as the little ones asleep in the wagon.

"Pop yourselves off to bed now quietly so as not to wake the others," she said. "It's my time to go on guard. Where's your gun?"

"Back there," Arthur admitted shamefully. That was the second time he'd left it behind him.

"Don't worry. It would have been worse if you had tried to crawl with it and it had gone off. You did the right thing. All right boys, you are relieved of your duties." She saluted them.

Snickering, they returned her salute and climbed into the wagon, snuggling into their bunks by the cookstove— Lester to his pallet of comforts on the lids of the stove and Arthur to his swinging bunk beside it. Sleep was not long in coming.

Arthur was yanked from a deep sleep by a scream of utter terror. It was Letha, at the far corner of a brush clump opposite where Mama was keeping watch.

All the Indians Arthur had discounted earlier, he now imagined behind the bush, grinning their mocking, painted, grins at his poor, defenseless sister. There they had been hiding waiting patiently just to attack her. Suddenly, she was very precious to him. He instinctively pushed his way through the wagon and jumped out the front. Peering through the darkness he could make out Mama struggling to lift herself off the ground. She had grabbed a gun in each hand as props, and was pushing herself toward the corner of the screaming bush. Letha's head collided half-way, smack into her mother's belly while her arms clutched as far around Mama as they could.

"Where are they? Where are they?" Mama shot the rapid-fire questions at Letha but held the heavy guns with barrels pointing to the ground.

"A snake, a snake! It bit me when I squatted!"

Indians vanished and in their places Arthur pictured hundreds of snakes, two-pronged tongues flickering wickedly in and out of red mouths like the one he'd seen that morning in the prairie dogs' hole.

Mama dropped the guns and bent to lift Letha in her arms and carry her to the shelter of the wagon. But as soon as she put her hands beneath Letha's buttocks the better to support her weight, piercing screams ripped from her mouth.

By this time everyone had climbed out of the wagon wanting to know what the matter was. Old Tudy was baying in circles about the lot of them.

"Get a match," Mama said to Arthur in an exhausted voice. An examination of Letha's private regions, despite her squirming to keep them from Arthur's view, disclosed scores of tiny stickers in the soft flesh.

"Looks like a cactus or a porcupine got you, not a snake," she chuckled. Match after match went up in flames in Arthur's hands as Mama, aided by Lester, tried to rid Letha of fishhook-like fragile thorns. Finally Mama gave up the idea of picking them all out and simply held her across her lap to comfort her.

"Go on back to bed, boys," Mama said. "And do what you can to get May back to sleep."

Arthur obeyed ready to return to sleep. Lester had been comforting May, so he climbed back into his bed, taking one last look out the peephole. Mama was sitting nearby, flat on the ground, the baby at her bosom, Letha lying across her lap with bare bottom sticking up.

Arthur now heard that brave morning chant in Mama's holy voice before they left the Comforts, replaced with a soft, simple plea: "Lord, help me. I am weak, I am lonely, I am afraid."

It took him longer to get back to sleep than he thought it would.

Chapter 7

Water: Friend or Foe

Breakfast became a meal of whines. Grace sighed with weariness.

Victor whined because there was no more milk for him to tug from her sagging breasts. Maybe, heaven forbid, this trip was beginning to tell on her, and she too, like Old Bessie was "drying up."

Arthur and Lester, reverting to boyhood, groused because they hadn't got to shoot the Indians. Or more likely because they hadn't got enough sleep.

Letha complained because her bottom hurt, because she couldn't sit down because Grace insisted that she should leave off her panties so they would not rub on the stickers, and because she couldn't lie down because then her dress touched the stickers. "Get them out, Mama."

"I can't get them out until they fester and get a little loose. I can see them better then too. And if you don't hush your whining I'll just spank them right in deeper, then you'll really have something to cry about."

"You'll just get them in your hand if you do," Lester said, always the one who stayed her threats.

May whined because the others whined. For nothing had disturbed her sleep during the night. She had slept through the whole hub-bub.

Even the horses seemed to complain—snorting, sniffling, and stomping—probably because they had stood up all night in their heavy harness. Or maybe for the same reason Old Bessie mooed her own version of whine—they all wanted water. Water to get their noses into, not just a wash pan of second-hand water! Water they could stamp around in with their feet!

Come to think of it, only Old Tudy was not grumbling. Grace looked about silently trying to locate him—wanting him to

61

put in his appearance even if he did whine. She was still looking for him when they began loading the wagon to break camp. Then she suddenly spied a grey nose stretched beyond a sage clump the better to sniff and catch the scent of these prairie roamers. Ears slowly came forward, below which were two bright and glaring eyes. It wasn't Tudy, but a wolf! At this point, she hurried everyone into the wagon. Looking in the direction of the wolf, she saw the grass sway in two directions at the same time, like a part being made down the middle of a man's head of hair. The beast was silently slinking away.

If only Old Tudy would come. They had to get started, but she felt as if she were pulling away and leaving one of the children. Yet she dare not call for him and have the children on her neck if the dog did not answer. She salved her conscience with the thought that he could and would follow their trail.

Her mind re-played each prairie sound that she had heard the night before to see if she might find a clue to the dog's absence. Crickets and grasshoppers and katydids and locusts serenading in the grass. Nothing there. A screech owl had interrupted her thoughts with its unsettling call—short eerie whistles that got faster and louder, suddenly stopping then dipping into a lower and longer trill—over and over and over until she wished somebody would come and shoot the poor bird so she could get some rest.

May was now seated beside her in the wagon so Letha could lie on the pallet with her dress tail pulled up airing her suffering bottom in private. Her thumb in her mouth, spreading her fingers with her nose dividing them into two plus two, May sat broodily watching her mother. Back in Blackwell Grace had vowed to break her of the habit, but now she was loath to deprive her of this simple comfort.

Grace continued hunting with her mind her beloved dog, who had always been her comfort. Then like a flash it came back to her. Last night, the howl of a wolf pack afar off to the north and Old Tudy's bay in answer. This morning, the slinking wolf must have responded to Old Tudy by coming to the camp.

She was sure now that Old Tudy was past trailing their wagon ever again. She thought of him nuzzling her that night by the creek, and suddenly without warning a tear dropped on Victor's upturned face.

"What you do that for?" May asked pointing to the big tear on the sleeping baby's face.

Grace said the first thing that came to her mind. "Maybe Victor wants a drink." It was the wrong thing to say.

"I do too," May said, and then the "I do too's" came from every corner of the wagon.

"Holy cow!" Grace exclaimed in exasperation.

At this outburst Lester popped his head through the peephole at the rear of the wagon. Returning he said, "No, Mama, Old Bessie is not holy yet. She's not wearing a halo."

Grace chuckled. If only Old Bessie was holy. But she was not giving any more milk. She and all the animals would have to be given water.

She stopped the team, got a tin cup, and stepping down onto the wagon tongue, she dipped it into the can of water. The horses smelled or heard the water sound, and they began to snort and stomp turning their heads right and left as if looking for its source. Then they chomped their bits and nodded their heads up and down as if saying, "Yes, we caught you at the cookie jar, but we won't tell on you if you give us one too."

Grace gave each horse and Old Bessie a wash pan of water, noting as she did so that the can was less than half full.

She began measuring it up in her mind. There'd be no milk for dinner. That would mean five cupfuls for the children, and a panful for each of the animals—after the family had used it for wash water, of course. Altogether that would take about three gallons at least. There wouldn't be enough left in that can for supper even with the milk Old Bessie might give. That left the ten-gallon can beneath the seat.

How wise Mr. Comfort had been to give them that second can of water. Surely they could make out if . . .

Here her contemplation was cut short by growing demands from Letha calling for her attention. She was tired of lying on the pallet.

Borrowing two safety pins from Victor's three-cornered trousers she pinned Letha's dress tail up where it could not touch her bottom when she stood up. She placed herself squarely in the middle of the wagon seat, put her two feet up on the dashboard so as to form three equal sized pens in front of the seat. She instructed Letha to get in the middle one between her legs where her drooping skirts would hide Letha's bottom from view by the others. Lester was told to occupy the north pen and Arthur the south one, the three heads forming a tit-tat-toe just above the dashboard.

May had already penned herself up behind her spread fingers and was now sound asleep in the swinging bed behind the seat. Victor continued to slumber in her lap.

Thus settled, they began another day's journey. To keep them occupied, Grace began to teach her three oldest nature's lessons as they presented themselves to their view from the wagon. Toads, lizards, horned toads, snakes, rabbits, large and small by the dozens, birds and bees, which Letha said she didn't care to meet again, thank you, and butterflies of every hue paraded obligingly by—each forming another illustrated page in a living science book. Nearly an hour passed happily with all forgetting their whines of the morning hour. All seemed content, but Grace kept turning over and over in her mind just how she would explain the absence of Old Tudy when the children discovered it.

Sadly, after an hour any lesson for children wears thin. They began to whine and quarrel again, so Grace decided to switch to a word-study game. Keeping them entertained on the long journey at least kept her mind from too much worry.

"Let's make some rhymes," she said.

They needed no coaxing, for that was their favorite game, and Grace's too for that matter. She started the game off by saying a line and the first one to end the ditty with a rhyming line would be the winner and would start off the next one.

"See that heat shimmer across the grass." And she pointed to something yet nothing that seemed wiggling just above the grass tops in front of the horses.

The children all watched this shimmering phenomenon.

"See it part to let our horses pass!" Lester shouted to be the first to finish with a line.

Sure enough, the grass did part to let them pass. Lester was so pleased with himself and Grace was too. She decided if this trip did nothing else it would get her acquainted with this silent lad so dear to her, but whom she had never been able to understand.

The wind had begun to blow a terrible gale from the south. It slashed the sage, twisted the tall dry grass until it wrestled itself out of the wind's strong grip and sprang back to its full height again only to be grabbed and twisted all over again by the next bullying gust.

Now it was Lester's turn to begin the rhyme.

"Wind, wind go away," he quoted the famous line.

"Don't come another day," Letha finished it off.

Grace could see they were on their way to self-entertainment so her mind returned to her worrying. What rhymes followed she did not know, but apparently Letha and Arthur had each had a turn since she had heard no fussing.

But then it was Lester's turn again, and all went quiet. When he began, the line he gave startled her out of her worries, and at the same time gave her an answer to them.

"See little green fingers down near the sand?" And Lester leaned over the dashboard and pointed with chubby fingers.

They all leaned over to look with Grace slowing the horses the better for all of them to see.

Sure enough, the new green at the base of each dried bunch of grass—last year's crop—looked like little fingers spread wide to hold the old grass from blowing away.

In a flash Grace completed the rhyme. "Holding its Mama fast in its baby hand."

They were all delighted, but Grace most of all. She had expressed, for both her children and herself, the source of the strength she would find to finish this trying trip. The small hands of her five held her to her purpose, and kept the old grass from being uprooted by the torturing elements.

She now had the answer, and sooner than she had expected, to her inquiry of the evening before—"Dear God what can be the outcome of this trip?"

The outcome would be the safe arrival at her father's farm.

She knew this beyond a doubt. She didn't know just when or what would happen in the meantime, but they would get there!

Grace saw a small clearing a short distance ahead. A fine place to make a campfire and cook their midday meal. She would promise the children a good meal soon if they would just quit nagging her about making camp.

As they came nearer to the clearing they saw another prairie dog town. If it was anything like last time, the children were not sure they wanted anything to do with the place. However, fed up with being cooped up in the wagon, they jumped down. The boys were soon finished with their regular camp chores—gathering fire wood, staking out the horses and the cow where they could get their midday meal—and began to look for something else to do nearby, while Grace fixed a meal."

Arthur, apparently still under the influence of the striking stage manners of some traveling entertainers he had seen shortly before the flood in Blackwell, decided to do a little play-acting himself. He walked boldly up to one of the very big mounds of earth, knocked with all the might of his fist on the top near the hole and said in mock manner of a mincing dandy, "Please dear sir, may we come in and visit you?" As he said this speech he bowed stiffly from the waist, one hand on his stomach and the other across his back.

Peals of laughter greeted this bit of melodrama. The others came trooping up and the four joined hands forming a circle around the mound. They dropped hands and all bowed as Arthur had done, but each with an eye peeled for anything that might decide to greet them at the door.

Receiving no sort of answer from the creatures hiding inside, the children began prancing about the mound—buzzing, flicking their tongues in and out, making big owl eyes with circled fingers, getting louder and merrier in their play until surely by now the creatures within had to go to the farthest recesses of their burrows to save their eardrums.

When they tired of the play, Arthur ended it.

"What strange company you keep, Mr. Prairie Dog," he said bowing again over the hole. "We've changed our minds about visiting you . . . so I bid you farewell."

Dinner was ready. At home they never presented themselves at table without first at least swishing their hands through a wash pan of water, sloshing it over their faces and then wiping the dampened accumulation of debris on a big roller towel. Now such niceties, along with Grace's fear of eating unseen germs, were easily replaced with the importance of conserving the dwindling water supply. They did, however, wash after eating, again giving the wash water to the horses and cow.

By this time the children noticed Old Tudy's absence.

Grace prided herself in the fact that she never lied to her children any more than she would want them to lie to her. It was her belief that the truth never hurt anyone. But this time she wasn't so sure.

Fortunately Lester came to the rescue with, "I bet he has gone back to be company for Papa." The longing in his face conveyed that he wished he could have gone along with the dog.

"Well, time to move on," Grace said, "and see if we can find water. We'll leave the prairie dogs to themselves."

The children couldn't argue with that, so they climbed dutifully back into the wagon.

After an hour or so of traveling west, Grace spotted the tips of a small cluster of scrubby trees sticking up out of what appeared to be a spreading gully.

"Water! Water at last!" Grace cried out as she climbed to her knees in the wagon seat and stretched her neck in order to see over the sagebrush.

Arthur and Lester sniffed over her shoulder like small thirsty beasts catching a scent from the breeze. May and Letha began bouncing on tiptoe on their pallet "Water, water, water!"

The flagging wagon team lifted their heads as one, and, with flared nostrils, pulled faster toward the water hole.

Arthur and Lester bounded out and outran the horses to get to the shaded inviting spot, but suddenly stopped dead in their tracks.

A rangy long-horned bull reared up from the shade and came bellowing head down to meet the boys. They were back at the wagon like balls on rubber strings. Each bounded to the top rim of a wheel on the side of the wagon facing the bull. Grace

67

yanked Lester into the wagon from his perch on the fast-moving front wheel, but Arthur, having climbed on to the back wheel, had no way to get in, no where at all to go.

The bull, being unable to change his course, split the difference and plunged head-on, banging his great horns and shoulders into the side of the wagon. The forward-rolling back wheel pitched hapless Arthur across the angry beast's back to the ground on the other side of him.

"Oh dear God, no, no!" moaned Grace as she bowed her head, fearing the inevitable. But so great had been the bull's thrust against the wagon bed, coupled with the weight of the great Majestic cookstove in resisting it, that it gave the wagon weight enough to knock the bull back on his haunches. The horses, taking the bits in their teeth, lunged to the right in their plunge headlong toward water. This turned the front wheel enough to bring the protecting cover of the wagon next to Arthur and at the same time keep the bull on his haunches as it pushed against him. He could not make another charge on Arthur, but turned his attention in another direction.

"Mama, Mama! He is goring Old Bessie!" came a shrill voice from the region of the horses' hind feet. She looked down to see the scared face of Arthur looking up at her. He was clutching the wagon tongue by which he was being dragged along until the horses reached the muddy brink of the water hole. By the time the horses had sunk their lathering nostrils in the muddy water, Arthur had pulled himself into the wagon. Grace knew what she must do.

"Hold the horses," she commanded Arthur handing him the lines. Pushing the other four whimpering children deep within the sheltering confines of the covered wagon, she got the big butcher knife with its foot-long blade. This she hurled point down so that it stuck into the ground just behind the wagon. She slid over the dashboard, and dropped as silently as the knife. Before she had time to think she found herself beside the knife on the ground. She put the big knife blade crosswise between her teeth—lips spread to avoid its sharp edge. Crawling stealthily beneath the wagon, she scooted around the chicken coop swinging beneath and climbed on to the back of the wagon. Then reaching up quickly, she cut the rope that fastened Old Bessie to the tailgate. The wildly mooing cow, thus released, backed away from her tormentor. The angry bull, spying Grace beneath the wagon, backed up to gain force for his anticipated charge on her.

Paralyzed, Grace sat staring as the bull snorted toward her. The smell of his hot breath in her face was a warning of what was to come but from which she had no strength to escape.

She was so frightened that she scarcely felt the bang of his head against her, but the impact of his great shoulders against the tailgate slammed the wagon forward against the rumps of the unwary horses and sent them forward into the cool depths of the watering hole.

There they stood, knee deep in mud, savoring their new source of drink, when a second butt of the bull's head knocked the water can from its shelf at the tailgate. It came rolling to the brink of the pool and poured out the remaining gallon or so of clear water into the muddy waters.

A third charge knocked Grace out from under the shelter of the wagon.

The bull, recovering his lost balance, backed up and charged straight at her amid the children's screams of terror.

With one swooping stroke Grace extended the point of the knife blade toward the on-rushing bull. The power of his head struck Grace on the chest, knocking her backward where she rolled in a state of stupor to the muddy bank of the pool under the wagon—but not before the knife blade found its way into the creature's gullet.

Puzzled as much as pained by this turn of events, the bull, like a stoic champion of a Spanish bullring, seemed to save face by saucily whipping his tail in disdain over his back as he trotted off across the prairie after his second choice target, Old Bessie.

Not because she wanted to do so, but rather because she had no strength left to do otherwise, Grace lay quietly on the bank of the water hole. After a little while she dipped her cupped hands into its depths to drag up some of the muddy brew in which she bathed her burning face.

In a delayed response, Grace heard the cries coming from the wagon. She lifted her tired body up and over the dashboard and

69

into the wagon seat with numbed arms. There she fell face downward in the seat while all five youngsters packed themselves upon and around her.

"I'm all right, I'm all right," she whispered to whomever might be listening. Having no more strength for sound, her sagging hulk shook with silent sobs while the children continued to soothe her. Finally she lifted her head and looked at each of them in gratitude. It was clear how much each of them needed her.

"We can't stay here." She barely breathed the words. "This is the only watering hole in miles and that won't be the only bull to know its whereabouts."

As she was talking she began gathering her abundance of black hair and fashioning it into one long braid down her back, instead of the usual knob on the top of her head.

"I'll leave the hairpins go. We'd never find them anyway in this mud."

"Gee, Mama, you look like a girl that way." Lester offered as he patted the muddy shoulder of her tattered dress.

"Mama, can't we just get our feet wet?" begged Letha as Grace prepared to "gee-haw" the now satisfied horses out of the puddle from which they showed no inclination to remove themselves. She looked toward the departing back of the bull finding relief for his agony by prodding the eastward fleeing form of Old Bessie.

To make sure it was safe, Grace stood in the seat of the wagon, shielded her eyes from the sun and looked long in every direction. Finding no enemy in sight in any direction, she said, "Yes, you may dabble your feet, but do be careful not to fall in. You don't all want to look like me."

The children's normal liveliness returned. They jabbered with excitement as they climbed out of the wagon, pushing and shoving each other to be the first to the coolness of the puddle.

Letha, who had forgotten about the stickers in her buttocks with the threat of the bull, suddenly recalled them when she tried to sit on the bank. She jerked, yelled—and slipped down into the mud at the edge of the water. She sat where she landed looking up at Grace with the expression "What's the use to get up—I'm already muddy." She would surely have cried had not Grace at

70

that moment thrown her a kiss on two muddy fingers, saying, "Now we are twins."

This pleased Letha so much that she giggled the first time since she had met up with the cactus. She got up and waded knee deep into the water. The other children followed her.

Grace, thinking that since she already looked like a girl, she might as well act like one, got down from the wagon with Victor in her arms. She sat on the ground and took off her shoes and long black stockings and dangled her feet in this prairie bathtub along with those of her children and the quiet resting horses, while Victor tugged at her mud-splashed breasts.

It was hard to pull themselves and the horses away from this great fun in the mud. But Grace expected at any minute to see a whole herd of thirsty bulls charge down upon them and urged them out.

In the hope of finding enough water in the fallen can to remove some of the mud from their bodies, Grace sent Arthur under the wagon to bring her the can. One scant panful remained, held back by the narrow neck of the can.

Grace remembered there would be no milk for supper now that the cow was given up to the wilds. "Poor Bessie," she moaned.

"Gone back to tell Papa on that bad old bull," Lester said.

Grace noticed that Letha had not complained once about stickers since her bottom got covered with mud. So she decided to leave this mud-pack on her when they used water from the precious supply to tidy themselves up a bit.

Mud-soaked clothes were exchanged for their remaining clean garments, with tall grass and sage serving as partitions for their traditional privacy. Then they climbed with revived spirits into the wagon to resume their journey.

After two hours Grace began to watch for a campsite. No shelter of any kind was available so finally she decided on the best possible open spot. As she stopped the team, they noticed a pile of bleached bones—gruesome reminders of failure to combat the elements, and the children instinctively huddled around her. To divert their attention, Grace pointed out a striking phenomenon in the west. Streaks of faint gray tinged with soft warm

71

colors streamed from the lowering sun to the horizon. Finding it a strange, inverse image, Grace said, "Look. The sun is drawing water from the earth."

"God is still busy answering people's prayers to take the floods away," Lester said quietly. "As soon as He gets them prayers answered then He will answer our prayers for some new water."

"Those prayers," Grace quickly corrected, but regretted it. Out of the mouths of her babes perhaps she would learn yet to be patient even with God—to take her turn instead of thinking God had only her prayers to answer.

When Grace unhitched the tired horses and Arthur had put them on the tether ropes to graze, she noticed that now it took several tries before either horse could roll over. Old Roany rolled only once, lying quietly on the grass a long time before deciding to get up and graze. Grace wished she could lie in the grass beside them, but there was work to be done.

When she started getting out the supplies she noticed that not too much meat was left—no bread and only three potatoes. She decided, much as she hated to, she had better kill one of the chickens and use that for supper along with plenty of flapjacks for bread. But when she looked beneath the wagon the chickens were gone. Only the empty chicken coop with its wire door hanging open greeted her sight. The intended meat must have escaped during the furor at the water hole or along the way since leaving there.

Well, if it isn't one worry it is two, she said to herself remembering that there would be no milk either. We've lost Old Tudy, Bessie, most of our water supply, and all of our chickens. But at least we're all still together if a little worse for the wear, she preached to herself, I must be thankful for that. And soon we'll be with my father . . . and someday John will be joining us as well.

She made plenty of flapjacks and fried the last of the ham, and the children did not notice the shortage of anything but milk. Grace ate sparingly. After all, she reckoned she had plenty stored in her husky body. But even Victor noticed the shortage of milk, for apparently she had been too tired to make a new supply for his supper.

They bedded down in the wagon at the close of day, Grace with the idea of sleeping "with one eye open" as she had tried the night before. But with the lack of sleep and the draining events of the day, she could not. Thankfully, the night passed peacefully. The next thing she knew, she woke with a start to face the bold sun of a bright new morning. Thankfully, her breasts ached with a new supply of milk for Victor.

Chapter 8

Lost Creek

Arthur woke slowly, gradually remembering his newly gained status of being the man of the family. He had been dreaming about his beloved Grandpa whom they would hopefully find soon. In his dream, Grandpa had been walking down a road looking for them. Had spotted them from a distance and was waving madly at them. But, sadly, it was only a dream because they weren't even on a road yet, and even if they were Grandpa was almost blind now and wouldn't be able to see them from a distance.

He lay there half-awake, thinking fondly of Grandpa. Although he'd grown up with two grandfathers close at hand, Mama's pa had always been his favorite. He had usually, though silently, sided with him and his compatriots, the rebels of the South, when he fought the Civil War with Yankee Grandfather Barnet—which happened almost every evening back in Blackwell.

"Didn't the North win fairly?" he recalled Grandfather Barnet's voice demanding one evening. He had meant with that question, to put end to all arguments, as he got up, walked down the brick path which led to his canoe moored on the dock, and unfastened it to go to his house across the waters. He'd had the last word.

"NO!" thundered Grandpa. "You didn't win fairly." This was like a cannon ball and it hit its mark more squarely than had it been fired forty years earlier on the actual battlefield—a fateful shot that had changed his family's destiny as truly as any shot fired during the Civil War.

"We did win fairly," shouted Grandfather dropping the canoe's mooring rope. The canoe began to float downstream as he charged back to continue battle with the enemy. "You and your

75

old muzzle loading Kentucky muskets lost the battle to us Northerners fair and square. Not only because we were right, but because we had sense enough to use a good breach-loading, repeating rifle against your old muzzleloaders. If you'd been wearing the blue uniform, you wouldn't have those powder burns in your eyes."

He might as well have waved a red flag in the face of a bull as a blue uniform before the old gray confederate soldier. The reference to Grandpa's failing eyesight due to those burns was the final shot. Mama had to pull them apart from their fighting in the creek, and after that, Grandpa decided he would take no more insults and left the next morning for western Oklahoma.

Arthur had hid behind the house and cried when he left. He felt bad that he'd not told him good-bye. Grandpa probably would have understood his tears, but he didn't want Papa or Grandfather Barnet to see them. He would make it up to Grandpa when they got to his house in Waynoka. He couldn't wait to tell him how he could now shoot his gun. Grandpa had given it to Mama because he couldn't see well enough to shoot anymore, but hopefully he would still be able to see well enough to tell how well his grandson could shoot it. If not, at least he could hear the shots, and hear the bottle shattering or the tin cans pinging that Arthur would set up along the fence.

Arthur lifted his head to the peephole and looked out. The morning sun struck his face like the fire through the peephole of one of the kilns back in Blackwell. Brilliant flames fanned out in a myriad of multicolored waves, a fiery promise of torrid heat for the day.

If only we had enough water, we could take the heat, Arthur thought. Well, we'll have to take it anyway, since there was no way out. But please, God, could they get to Grandpa's soon.

Arthur got up, put his shoes on and found Mama at the wagon, rummaging through the remaining stores of food, muttering and taking inventory. "Only enough bacon for one meal, three potatoes, a quart of flour and a small jar of grease left from last night's fried ham. Just seven gallons of water. No milk and no eggs. A jar of applesauce, and a jar of jelly.

"I guess we'll have flapjacks," she announced to Arthur.

76

"Get Lester and see what you can find in the way of fuel."

There was plenty of sagebrush for starting the fire, but the only fuel they could find to make enough fire to cook the flapjacks was the bleached pile of aging bones. Once they got it started with dried sagebrush, it burned a steady, intense heat—perfect for flapjacks.

They ate breakfast quickly, then loaded up, anxious to pull out of the bleak campsite. Mama clicked the reins and they moved on, leaving the remaining stack of bones, topped with a skull, to stare back at them as they drove off.

Arthur found himself welcoming the familiar jostling, jolting and swaying of the wagon.

As the temperature climbed, Mama countered the usual mid-morning bickering by spreading a layer of jelly over a leftover flapjack for each child, folding it over, and tossing it to each of them as a bone to a dog. The jelly, crumbs and grease were soon spread over their faces and clothes. Amazingly for Mama, cleanliness no longer seemed important.

Arthur sat in his new lookout post, but as Mama drove the team, the tall brown grasses, swaying gently in the hot wind as if to a lullaby, all but rocked Arthur to sleep.

Suddenly he spotted something in the distance—a racing feather of dust winging its way from the west directly toward them. He stood full height in the seat the better to see what caused it. Two horsemen were racing full speed across the prairie and were now separated from them by only a shallow ravine.

"Indians again," Mama stated calmly. She sat down quickly, snatched the muzzleloader with her right hand from the front of the dashboard, while passing the baby like a hotcake with her left hand to Letha.

When the riders crossed the ravine, they zigzagged back and forth, crossing and re-crossing each other's path so that when one came toward the left of the wagon the other came toward the right of it. The maddening thing was that neither stayed on one side more than three horse leaps before exchanging sides with the other.

Arthur, still in somewhat of a stupor from the swaying grasses, now became completely mesmerized. Mama dropped the gun across her lap, stopped the horses and seemed to brace herself for the inevitable.

"You children are to say nothing, absolutely nothing, just as Mr. Comfort advised us. Do you hear? Say nothing at all! Show no fear and don't move a muscle. I will answer any questions they ask if I think they need to be answered."

Once they had agreed, she added, "Now close your eyes, bow your heads and repeat with me "The Lord is my Shepherd . . ."

They bowed their heads and chanted as the riders approached.

"He maketh me to lie down in green pastures. He leadeth me beside the still waters . . ."

But a sudden movement caught Arthur's eye and he gasped in spite of himself. Stopping at the heads of the horses, one of the riders jerked the lines from Mama's hands. He now had hold of Old Sam's bridle as he posted his pony between the heads of the team, his gun in hand.

The other man grabbed the gun from Mama's lap. She raised her head slowly and looked him squarely in the eyes. His eyes dropped to the old muzzleloader. He turned it first one way and then the other, trying to find the cartridge breach.

Arthur remembered Grandfather goading Grandpa by saying that not even an Indian would be foolish enough to use an old blunderbuss like his—it was too heavy and too awkward to load. Apparently he was right. This man had obviously never seen one of them. When he could find no breach to open, he growled and attempted to break it across his upraised knee. The jolt fired the gun with such a loud and unexpected bang that his pony bolted throwing him into the tall grass.

The pony began running in circles with shrill neighs. His owner put two fingers to his mouth and gave forth with an ear-splitting whistle that brought the pony prancing dutifully to his side.

Mama sat wide-eyed and silent. Arthur and the rest of them, except the screaming baby, followed her example.

The Indian re-mounted his pony and came back to the wagon. He peered across Mama's shoulder into the back where

Lester and May were crouched, and with squinted eyes searched the layout, while his silent companion remained on guard at the heads of the horses.

"Where is your man?" he demanded.

Mama made no answer, no move.

"Where is your man?" he asked again, this time his question accompanied by a sharp jab to her ribs.

Assuming his same tone Mama answered, "He is coming—from the East. He follows." Of course, Mama didn't tell him that they didn't know how long it would be before Papa followed, nor by what route he would come.

The Indian wheeled his pony, jabbered something to his companion, and they both bolted toward the east.

"Indians," Arthur scornfully said out of the stillness. "Who's afraid of Indians?"

"The Indians are afraid of Papa!" said Letha, proudly. "When they heard he was coming they ran like 'fraidy cats."

"I'm thirsty," May whined.

Mama gave each child a sup of water with a promise of a cupful for supper.

She urged the wagon westward again. As they topped a sudden rise, Arthur stood up in the wagon seat again to scan the prairie in all directions. No more Indians were in sight. These must have been the same two they had seen before and the two who in the night had come back past their camp. Maybe they were just curious. Apparently they meant no real harm.

No sign of life at all now—man or beast. But then, what was that he saw? Yes, treetops in the distance! He pointed them out to Mama who grinned and clucked the team forward. But the poor tired beasts would not be hurried.

Over a few more slight rises in the terrain, the treetops now appeared tall but scraggly with few limbs and a few sickly leaves. Hopes of finding water diminished as the distance closed between them. They could now see white sand, marking the bottom of what had been a small creek. A lack of small trees and brush along the bank confirmed that it had been a long time since any water had passed there. A crudely printed wooden sign was nailed haphazardly to one of the ailing chinaberry trees.

"Lost Creek," Mama read out loud, "Or does it say Last Creek?"

"Which is it?" Arthur asked.

"Well, I would say it is certainly lost. We can only hope it is not the last one," she replied.

"So we are lost, aren't we Mama?" The fatalistic tone of Arthur's voice expressed the weariness they were feeling. Past the stage of being disappointed at not finding water, they were almost to the point of it not making any difference if they were lost. They hardly felt anything at all.

Arthur had been thinking all day that they might be lost. Back in Blackwell, Mama said she expected to make the trip in six days at most. This was the middle of the sixth day and no sign of civilization was in sight. Arthur checked the shadows. Yes, they were headed due west.

May was crying for food and another drink of water. Arthur noticed the lather under the horses' harnesses. Mama must have seen it too.

"We will eat here and you may play in the white sand," she announced.

They all climbed out, but with no enthusiasm for the dry sand.

Arthur unhitched the horses and gave each a panful of water before he tethered them out to grass. They both lay down, but neither of them tried to roll. Arthur looked at them worriedly.

He helped Mama build a fire in the sandy creek bed with some fallen branches and gnarled roots she chopped from the dead trees. Some strips of bacon, three potatoes fried and some flapjacks—that was their dinner. According to the morning's inventory that left only the jar of applesauce and a little jelly to go—with more flapjacks for supper. Breakfast? Well, that is another day. Maybe evening would see them at their destination.

They ate, but it was not a happy meal. Even Lester was beginning to get sullen and, if crossed at all, they flailed out at each other with fists as well as words.

They had a cupful of water each and the poor horses were served the wash water as their second helping, which they seemed to like, asking for more.

80

"Scarcely a gallon of water remains," Mama told them as they climbed back into the wagon. "You may have no more now."

Less than a mile westward, just as they crossed another erosion gully and started up another rise, steeper and higher than any they had come to before, Arthur spotted tall spires of smoke rising above the hills beyond. Waynoka was a railroad town. Perhaps that was smoke from an approaching train!

A flick of something bright caught the tail of his left eye. He swung his head in that direction. Around the sloping south end of the hill—a fire! In a flash it came roaring along, leaping and careening, flying on wings of soaring, dipping, twisting prairie grass, whipped by the wind, heralded by rolling fiery balls of tumbleweeds spit out from the mouth of the raging, smoke-blinding fire.

Across the draw to the south of them it bounded, its bright flames reaching out in front licking its lips as it devoured the dry grass before it. Wild animals: wolves, coyotes, rabbits, large and small, birds, lizards, snakes were in full flight before the roaring inferno, paying no heed to their natural enemies.

The family joined the stampede. Mama turned the horses around and headed them eastward swatting their backs with resounding whacks using the flailing lines in an attempt to get them into a lope.

They must get to somewhere safe—and quickly!

"To the creek, to the sandy creek bed," Mama shouted. But the team was too spent for speed.

At that moment, ahead of them dashed the two Indian riders again, leaning forward on the forward-stretched backs of their mounts like streaming arrows pointing directly into the oncoming rushing flames. They ripped off their shirts, bent down and dipped them in the fire, then swooped towards the sandy creek bed. Dragging his flaming shirt, one of them created a huge circle of fire. The other dashed within it and lit a smaller circle of flame. He escaped to the north just before the ends of the larger circle joined hands.

Leaping flames were now fanning out around the hillside towards them. At the top of the hill fingers of fire seemed to

81

point toward the stranded family saying, "Over there they are—get 'em, get 'em."

The riders dashed to the covered wagon with such speed that when they reined in, their pop-eyed ponies reared straight up with snorting spires of nostrils, twirling on hind legs. They then closed in one on each side of the now panicked wagon team. Each rider grabbed a ring at the end of the bridle bits, hugged their ponies close to the sides of the leaping team, and pushed them against the wagon tongue. Under the plunging strength of all the animals, the wagon moved forward.

The men steered and dragged the wagon within the still smoldering circular spot they had just burned, and to the sands of the creek bed. As the wildfire reached their burned circle, it parted as dancing partners do, bowing right and left, and swept around the small burned island, joining hands again as it passed the circle—leaving the precious cargo cringing in the center engulfed in smoke, but unharmed.

While Mama had been turning the team around, Arthur had pulled baby Victor from her lap and, sliding him into the swinging bunk behind the seat, was now hovering over him. Lester and his two sisters were huddled under the wagon seat silent and immobile as baby quail.

The leaping team had knocked Mama over backward on top of Arthur and Victor. There she lay too exhausted from fright and exertion to move. Screams from the baby brought one of the riders to investigate.

"Fool squaw," he said as he grabbed Mama by both legs and dragged her weight off the two children and back onto the seat. Then he reached into the bunk, pulled Arthur back, lifted the baby by the front of his clothes, dropped him with a thud into Mama's lap, then returned to help calm the team still rearing, pawing and stomping in the sands beneath their feet.

Arthur jumped out of the wagon and threw himself face down on the sands of the Lost Creek, his arms outstretched as if hugging an old friend. The men unhitched the team, tethering each horse to a tree. That done, they proceeded to ransack the contents of the covered wagon, making every possible tone of disgust at the family's lack of provisions.

Then one of the men rode off, while the other stayed with the family by the wagon. Mama sat still, letting him take charge showing in her face a strange mixture of fear and gratitude. After a while he signaled Arthur and the children to go with him to gather fuel for a fire to cook supper. Everything around them was burned save some recent, moist cow chips they found in the sandy creek bed. The Indian pointed to the chips, ordering his little scouts to pick the chips up and carry them back to the campsite.

The Indian stood straight and tall, watching his adopted tribe do his bidding with the same air of detachment as an army officer commanding his foot soldiers. When he signaled that sufficient chips had been gathered, he made a large pile of the driest ones, set them on fire by kicking some smoldering embers and replenishing the fire with fresh chips as needed.

By this time the other man returned walking along the creek bed with two singed rabbits fastened together and slung across the withers of his pony. Old Bessie lagged behind singed-to-the-hide, led by the frayed remnant of the rope Mama had cut the day before.

The whole family danced with jubilation around the quiet cow, reaching out to feel her sagging udder and pulling on her smoke-blackened teats—rejoicing gleefully when drops of milk obliged by oozing their way out. Then Mama lay on her side in the sand, baby Victor busily tugging to find his own comforting drop of milk.

Suddenly the two dead rabbits landed squarely at Mama's feet. Mama sat up startled.

"Clean 'em!" said the donor.

What was so surprising was not only the order, but the sound of the voice giving the order. Those two clipped words told Arthur that the man was no Indian—just plain Yankee!

Then his eyes fastened on the hand that released the rabbits. It was missing a thumb and one finger. Three-fingered Dick, the outlaw!

Mama was staring at his hand too, but she kept calm. "I've not got the slightest notion how to clean them. Show me and I will do it."

Without a word the outlaw jumped from his pony, grabbed a rabbit and skinned it with lightning speed. Mama leaned forward to watch. She stood up, putting the baby on the sand, grabbed the other rabbit and gave her best effort to imitate the man's deft movements. Her feeble efforts did nothing but scatter fur into the moist exposed flesh of the rabbit. With exaggerated disgust, the man pulled the rabbit from her and completed the chore.

He didn't bother asking her to remove the entrails, but pulled a jack knife from his pocket, slit the rabbits' bellies with sweeping strokes like an apt farmer at butchering time. Arthur watched his every move. With like speed the man pulled out the guts of the animals, tossing them away from the campsite. Mama shivered but kept her gaze on the dripping forms of the hapless rabbits.

The Indian, squatting on his heels by the burning embers of the campfire, received the naked rabbits in his soot-grimed, cow chip soiled hands and laid them on the embers of the fire. He took an unburned cow chip and, using it as a coal shovel, heaped some of the embers on top of the sizzling, smoking rabbit flesh. Then before Mama's horrified eyes he covered them with some of the moister cow chips, forming a smoldering fireplace in which to braise the meat.

The Indian was squatting on his heels poking at the fire when he suddenly jerked as he felt something crawling up inside one of his pants legs. Quick as greased lightning he undid the buttons down the front of his pants, jumped out of them in one leap and stood before them all completely in the raw from the waist down. Mama shielded her eyes. He shook the pants and a tarantula with singed legs dropped out. "Damn," said the Indian as it hobbled its way into the grass.

Little May had followed the sailing entrails to their landing spot. Arthur, Letha, and Lester now ringed around the discarded viscera, watching every movement caused by little May as she probed them with a charred stick, trying to discover what had once made the dead rabbits alive.

"Children!" Mama's scream startled them so much they all but fell headlong into what they had been so intently examining.

84

"Come here this minute!"

They came, but reluctantly. Why was Mama, who encouraged them to explore the mysteries of life, suddenly so angry?

The Indian was leisurely climbing back into his trousers. Once buttoned, he pushed the smoking, smoldering cow chips from the charred rabbits. He stuck his long knife blade into one of them and removed the speared flesh to cool. His companion speared the other carcass and the two rabbits found their destiny as twin offerings lying across the wagon tongue.

Mama was ordered to milk the cow. This time she did not need to say that she did not know how. She tenderly approached Old Bessie, no doubt wishing she could wash her first as usual, but set straight to work milking. The silent, brooding cow was too weary to resist, but she tensed to the tugs on her scorched udder and teats. Try as Mama might, only about a quart came out.

Still, a quart is a quart in any liquid, and she happily divided it into four parts. The three-fingered man picked up each tin cup and poured a little from each into a fifth. He picked up the wailing baby and put the cup to his lips. His stance showed that he was prepared to do so, but he did not need to force the cup's contents down the hungry throat. He put the child back on the sand and went to help the Indian carve up the rabbits.

As a charred piece was removed from a carcass, Arthur could see that the flesh was still red inside. Mama would not approve of this.

A piece was handed to each of them ringed about like hungry puppies. Had they tails, no doubt they would have been wagging them. After the children were all served, the Indian picked up in his grimy hand what remained of one rabbit and thrust it at Mama with a grunt. She drew back, would have refused it, but his eyes told her he would do to her what his companion would have done to the baby had he refused the cup of milk. She glanced over at Victor now fast asleep on the sand, his aching stomach full. Mama knew he needed her nourishment.

She took the meat gingerly from the Indian and began turning it this way and that in her fingertips. She looked at the pieces being devoured by the rest of them so greedily. They certainly saw nothing wrong with it. Still she examined the food carefully, as if at any moment she expected to see a giant dinosaur germ crawling about on it.

The Indian, apparently thinking Mama so ignorant she didn't know how to eat the meat, grabbed up his piece in both hands, and bit viciously into it with his yellowed teeth, pulling with all the might of his jaws, grunting as if to say "do like this" and chewed lustily on the big piece of flesh.

Mama closed her eyes and took a tentative bite of rabbit, then another. Obviously her stomach was not as squeamish as her mind. She devoured it.

There was no wash water, so the family wiped their smeared hands on their clothes as did the Indian and his companion.

Silent now, stomachs filled with real life-giving food for the first time in twenty-four hours, all sat or hunkered about on the sand in the empty creek bed. They were content for the first time in days. May began to hum a little tune.

Grace, now humbled but fed, listening to her daughter's humming, felt strangely relieved. For the first time in their long journey, she was no longer in charge. She sat pensively, looking over her benefactors. The bronzed greasy face of the Indian was ugly to her, with no part of it outstanding in ugliness beyond another. His clothing, with at least several weeks' supply of sweat, dust, and food drippings, was disgusting. But his body, now reclined in the sand, was a symphony of composed ease, quiet, yet, she knew, capable of lightning swift movement at the right cue.

But it was in his hands that her eyes found real interest. Her enormous love of beauty could appreciate the long, pointed and sinewy fingers beneath the grime. Their joints were as small and flexible as a woman's yet held the strength of a man's.

She suddenly saw him as a person as generous as any she had ever encountered. While she would gladly have sacrificed herself, as would most women, for her children, this "uncouth" creature, roughened and pummeled by harsh circumstances not of his own making, risked self-sacrifice for a family that had been nothing but hostile to him.

She thought of the men who had come and gone as oil field workers near their brickyard at Blackwell. She had despised them all for their untidy appearances and uncouth manners. She wondered if she'd been too quick to judge them. Maybe a clean exterior and polished manners didn't make the man after all.

Her reformed attitude, however, did not extend to the Indian's companion. Three-fingered Dick seemed but a faint carbon copy of his Indian friend, fuzzy about the edges. But since the Indian was clearly in charge, she gave up worrying about having an outlaw in her company.

Nightfall came like a friend. Mama would have put the children to bed in the wagon as usual, but the Indian looked up at the stars and smiled. He went to the wagon, got the family's bedding, and spread it upon the inviting sands of the creek bed.

The members of the family stretched gratefully upon their pallets without objection or fear. Somehow the commanding presence of the Indian was reassuring.

Three-fingered Dick stretched out as guard at one end of the continuous bunk, and the Indian at the other end. And it mattered not at all that the Indian began snoring only five feet away from where Grace lay, where she could get full scent of his sweaty body as she slept soundly all night long.

Chapter 9

West End of the Rainbow

Rays from the rising sun flickered through Grace's wavering eyelashes like soft tickle grass teasing a sleepy-headed child to wakefulness. It was but a dreamy illusion. She opened her eyes to see only tiny sprouts of green fingers stiffly holding the burned stubble of the prairie grass. Then, she remembered the terror of yesterday and the reason she was sleeping outside.

When she tried to pull herself from her hard pallet, every muscle in her still-tired body screamed in protest. She propped herself up on her elbow and counted the sleeping children. Yes, they were all there.

The men and their ponies were gone.

She bolted upright as if she had swallowed the ramrod of the muzzleloader. Her clamped jaw worked to hold it there and push the terror from her mind.

She boosted her heavy, aching body to her feet and looked about quickly. Thank God, the team of horses was still there, straining against the pull of their ropes to nibble on the new growth.

The cow was lying placidly chewing her cud amid the circle of her grazing spot now stripped of its green sprouts. Surely this would help her milk supply.

The words of the Lord's Prayer sprang from her lips. When she came to "forgive us our debts as we forgive our debtors," she could go no further. The two men she had judged so harshly by their appearance and manner had turned out to be their benevolent keepers. She might never be able to repay these strangers, but she prayed that from this day she would look first for good in people instead of expecting to be wronged.

She knew without looking that the small quantity of food—the quart of apple sauce and a few cups of flour—would be untouched in the wagon. Their benefactors would not give so generously with one hand and take away so little with the other.

The children came to life on their pallets, sniffing the morning air like small puppies trying to identify the odor left over from the night.

"Where are the men?" Arthur asked, as all the children looked wonderingly about at the peculiar world in which they found themselves.

"They have gone to find us some food and water," Grace tried to say reasonably. And she knew—hoped at least—that it was true.

"Will we starve if they don't come back?" Letha demanded to know.

"I'm hungry. Why can't we eat now?" May said before Grace could find an answer.

Lester had climbed into the wagon saying nothing.

Not wanting to transmit her fear to the children, Grace struggled to make a reasonable reassuring answer to both Letha and May. But before she could answer, Lester called out. He stood in the wagon, a big smile on his face, gallantly holding aloft a jar of applesauce. Lester, the quiet one, never demanding an answer to the unanswerable, but never accepting defeat. No, Letha wouldn't starve, and May would have her food. Mama's heart filled with pride and love for him.

"Flapjacks and apple sauce," Grace said happily as she handed the baby to May, grabbed the milk pail and ran hopefully to Old Bessie. Sure enough, fresh milk squirted into the pail. While she milked, Arthur re-staked the horses where they could breakfast on the new grass. Then with Lester's help he gathered the dry grass stubble to kindle a cow chip fire. As Letha bent over to blow on the fire, great chunks of dried mud cracked and dropped from her bottom. May giggled and pointed, but no one said anything.

The huddled family was eating happily at last when they saw the Indian returning across the prairie. He rode up and before his pony had even stopped, landed on his feet by the smoldering campfire. In his hand he held what Grace took to be a squirrel without its bushy tail.

"Ground squirrel," he said. "No rabbits. No nothin' left. Wolf, coyote come back in night, eat all dead ones." He shook his head as if in apology as he looked at his meager contribution to the meal.

After a glance at Grace, he quickly skinned and cleaned it himself. He buried it in the red-hot coals of the fire while Grace cooked him some flapjacks in the skillet on top of them. He watched the operation dubiously, but after a tentative first bite, ate the flapjacks and applesauce like a much-pleased baby with its first sugar teat.

When he had finished he pulled the ground squirrel from the fire, but it had shrunk to almost nothing. He tore flesh from the tiny bones handing a bite to each child. Grace cringed as he carefully licked his fingers between each tearing, handing her the last bite. As he began to gnaw the bones, he looked at the kicking baby lying on his pallet. He pulled off the leg bone and stuck it into the baby's mouth.

Grace gritted her teeth but said nothing as she silently choked down her own bite of meat. Victor himself could not have been more pleased, cooing and drooling over his prize.

The Indian made no effort to help them get ready for departure. He made no explanation of Three-fingered-Dick's whereabouts or why he did not return for breakfast. He simply hunkered on his heels, leaned against a tree and carefully looked over each and every member of the family, the dilapidated cow, the obviously thirsty horses. His eyes kept following the small clods of mud that continued to fall from beneath Letha's dress. He picked up a piece and crunched it in his hand. He picked up a piece of cow chip and did the same comparing the two. Then, like a stroke of lightning he reached out and grabbed Letha, turned her over his legs and flipped up her dress tail.

Letha screamed and kicked, but he pinioned her legs between his own and continued to examine her inflamed, festered spots.

All the children screamed at the outrage. Mama lunged for him like the bull at the waterhole had charged at the boys.

"Obscene brute!" she yelled.

He scarcely looked up at Grace as her feet landed in front of

91

him. He hooked a foot behind hers, jerked them forward and simultaneously gave her a brutal shove with his widespread hand. She was flat on her back on the ground before she knew what was happening.

"Damn fool!" he shouted.

At this moment Letha bit him on his hip.

He jumped up and released her, sending the girl sprawling on top of Grace.

"Damn!" he exploded, feeling the place where Letha's teeth had taken hold. He jumped back from this human pack now howling like prairie wolves. He whirled around and barked back over his shoulder, "Damn—I try to help."

It was well he seemed to know only one American cuss word, Grace thought. She could think of a few more herself at this point, but she decided not to add to his vocabulary.

They all stood helplessly watching what he might be doing now. He stooped over a spreading cactus, deftly snipped off several lobes with his jack knife, jabbed the blade through all of them and carried the lobes past them toward the wagon.

He moved to the wagon and she followed him, the children hanging to her torn and tattered dress tail. He laid the cactus lobes on the wagon tongue, neither looking up nor acknowledging the family's presence.

Shame crept over Grace. Only an hour ago she had silently promised she would be less quick to think evil of someone, especially a man who had gone to such extremes to show kindness. And here she was again—her children too—fighting this one who only wanted to help.

Having skinned the cactus lobes, he took the blade of his knife in his hand and pounded with the handle, beating the cactus flesh into pulp. Done, he reached for Letha again, but she screamed and he dropped his hand to his side. He looked at her with eyes of flint, and turned to Mama.

"You," he said, "take stickers out." He pointed to the cactus pulp with one hand and put the other to his own buttocks.

Grace resolutely went to the wagon and got one of Victor's diapers. She walked back to the wagon tongue and sat down on it with her back to the others.

92

"Letha Faye," she said. "Come here."

Letha crept past the Indian to her mother.

"Lie across my lap so I can put this on you, and don't let me hear a whimper out of you. This is medicine to take those stickers out and make the sores get well."

With a sigh of defeat Letha lay across Mama's lap. The Indian leaned across her shoulder and occasionally lent a hand in pushing the pulp tight against Letha's flesh.

When Mama put the diaper on Letha to hold the poultice firmly in place, her usually brave daughter whimpered in humiliation. But the soothing ointment soon made her smile with relief.

Thus, Grace added a procedure to her internship toward a degree in prairie medicine.

As Grace prepared again to start the day's journey, the Indian inquired, "Where go?"

"West to Waynoka," she pointed.

"No," he said, and he flicked his hand northwestward. He mounted his pony.

"Come," he said and led in the direction he had indicated. Without a word, she and the children climbed into the wagon and followed.

A two-hour drive brought them to the crest of the highest hill they had yet climbed. He stopped and Grace drove up beside him. He was studying the westward landscape with hand shielding his squinting eyes.

Grace stood in the seat and did the same.

"Prairie fire," she moaned as she saw a flowing line of smoke.

"No. Look!" the Indian replied. "Iron snortin' horse. W'nuka," and he pointed in the direction of the streak of smoke.

"The railroad! Waynoka!" Grace screamed forgetting to control herself before her children. She pointed out the streak of smoke to the children, laughing and yelling hysterically as she remained standing on the wagon seat. "Grandpa's claim! It's but a few hours drive away!" Only Lester's voice brought her back to her senses.

"Mama, we didn't even say 'thank you' to him."

93

When she turned in gratitude to their Indian guide, she saw him streaking eastward across the burned stubble.

She tried to urge the horses on, but they would not be urged. They had not received even a panful of water that morning and had had only a sniff the night before. Heads and tails drooping in fatigue, nostrils dilated, flanks heaving, beady dull eyes staring, the horses plodded on until they reached the dusty street of the railroad village with its scattered assortment of makeshift buildings.

Arthur, straining ahead with Mama, spotted a big waterspout poised over a large tank on the ground at a crossroad ahead.

"Water!" he cried.

With that one word, the three eldest piled out of the slowly rolling wagon, ran to the tank, bent over and cupped the precious liquid into their hands, and started to lap it up with their parched tongues.

"Don't drink that water!" Mama yelled at them. "Wait 'til I get there!"

The horses could not hurry even with the smell of water flaring their nostrils. They plodded to the tank and dropped their heads into the water like a steam shovel. They gulped the water, lifted their noses for air and gulped again and again.

Arthur, Letha, and Lester hoisted themselves up and perched on the rim of the tank, kicked off their shoes, and plunged their feet in the water.

Mama sat May down between Arthur and Letha, and holding the squalling Victor under one arm like a feather pillow, she pumped fresh, cool water from the spout above for the children to drink. Once she got it going, it fell in a steady stream into the tank. The children squeezed up together on the edge of the tank like thirsty chickens. The water spilled down their faces and over their smoke-laden garments.

Not having the heart to send Arthur from the cooling spot, Grace untied Old Bessie from the back of the wagon and brought her to the water tank. The silly cow plunged her head into the water up to her eyes.

Grace began pumping more water to replenish the supply in the tank. She reached her hand into the stream coming from the pump and sloshed great handfuls of it across her tired, smoke-covered face. The children began to do likewise, and soon they began to look like striped zebras.

She tried to pull the team away, but they would not be budged. Neither could Old Bessie. Nor the children. But Grace wanted to find out if this place really was Waynoka, and if so, to find out where she could find her father's claim.

All at once Grace became aware of rollicking guffaws, coming from the front of a general merchandise store a short distance away. [1]

She turned to face them, ready to squelch whoever was laughing at her and her children. So what if they had grimy faces, dirty clothes, dirty bodies and disheveled hair?

Then she remembered her sacred promise—already broken—not to condemn or think evil of her fellow creatures too quickly or unfairly.

She saw a dozen or so dark-skinned men. They were not Indians—of that she was sure. But they were definitely laughing at her family. How dare they laugh when they were dirty-looking themselves? Anger seized her. She pushed it back. A promise was a promise and this time she meant to keep it.

She smiled at them and turned back to the children.

With her turn, screams of laughter and hip-slapping hilarity came from behind her.

Grace wheeled back toward that group of brown men, all thoughts of her promise thrown to the winds.

"Oh, Mama!" Letha said as she pointed to her backside, "your dress is all torn and they can see your flour sack panties!"

Grace grabbed at her skirt and looked. There blazoned across her ample buttocks was a big sunflower, which had been too stubborn to respond to the lye bleach, and just above the sunflower was the equally stubborn brand name, "Pride of Kansas."

For one moment she smoldered with enraged humiliation, but before she could decide which man to attack first, God's grace and humor came to her rescue. She laughed heartily and the children joined her in the joke. Perhaps her prayer did work after all.

She borrowed a safety pin from Victor's diaper, puckering

95

the material to the waistband of her dress where she pinned it.

This done, she literally pulled the horses and Old Bessie away from the watering tank. They came out snorting and blowing the water in heavy spray all over the already bedraggled children. She pulled the team to a hitch post in front of the store and tied them. She tied Old Bessie again to the back of the wagon where some of the curious gang snickered at the almost hairless cow.

Lifting her head regally, Grace walked quickly into the store without a word.

The lounging men outside the store were joined by others who came from every direction within hearing to see what the laughter might be about.

As a regiment following a marching leader, the children trooped after her into the store, followed by the crowd. For the most part they were now silent. But Grace refused to acknowledge their presence by the even slightest sign.

The storekeeper came out from the back of the store to greet this strange procession.

"Is this Waynoka?"

"Yes Ma'am. And what can I do for you?" The man's eyes implied he thought there was plenty that ought to be done.

"I am AdamYourt's daughter. Can you tell me how to find his claim?"

Surprise came to the man's face. He wheeled to the crowd.

"Unless you want to buy something, leave this lady and me alone to talk," and he nodded meaningfully toward the door.

The men strolled away silently. "Mexicans," he explained. "They are section hands for the railroad. They tend to hang around here when they've got no work. They mean no harm."

"The farm—where. . .?" Grace began, so eagerly she could not speak coherently.

"Oh yes," and he led her out of the store, past the loitering men and to the corner. Pointing west he said, "See that hotel at the end of the street? Turn to the right there until you come to the road that crosses it and goes over the railroad track. Turn left on that road and drive west just about two miles. The Yourt farm is on the north side of the road. You will see the neatly painted

96

white house before you get there."

"Thank you. Oh thank you," Grace said.

"Only two miles, only two miles, only two miles!" She galloped to the wagon in time to the words, "only two miles," the children joining in the chorus behind her. She jumped into the wagon with them, the girls in the back, the boys by her side. The replenished horses at last began picking up their feet.

The herd of men followed, accompanied by numerous dogs which sniffed about their feet.

As they passed the hotel they saw a tall, gaunt woman sitting on a long veranda which ran all the way across the south side of the hotel. As the woman grinned at the strange parade that was passing by, her mouth flashed of gold. Grace took quick stock of the woman displaying herself and her teeth on the hotel veranda and decided that it wasn't the passing of years alone that had made her look so worn out.

Mentally she slapped herself. Here she was thinking evil again with no reason other than her imagination. She turned toward the woman and smiled back at her. The woman grinned even more broadly and sure enough there were gold teeth standing end to end like brick in a drying area filling the expanse of her smile as far as the eye could see.

"And I thought we kept all our gold in the government's vault," she muttered.

"No, Mama," Arthur whispered. "It's in the river down by the brickyard. Don't you remember the outlaws lost it there when they took it from the bank?"

Grace laughed, once again grateful for humor.

As they crossed the railroad, she noted many lean-to sheds and patched up small hovels on the west side of the tracks in a fenced portion of the railroad right-of-way. Children, brown-skinned like the men following her, played in the dust or sat on doorsteps silently staring. Skinny brown women leaned on shanty sides or sat on doorsteps before doors that hung askew. They stared listlessly at the wagon as it passed down the road.

The men, still silently following her, began to drift in the direction of the shacks along the railroad track.

"Are those their homes?" Grace wondered, feeling superior.

Then shame and humility came over her. Though her former half-dugout may have been a mansion by comparison, now it was gone. At least these people had some shelter. She did not—not of her own at least. She only had the hope of her father's home.[2]

She urged the horses on.

"We are almost there," she told the children. They all strained their necks to see the house sooner and kept quiet as if any noise might scare the house away.

At last a house came into sight—squat and square it sat, neatly painted white. They all leaned forward breathlessly as Mama guided the horses into the road leading between the house and barn.

On the stoop of the house sat a square, squat man whose head was thatched with long white hair that hung to his shoulders. A white beard covered his chest. He was as neat as the house. Beside him sat a square, squat, white dog with a few black spots dropped here and there to distinguish him somewhat from the house and man.

A lone locust tree shaded the pair on the stoop from the bright rays of the noonday sun. The dog sat quietly with his muzzle laid across the knee of the man who was peacefully rocking back and forth.

The excited children began to squirm in their eagerness, like sprightly colts waiting to dash from the corral gate as soon as it is opened.

"He looks like Moses!" Letha said in wonder.

"He's Santa Claus without his red suit on," Lester said, and Grace thought how right he was as usual.

Soon Arthur jumped from the wagon and ran toward the house, screaming to the top of his lung capacity, "Grandpa, Grandpa," with every step he took.

The dog got to his feet, stood exactly in front of his master and growled menacingly, his tail stretching stiffly out behind. The man groped for the arm of his rocker, picked up the cane hanging over it and started haltingly forward.

He's gone completely blind now, Grace realized with a jolt. She paused there taking it in, one foot on the rim of the front wheel and the other yet in the wagon.

"Down, Noble. Down boy," Grandpa commanded the dog. The dog sat on his hunkers and whined, wagging his tail.

Arthur met Grandpa's outstretched arms with such force he all but knocked the staggering man down. Grandpa lifted him up so high his feet dangled.

"Arthur," he said as he set him down and crushed the boy to his chest. "You've grown so big." Then he began to shuffle off the stoop, Arthur finally leading him.

By this time Lester and Letha were out of the wagon and on their way to meet him. May's "I want him for my Grandpa too," brought Grace out of her trance. She took hold of May's out-stretched arms and swung her to the ground, and chubby May started her legs running.

Grace picked up Victor and followed her, sobbing, "Oh, Pa, Pa," with every step she took.

As father and daughter met in the sandy road, she placed the baby in his grandpa's arms where they both hugged him and each other, while the happy upturned faces of the children formed a jumping four-leafed clover about their legs. The dog sat on the stoop and beat the floorboard tom-tom with his tail in time with the children's steps.

"There, there, daughter," Grandpa said with comforting pats on her shoulders while Grace lay against him, her sobbing face mixed with his flowing beard.

"I'm so glad you came," he said. "But John—where is John?"

"Oh, Pa. He isn't with us," she sobbed anew. And then she rushed on saying, "The river washed away everything we had, and we were doing so well, I'll just have to tell you some other time," she finally said. "It was so awful. And you know how John is—so proud. He said he would come for us as soon as he makes enough money he won't have to come as a beggar."

They were walking toward the house. "I'd been wanting to see you again for so long," she continued, "So John agreed this was as good a time as any to do it."

His steps faltered by her side. She reached up and touched his eyes gently with her fingertips.

"Why didn't you tell me this?" she asked.

"I wanted you to come of your own free will whenever you could," he said, "not out of pity. I can fully understand John's pride."

"Yes, you two are peas in a pod. Why do you think I was drawn to him in the first place?"

Laughing gently he said, "Neither of us has ever been able to swallow past the place where pride gets stuck in our throats."

She kissed her father again for his forgiving nature. If only John were here. But would John ever be able to swallow his pride and come here to the farm?

"As for the flood, if it hurts you too much to talk of it— don't. Some things are best left unsaid," he told her.

They went inside and put Victor on the bed for his first luxurious nap in days. Suddenly Arthur burst into the house screaming, "Mama! Mama! Come quick. Old Roany fell down and is groaning. She is pulling Old Sam down too!"

Forgetting Grandpa, Grace dashed out to where the horse lay in the road. She'd never seen anything like it. Then, with a great snort, followed by shudder, Old Roany stretched herself in the sand of the road, and became motionless.

Arthur had led Grandpa to where the moaning horse lay. Grandpa leaned over, found a spot just back of her front leg and placed his ear on the horse's side. After a moment he lifted himself up and pronounced the horse dead.

The four children screamed in unison. Grace gulped as she felt the terrible pit of her stomach.

Usually stoic, Lester threw himself across the still form of the horse, and broke into uncontrollable sobs as his chubby arms hugged Old Roany's lifeless neck.

This will never do Grace thought. She lifted her quivering voice in song. "Praise God from whom all blessings flow, Praise him all creatures here below . . ."

All save Lester joined in the song.

Lester sat up and glared at all of them until they finished singing. "Why do you praise God for killing Old Roany?" he demanded.

"God didn't kill Old Roany," Mama said calmly. "I'm

100

praising God for keeping her alive until He got us here."

"I think you should praise Old Roany for that," Lester said as he pulled away from Mama and lay tenderly across the horse's side again, patting her lovingly.

Grace was puzzling over an answer when Grandpa came to her rescue. "Old Roany gave her life to get you here. Should we not praise God for giving us so wonderful a horse?"

Switching instantly to a believer, Lester jumped to his feet. "Then if Old Roany died for us just like Jesus did, I want to put a cross up for her, too!"

This posed a real problem. None of them could dig a grave big enough for the animal. Nor could they tell the child he could not mark the grave of the much-loved horse.

Old Sam was straining across the wagon tongue to nuzzle his lifeless mate. Again Grandpa's thoughts came quicker than Grace's.

"Let's take care of Old Sam before something happens to him," Grandpa said. Good thinking. This would give them time to decide just what was to be done about the other horse. But she knew she had better watch out or she'd be leaning on him for decisions she should be making herself.

Arthur, obviously determined to be his grandfather's eyes, led Grandpa, while Lester led Old Sam, to the barn.

When they returned to the house the spotted dog was standing guard by the fallen horse. The whole family loved him completely from that moment.

"What's his name?" May had to know.

"I call him Noble," Grandpa said. May tried to say the name, but what came out was "No-No".

Mama said, "Poor little May has heard 'No, no' so many times in her short life that any word that begins with "no" will probably always be No-No."

"No-no" became the dog's name from that time on.

But still there was the problem of the horse.

"Arthur and Lester, will you walk with me up the road a ways?" Grandpa asked. "We will get one of my neighbors to take care of Old Roany."

"Me go too!" said May.

"Say, I not me," Grace automatically corrected.

"May, darlin', why don't you stay here with the others and get dinner?" Grandpa said. "Arthur and I might come back mighty hungry. You can explore your new house."

Grandpa seemed to have a way with everyone. For they were indeed eager to see what was inside the front door.

That night a neighbor hauled Old Roany away and small Lester never knew that the mound on which he placed his crudely constructed cross the next morning was as empty as Christ's tomb.

Mama Grace
Part Two
1907-1917

Chapter 10

Grandpa's Claim

Grandpa was sitting in his rocker, but he couldn't rock. He sat in surrendered stillness, allowing his grandchildren to braid his flowing white locks. May was sitting astride his right leg. His right arm, resting on the arm of his rocker, encased her small waist. Lester was likewise seated and enfolded in his left arm. Between them they shared his beard, twisting and crudely weaving it as only small hands could do.

Arthur and Letha stood behind the rocker sharing the hair on his head—not always peacefully or equitably.

His worries that he wouldn't be able to keep the children straight in his mind had ceased. He was amazed at what a unique statement each child was. He didn't need eyes to tell.

Could he not tell by the very pulling that Arthur thought he loved Grandpa the most, and that he should have the larger share of the hair of his head?

Could he not tell by Letha's reluctance to concede such division that she contested Arthur's share—of love and hair—but was willing to concede either or both after a while for the sake of peace and her Grandpa's scalp?

Could he not tell by the peculiar twisting of his beard in tiny May's hands that she was not thinking one whit about how much hair was in her hands, but rather why his was the only face among them with the likes of such a glorious beard?

Could he not tell by the gentle manipulation of the beard in the hands of quiet Lester that he knew the hair was not divided equitably among them, and that he perhaps was not doing as good a job of braiding as Arthur and Letha, but that he was doing the very best he could and knew his Grandpa loved him just the same?

Could he not tell this business of braiding and re-braiding

was also a balm to the restlessness of his dauntless daughter, Grace. She who attempted to cover up the longing in her heart—the frequent trips throughout each day to the front window or door—by her almost constant and sometimes overloud singing of hymns.

So he just sat there taking comfort in the busy little hands and the babbling voices that were magical to him no matter what nonsense they spoke.

Baby Victor, too, he often took in his lap. Then he rocked, but for the baby's comfort, not his. And when Victor snatched his beard and it went in his mouth, he was content to wipe off the slobber later.

He had no toys for his grandchildren, but they didn't seem to miss them at all. Whenever they were restless, they played with his hair. They made rag dolls of it, weaving in scraps of material for colors, and played with these dolls on his lap, up his arms, and dancing on his shoulders.

This time they were fashioning his hair into Indian braids also entwined with colors, as Indian hair should be. Arthur and Letha went out into the yard and collected chicken feathers to aid in the over-all effect. He was their honored chief.

Noble, now answering fully to the name No-No, sat dutifully at his feet, accepting the gentle onslaught because his master did.

Sometimes Grandpa would announce that he wanted to take a nap, and stretch out on the floor. Then the children would lie beside him observing the spot on Grandpa's diaphragm he jokingly called his bellows, watching it rise and fall, expanding and receding with his great breaths made greater still because it made them laugh.

The sitting room with the rocker was the sacred place where they also gathered of an evening to play games— learning games of Grace's devising. It was also the room where they sang together. The room where the Bible occupied a place on the handmade lace doily on a box for a table, and featured nightly in Grace's teaching-learning activities.

Next to the sitting room was the kitchen, where Grace's big Majestic cookstove had happily been installed with help from the neighbors. There it lorded over all else in the room including the substantial plank table at which the children happily sat on benches or upended store boxes to eat their meals.

"Your Mama is a good cook," he often told the children. "Even if she can't skin a rabbit," and he winked in Grace's direction causing the children to giggle.

Homemade wooden beds now occupied the other two rooms of his house. Arthur, without leave from anyone, claiming his first right as Grandpa's guardian-guide, crawled into bed with him.

Lester, Letha and May were assigned the bed in the other room. Crowded in the room beside them was their Mama's four-poster, the envy of them all. For Grace had resourcefully rigged up a bed for herself and Victor. She used the sideboards of the upper deck of the covered wagon bed. These she nailed to the sides of four hackberry fence posts from the farm.

Over this frame she stretched a double thickness of the wagon canvas. This became the springs and mattress when she stuffed it with sweet smelling prairie hay. The hay was carried to the house in eager arms, the leavings trailing behind throughout the house. Grace didn't scold them for it, simply swept it up to add to the bed. Grandpa had raised his daughter to be resourceful and thrifty, and that she was.

To Letha, Grandpa's four-room house had seemed a mansion after being cooped up for over a week in the covered wagon. It remained so even during the summer while doors and windows were open—while all were busy in field, garden, cow lot or at play outside. But somehow with the coming of fall rains and winter snows, the rooms seemed to have shrunk.

Lucky Arthur got to sleep with Grandpa in his room, enjoying peace and quiet, aside from Grandpa's snoring, which Letha could hear clear into the bedroom stuffed to the rafters where she slept. Sharing a bed with Lester and wiggle-worm May was not easy. Cold nights brought on much bickering among the three of them as they wrestled with the blanket that covered them.

Because she was too small to hold her own in the tug-of-war over the blanket, May squeezed into the space between Letha and Lester. Letha and Lester settled on arranging themselves

107

jack-knife fashion in the bed. When they wanted to turn over, they had to do it in unison. As they tugged at the sparse blanket the better to cover whichever posterior was outermost at the moment, poor May was shivering in a tent between them.

When May began to whine and whimper, Letha and Lester took turns trying to shush her by putting their hands over her mouth. May retaliated by pinching any part of either of them which came within her reach.

Mama, trying to rest after a tiring day, soon grew tired of their cavorting in bed and they found themselves the recipients of lessons in proper, crowded, bedroom manners from Grandpa's long-unused razor strap.

After that, they had to solve their problem by pinching, kicking and pulling covers in near silence. Finally May hit on the scheme of crawling to the foot of the bed and sticking her cold feet between Letha and Lester. After they got used to this arrangement, it made sleeping three in a bed not so bad after all.

Sleeping together was just one of the adjustments they were forced to make at Grandpa's. They also had to learn a new way of talking to Grandpa so that he understood without seeing. Mama had explained that they needed to start making their words paint the picture of what they wished Grandpa to see and understand. Letha picked up the new language as easily as she would have chicken pox, and soon the rest of them caught it too.

Since Arthur had become Grandpa's seeing eye, and Grandpa loved to hear about beautiful things, many was the time Grandpa stood, feet braced apart, chest out, head up, enraptured as Arthur described a sunset, a sunrise, a prairie flower or bird. "How beautiful it is," Grandpa would exclaim. Letha was amazed and jealous of Arthur's devotion to Grandpa.

Once, as Grandpa stooped to smell a flower May had discovered, Letha was able to contribute something from her store of experience.

"Watch out! Watch out for that bee, Grandpa," she yelled. "He will sting you most awful." And she bravely, though cautiously, shooed the buzzing insect away.

"Do you know why you must be careful?" May inserted. "'Cause he sting you there," and she pinched him on his backside, "like he did Letha." Grandpa put on an exaggerated display of fear, surprise, and wonder much to the delight of them all.

Life with Grandpa was happy, but something was missing. As winter approached, still no word had come from Papa.

If Grandpa was puzzled, he never let on. Nor did Letha ever hear Mama mention any doubt that he would come. But, with time, she noticed Mama making more frequent trips to the door whenever she heard a sound and heaving out deeper sighs when she found nothing.

The other children missed Papa, of course, and they were less tactful about it than she and Grandpa.

"Is Papa here now?" they would yell and run to look, pushing Mama rudely aside when she went to the door, or to the window as the weather became chillier.

"Why he not come?" May asked.

"He has to get some money first, silly," smart-aleck Arthur replied.

Maybe he was helping the umbrella man hunt that gold in the river, was Letha's wishful thinking. Papa might be late, but when he did come, he would lug in a saddlebag of gold.

Lester made no reply, but the look on his face conveyed his opinion—Papa was wasting his time looking for money. They were happy here without it.

Grandpa was proud that the food he could offer them was plentiful. Several years of plowing the same fields near Waynoka had left him with a sixth sense of the lay of the land. He could plow the place despite his blindness. His faithful team, Sandy and Blaze, could possibly have done the job without human hand to hold the plow in the soil. Many times they had plowed the furrows, curved, rather than straight, because he had decided they would hold the "here-today and gone-tomorrow" prairie soil better that way.

He had not been alone before Grace and the children arrived. Neighbors, kindly all, had lent him a helping hand to get the crops planted the year before. They had planted corn for hog feed and some to dry for human use, kaffir[1] for chickens and cows, oats for horses. None too happily, the horses shared the

109

oats with the chickens—they couldn't keep the cackling greedy things from their manger and feed boxes.

Even now the corn and kaffir spots were green with wheat they had planted for winter pasture, and the haymow[2] was full to its pointed roof with prairie hay. Nor did the neighbors' efforts cease with the coming of six good pair of eyes, for it only meant more mouths to feed.

Grace, however, was not happy with the neighbors constantly nosing around the place. They never asked questions, but their knowing looks and too kindly voices made her uncomfortable. Even when she went to church, she felt their eyes on her and she longed to be able to hold her head up high with her husband at her side.

In time, however, Grace began to accept that she was going to have to make a life with her father for some time. She could no longer be a guest. She had to earn her keep. After all, she had her pride too. This spring the children could help with the gardening. Already last summer Grandpa had taught them to thump watermelons: that a "plink" meant not ripe and a "plunk" meant ready to eat!

After a winter of watching and waiting—and seeing Grandpa's fabric purse grow lankier—Grace decided that, although the arid soil produced what it could, there were other needed things it could not supply. Sugar, salt, coffee, even flour required cash. And she longed to bake nice things again in her marvelous Majestic.

With three cows now, there was more milk than could be consumed by the family. The hogs could slurp it up, yes. But they could very well do without it, too. Instead, the pigs could grunt, fight and guzzle the unlucky watermelons pronounced "plink" by the young "farm hands." And since Grandpa would never challenge their judgment, there were plenty.

Grace decided to take the excess milk to town and sell it. But how to get it there? Grandpa could not spare his team. Their one horse, Old Sam—fat and sleepy now from months of disuse and overeating—could not pull the wagon alone.

She was reduced to accepting help from a neighbor. One of

110

the post-adolescent young men, who had graduated from a pony cart to a buggy, lent her the cart to help her with her enterprise. Old Sam could easily furnish the one-horse power needed for this vehicle. With milk in a can set beside her on the seat of the cart, hope in her wistful heart, and a song on her determined lips, Grace set out for town.

Waynoka proved to be quite a different town from what she had experienced back in Blackwell. There, where most families were concerned with their struggling industries, they were happy to buy their produce.

But in Waynoka, everybody who was anybody had a cow of his own which pastured on the back of the family lot or was staked at the edge of town during the day. They had chickens, too, to gobble up their garbage and general refuse. Seldom would anyone in town need more milk or eggs than he or a neighbor could furnish.

This was a blow to Grace's financial ambitions. It took the song from her lips and set them in that same determined line displayed when crossing the prairie.

"There will be something," she said with clenched jaws.

She managed to sell a quart of milk for a nickel here and there with the promise of perhaps other quarts if the neighbor's cow began to dry in preparation for calving and could not supply their wants.

Grace started back across the railroad tracks with her can of milk, sloshing—destined for sour pig swill—and perhaps a quarter in her purse.

Along the railroad track once again she saw the sad, hungry, listless looking women and children in the Mexican quarter. That gave her an idea. If she couldn't sell the milk, she would *give* it to these poor families!

The idea made her happy, not because they were less fortunate than she, but because she had something to give them that no one else seemed to want and that she didn't need either. She could not stand to see anything go to waste.

Joyfully she offered the milk to the women who were as obviously hungry as their children were. So it came as a shock to her to find that these people, living in hovels she thought not fit

111

for Grandpa's hogs, had their pride too. The women refused to take the milk unless they paid for it, albeit with pennies.

Grace picked up a cent here and a cent there until her horse sense told her she had at last found a trail. Not too warm a trail, but if she followed it, it might yet bring her to enough cash to buy the necessities they could not raise on the farm. She remembered Benjamin Franklin's sage advice, "Take care of the pennies and the dollars will take care of themselves." She resolved to do just that!

The few pennies jingling against a few nickels in the sagging purse made a tuneful sound as she started toward home again. It was an odd thing, she mused, that the people whom she had scorned when she first arrived at the Waynoka water tank had now become her prized customers.

Suddenly, she had an inspiration!

"Those dry cows!" she shouted.

Old Sam's ears flicked back as if asking, "Yes, what about them?"

In reply he found himself being abruptly turned around in the sandy, dusty road.

And with a smart swat of the lines on his back, he broke into a brisk trot back to the homes where she had first sold the milk.

On the return, Grace did not urge Sam to trot because behind the cart ambled two cows heavy with calf. They were to be fed in the green pastures on Grandpa's farm, sharing the kaffir heads and fodder with their own cows until they freshened. The pay for their keep? One of the calves. She would thus build up her own herd at no cost. Of course the calf might be a bull, but that would be meat! Meat, which if not needed at home, could surely be sold in town.

Maybe God was a little short providing food, but he gave her a brain and she'd use it.

That spring Grace and her old Majestic were in their glory once again. The children sometimes had cookies, occasionally a fruit pie made from wild plums, grapes or gooseberries canned last summer and fall.

Grace put back the weight she had lost on the prairie—and then some. But did it matter when John was not forthcoming?

112

She might as well enjoy one of the few pleasures in life left to her!

As she cooked and ate, her mind churned over plans for her family's existence, wondering bitterly what her absent husband might be doing to recoup their finances—or further deplete them.

Maybe it wasn't neglect after all. Maybe he had such bad burns from the kiln fires that they had become infected and he was at death's door. But past that, she refused to go. She stopped in the middle of her work to say to herself, "He just can't be—"

No, of course he couldn't. He was alive and doing something for them and he would soon come. Maybe like Letha said—with a saddlebag of gold.

Hope! Silly hope, to soothe her jagged nerves.

During the first months of her waiting and watching as she went about the family chores, she thought perhaps John might have reestablished the brickyard at Blackwell. Or, if not that, then he was working in another brickyard nearby. Or had even stayed back east where he had taken his father's body.

With each passing month and no word of earnings, she began thinking darker and sillier thoughts. Maybe he's already reestablished the brickyard but is remaining in Blackwell because he is too busy having fun and spending our money cavorting with that shameless schoolteacher who still flashes her biggest and most fascinating smiles at the man whom I only caught on the rebound. The hussy's "good marriage" was just a public facade for the school board that hired her. John was still her secret lover.

If he wasn't with that woman, she reckoned John was spending his money on booze and cock-fighting. Her indignation boiled. She imagined a cockerel in the fighting ring, twisting himself this way and that, not only in his efforts to protect himself from his blood-thirsty antagonist, but to get in position to attack a weak spot in his adversary to his own blood-thirsty advantage. Sometimes she felt like one of those cockerels herself.

But somehow she would find the strength of body, mind, and spirit to carry on through the coming of the second winter on Grandpa's farm.

113

Chapter 11

Old Roany's Ghost

Grandpa felt the warm autumn sun upon his back. He was in the garden giving instructions to Arthur, Letha and Lester on how to gather the dried pods of beans so as not to crush them and spill out the beans inside.

Arthur bent over the bean bushes, following his instructions to the letter, and filling his gallon lard pail rapidly, his pods plopping rhythmically into his pail.

Lester, by contrast, stopped to rattle the beans in the pod before dropping them in his pail.

We all have more time than brains, Grandpa reminded himself. So he left the boy alone to gather the beans his way.

He knew by the sound coming from her pail that Letha was picking fewer beans than Arthur, but more than Lester. Sometimes she kept pace with Arthur, but often she stopped to rattle a pod with Lester, adding a girlish giggle. This didn't bother Grandpa either, for he figured that was the way she was bound to do things, being sandwiched in between the two boys and often the peacemaker between them.

May's hands were too small not to crunch the dry bean pods, so she soon became distracted. She squatted in a barren spot in the garden, intent upon something in the ground.

"Every little while, she hops forward like a rabbit," Lester reported as he stopped picking pods to see what was keeping her so occupied

"Why it do that?" May earnestly asked of Lester hopping beside her. As usual, Lester withheld any answer until he studied it a bit.

Grandpa heard May's question and strained to hear Lester's response.

"It's a funny streak of ground wiggling. It wiggles. It stops. It wiggles. It stops."

The two children continued to hop with each wiggle, and

115

stop with each stop.

"A mole must be under there." Grandpa told him.

"Mole? What's that?" May asked.

"A mole is a soft little animal which can't see in daylight, so he stays underground," he said.

"Like you, Grandpa?" May wanted to know.

"Grandpa doesn't stay under the ground," Lester corrected still focused on the moving streak.

But Grandpa smiled at May's quick observation. Those rapidly multiplying moles were the curse of his existence. They destroyed the fibrous roots, stole the field seeds as well as the garden seeds. There was no choice—the soft little creatures had to be destroyed. He had to make a living from his acres. He loved life of all kinds, but the moles, like weeds, must go.

"Which way is the little fellow going?" he asked.

"That way," pointed May.

"She means the way the eight o'clock train is going when we have to wait for it when we go to town," Lester explained.

Grandpa knew that meant the mole was going due north and that he was standing close to the west side of its lengthening burrow. He reached down and put a hand on Lester's forearm.

"The next time it wiggles, point to where the ground moves," he said to Lester.

As quick as Lester's point, Grandpa's foot shot out and he crushed the heel of his shoe down on the burrow behind the mole, leaving it trapped. It could not get past his heel to go in the direction it came from and was too cautious to burrow further.

He poked a hole with his cane into the soft earth in front of where his heel had been. He took a grain of corn from a section in his pocket purse where he would have kept folding money if he had any. Handing the grain to Lester, he said, "The mole is hungry and he is hunting something to eat. Put that grain of corn into the hole I made and cover it well so no bird or chicken will take it away."

It was corn he had soaked in water and arsenic for precisely an occasion like this. His conscience was not eased by the whimpers of little May.

"He's my mole. I want to feed him."

116

Lester would do strictly as bidden with the corn. But May could happily eat her weight in hominy. She might fudge a bit and put the corn into her own mouth. Or plant the corn and then put her fingers in her mouth to suck. However, he could not refuse the little fingers now prodding into his pocket to get corn.

He made another hole in the mole track with the guidance of the cane by Lester. He put a grain of corn into May's soft baby fingers and never relinquishing hold of hand or corn, guided its planting and covering. Then he wiped any trace of poison from her fingers onto his bandana handkerchief.

The children were happy and satisfied with their efforts to keep the mole from going hungry.

"Come on little May," he said, "Let's lie down for our nap now, and listen for moles." He spread out his jacket, and she snuggled beside him.

"Can we go to the peanut patch now?" asked Letha and Arthur who brought their pails and placed them beside Grandpa.

"Just remember what I said—don't eat any peanuts while they're still green."

Letha loved the way the peanut plants were piled and twisted with their bottoms turned up to the sun.

"Grandpa said they must be *cured* before hanging them in the haymow," said know-it-all Arthur.

"Cured of what?" she asked. Arthur just laughed at her.

Lester looked at the peculiar looking, swollen knots on the roots of the plants—a mixture of gray and brown.

"They don't look green to me."

"Go on, then. Take a taste," Arthur dared him.

Letha looked back and forth between them, and before she could decide what to say, Lester took a bite.

"Not too bad," he pronounced, and to prove it, ate a few more.

"Come on," Letha pleaded. "We'd better get back to Mama and do our before-dinner chores or we'll be in trouble."

They passed Grandpa and May happily curled up together in the warm afternoon sun.

Must be nice to be really old or young and not be Mama's

117

slaves, Letha thought. They picked up their pails of pea pods and trudged toward the house.

Just as Letha had expected, Mama was more than ready for their services. Being left alone in the house with Victor was becoming increasingly difficult. He was running all over the house now getting his hands into everything. She could barely keep up with washing dishes, milk buckets and cans, not to mention the family laundry. She complained she could hardly think whenever she tried to write out her grocery lists.

"Put your pails there by the door. Where's May?"

"Taking a nap with Grandpa."

"Here, Lester, you play with Victor," handing the baby to him. "Arthur, go take care of the animals, and mind the new cows . . ."

"Letha, you can help me get the front room ready for the evening's lessons." Putting materials in place for Mama's teaching-learning game was one chore Letha actually enjoyed. First there must be pennies to count and add for number lessons. And buckets for each child—even for little May—in which to put the shelled and counted beans. There must be a gunnysack for the discarded hulls to feed to the pigs since they were being deprived of their milk swill. She didn't forget the broom for clearing up the litter they would drop on the floor.

Letha spread a colorful Sears Roebuck catalog on the table before her. It made a perfect lesson reader—illustrated colorfully and profusely—combining the teaching of numbers and reading, ending with order blanks to complete for practicing their penmanship.

Every evening, after supper, no matter how hard or busy the day, the whole family gathered in the sitting room for lessons and fun.

Arthur as always stood on Mama's right side—the better for her to use her right hand to help him with his work. Letha stood on her other side, getting such help as Mama could give her from her left hand.

Lester had long ago pushed himself into the learning group. "In a little while I will go to school, and I need to learn something! You want me to go to school and be a little half-wit?"

"But can't you see, Lester, there just isn't room beside me for another learner."

"But Mama," he pointed out reasonably. "I can just sit right here." And he quietly stationed himself across the table from the others. And there he remained at every lesson.

As he sprawled across the table looking at everything upside down, he learned on his own. Unabashed about receiving no help, he made childish scrawls on a slate Grandpa had bought for him.

Mama had no time to test Lester's knowledge. Her job was to see to it that Letha and Arthur learned. They must not be behind their contemporaries when such time came that decent clothes were available and they could go to regular school.

Usually, Lester was content just to be there. But after dinner that night Lester was quarrelsome, something rare for him. He complained and cried, neither of which he ever did without just cause.

Mama took his temperature by putting her finger into his mouth, feeling under his arms, feeling the palms of his hands.

"I'm not sure. Maybe you have some fever. Maybe you should go on to bed."

Grandpa took him up to bed, while the others finished their lessons. He felt Lester's head, and it was indeed very warm. But poisoning doesn't give fever, he rationalized. He sat beside the boy, stroking his hair.

As he lay there listening to the boy's increasing groans, he was in agony himself.

I should have guided Lester's hand in the placing of that poison grain of corn just as I did May's even if it hurt his pride. Like his daughter, he sat and embellished on the thought, twisting his hands, pulling his beard, combing his long hair with agitated fingers.

Soon the rest of the children came up to bed. As the girls made ready to climb in with Lester, he could stand it no longer. He went to his bedroom door.

"Arthur, get up and dress quickly. We are going to town for Dr. McGinnis."

With Arthur driving them to town in the cart hitched behind Old Sam, Grandpa's thoughts kept pace with the steady beat of the horse's hooves in the sandy road. With each beat, he bent his head over further until his face was buried in his flowing beard.

Fortunately, Dr. McGinnis was home and set out with them immediately.

"I was careless this morning," Grandpa then confessed to the doctor as soon as they were back and Arthur had been dispatched to take care of Old Sam. "More than careless—criminal. I put into the hands of my dear little grandchild a grain of poison corn to put in a mole's hole. I felt sure he followed my instructions—he is a good lad—but it must be he did not. He must have eaten that grain of poison corn himself."

The disclosure must have worried the doctor, but Grandpa felt the doctor's words and voice were as steadying as the hand he felt under his shoulder. "You lead the way to the mole trail," the doctor said. "By the light of my lantern we will see whether that grain of corn is there—or the dead mole."

Grandpa tried to lead the way toward the garden spot, but his legs would scarcely hold his weight. The doctor held him up, pushed him along.

When they arrived at the spot, the doctor dug with a stick until he uncovered the body of the dead mole. Grandpa began moaning.

"There now friend," he said patting him, "your fears may be completely unfounded. Calm yourself."

"I gave May a grain to put in there. I held her baby hand and saw to it that she planted the grain, as I should have with Lester, and wiped any lingering trace of the poison from her fingers."

The doctor went back to probing in the soft soil. No grain was to be found.

"True, only one grain would have killed the mole, but he no doubt ate both before finishing his meal," the doctor said.

"Or else Lester—" Grandpa's voice broke.

Leading, dragging and pulling the old man, Dr. McGinnis got him back to the house as quickly as possible, guiding him to his bedroom, Grace at their heels.

"Put him to bed while I examine the child," the doctor told

120

her. "Give him one of these."

Grace did as the doctor directed, giving him a pill, trying to soothe, comfort, and assure him. "It's all right, Pa. Why are you so upset? The doctor is here."

He could not bring himself to tell her about the poisoned corn. He asked her instead to go to Lester's bed where the doctor was completing his diagnosis.

"As soon as you know anything, come back and tell me," he begged as he pushed his daughter away from his bedside.

He heard Arthur coming into the house from tending to the horse.

"Arthur, go to your room and stay with Grandpa," he heard Grace say. "Keep him in bed even if you have to lie across his body to do it."

Arthur came running to the bedroom. But Grandpa didn't need to be restrained by anyone. He was completely limp, without the strength to respond at all to Arthur except to snuggle against the boy as he climbed into bed beside him.

He lay there listening to what was going on. Grace ousted May and Letha from the sickroom so that the doctor might make a diagnosis without interruption with their "whys." They were in the kitchen taking care of a wailing Victor.

Grandpa strained to hear Dr. McGinnis' examination in the next room, but it seemed the doctor was getting no useful information from Lester. In fact, he seemed to be giving up, leaving the bedroom and walking with Grace toward the kitchen.

"Too bad we don't know what caused it," he said loudly. "I guess we'll just have to leave Lester alone to die."

"Like Old Roany?" Letha wailed at the doctor.

"PEANUTS!" came Lester's terrified voice from the next room.

Arthur threw the covers back and ran from the bedroom as if he could chase death itself away.

Dr. McGinnis walked quickly back to the bedside of his young patient, Grace close behind.

"I will not have you putting fear into the heads of my children," she yelled at him belligerently.

There was a moment of silence then came the doctor's voice

in an even tone. "Madam Barnet, do not try to tell me how to practice medicine. I have been at it since before you were born. Fear has a wholesome place in medical practice as well as in life. I daresay you use it as a parent. Fear is mentioned in the scriptures more times than love—and most of those references commend it to us."

Grace retreated to her father's bedside.

"I heard everything," he told her. "And I thank God that's all it is, for I thought I had poisoned him." He proceeded to tell her everything, at last sharing his silent burden. When he had finished, she took his hand and held it, while he drifted off into exhausted sleep.

Grace sat quietly beside her father, trying to get hold of herself. Never before had her knowledge—her interpretation of the Bible—been put in a questionable light. But according to the doctor's measuring stick, she knew herself to be somehow wanting. She knew it was not intentional, but she was wanting nonetheless.

She tucked the covers Arthur had left awry around her father, and headed straight for the well-worn Bible on the table in the sitting room. She brought it to the kitchen where May was being little mama to the whimpering Victor. Taking them both into her lap, with the Bible between them, she sat down at table and consulting the concordance, began getting acquainted with fear as taught in God's word.

Dr. McGinnis came from the room where Lester was at last asleep.

Grace carried her two youngest into the bedroom, unloading them from her arms into their respective places, returned to the sitting room and feeling shame over her outburst, shook the doctor's hand, resting her other hand on top of his.

"I'm afraid this is all the pay I can give you this time.

"Many's the time a doctor receives much less."[1]

"I will take you back to town," Grace said.

But before she could grab her wrap, a strange whinny announced the approach of someone.

She froze. Could it be John?

"I left word for the livery stable boy to come for me when he closed for the night," the doctor said.

"Of course," she said trying to keep the disappointment out of her voice.

She stood a while listening to them gallop away, then slowly turned to sit at the table and continue reading the scriptures about fear.

Arthur and Letha were hiding in the sanctuary of the hay-mow where they had taken refuge when they heard Lester yell PEANUTS. They were engaged in a careful review of the words pronounced by both Grandpa and Lester.

"I don't see why Grandpa thinks the peanuts are green," Arthur said. Letha heartily agreed.

They consoled each other with the thought that they really hadn't intended to harm Lester by encouraging him to eat the peanuts. It was just an experiment that had backfired.

They heard the horse drive away, and they knew the doctor was gone, but they decided to keep themselves buried in the sweet smelling hay and wait for developments from the house. No one called them. Why? Finally the stillness and the pitch blackness overtook their fear of the consequences. They climbed silently down the ladder from the haymow, stood by Old Sam's stall for a moment to feel his warmth, then slipped into the house and crept off to bed.

Arthur climbed back into bed with Grandpa. He could not understand not being reprimanded in some way. Mama had been sitting there in plain sight at the kitchen table reading her Bible. She didn't look up as they came into the house, said not one word to them.

Knowing Mama, she would come up with something and he would find out what it was in the morning. It was some time before he went off to sleep.

Chapter 12

Dashing Stranger

The next morning Arthur lay in bed long after Grandpa had risen, dressed, and gone into the kitchen. By now Mama would have figured out what their punishment for letting Lester eat green peanuts would be. He dreaded making his entry into the kitchen to hear the pronouncement, but he heard his stomach growl and he definitely needed some breakfast.

How could Lester have been so silly as to eat the peanuts? And people were always saying Lester was the wise one. Was it because he had dared him? How could Lester have been so stupid as to fall for that?

"How are you this morning, daughter?" he heard Grandpa say. Arthur slipped in while they were talking.

Letha was sitting at the table looking as miserable as he felt.

"Say, look here—you're putting on a little weight," Grandpa observed.

"Ah, I thought I could get away with it now without your ever noticing." She laughed, but no real mirth was in it. "As for how I feel—numb and dumb. How do you feel, Pa?"

"Daughter, I feel like a cow after eating loco weed."

"Well, you look like one too. Walking bent to one side like one leg was shorter, practically walking in circles."

At that point Lester entered the kitchen. "Here comes another wobbly. You'd think he had eaten loco weed instead of green peanuts."

"Better loco than dead," Lester said solemnly.

Mama started, then laughed. She gave him a little swat that signaled to him "I'm glad you're alive and you learned your lesson, but don't ever scare me like that again." He shot a glance to Arthur, who began to relax a little. Maybe they were off the hook?

Letha got up from the table and picked up Victor, and placed him astride her hip, her arms about him.

125

"Letha, I've told you not to carry Victor. He's getting too heavy for you—especially on your hip."

"First thing you know you'll be walking in circles like a loco'ed cow, too," Grandpa teased her.

"Oh, I think this whole family is loco," Arthur said.

"All but you, of course," amended Mama.

For breakfast meditation, Mama read Isaiah 14:3. "And it shall come to pass in the day, that the Lord shall give thee rest from all thy sorrows, and from thy fears."

She made no comment.

Arthur and Letha exchanged glances. Neither said a word.

Grandpa sat in his high-backed, cane-bottomed chair. Lester pulled up his box beside him. Arthur noticed how blue veins stood out at Grandpa's fair-skinned temples. The fingers of his delicate though worn hands nervously interlocked and then unlocked on the plaid tablecloth. As Lester leaned up against him, Grandpa put a shaky arm around his shoulder.

Mama looked at the two of them and announced, "I don't think either of you is in a condition to go outdoors today."

May was busy feeding Victor graham gruel, dividing equally with him the bites from her bowl. She loved to spoil her baby brother.

"Victor can feed himself," Mama said to her.

She took the spoon from May and handed it to Victor.

"Here, Victor," she said. "Take this spoon like a man and feed yourself." That was the line she always used on Lester and Arthur, but would it work on Victor?

"May do it," he demanded.

"Looks like we're bringing up one man who will like to be waited on," Grandpa said, laughing.

Mama frowned at him and said evenly, "I don't want to encourage it. He never does anything for himself if he can get someone to do it for him. Like riding piggyback, when he has two perfectly good legs."

Mama was right. The girls had spoiled him. He held out his hands and pointed to what he wanted. They got it for him. He wheedled, whined, batted his big blue eyes and long lashes in order to get them to do whatever he wanted. Especially May,

126

who with Victor's current demand, quickly came to his defense.

"He take too big a bite by himself and get the bellyache," she said, continuing to feed him.

"Say, takes—he takes," Mama corrected, "and don't say bellyache—say stomach ache."

"The doctor said bellyache," Letha pointed out.

Mama got up from the table. "When you get to be a doctor, you may say bellyache," she said crossly. "Until then, say stomach ache."

Letha seemed struck by the possibility. "A doctor?" she considered, followed by a definite "No. I want to be a teacher."

Mama walked over beside Grandpa to refill his coffee mug. She sighed deeply, wearily.

"Why don't you write another letter . . ." Grandpa began.

"All my letters have come back from Blackwell marked unclaimed. It's no use."

Grandpa reached out and put his hand gently on her arm.

She fled toward the door and opened it to escape.

Letha followed her. "Is Papa coming, Mama?" she cried, as she tried to find space beside Mama in the doorway.

"He is not coming!" Mama said fiercely.

Letha returned to the table. Once again, Mama had spoken. But this time, it bothered them more than usual.

Mama stood straight in the doorway scenting the autumn air, listening.

Grandpa went to the door and stood beside her, his arm around her shoulder.

"I do wish I had given your address to someone else in Blackwell," she said to him.

She turned to him. "Trade places with me today, Pa," she said. "I have been staying in the house too long. I need to get outdoors. Get my fingers into the soil. Clear my thoughts. Decide my next course of action," she said.

"Of course, daughter. Do what you need to do."

Mama busied herself clearing away the breakfast things while giving them their instructions.

"Here, May, you wear my big apron today." She folded the apron around the waistband three times to make it short enough for May and tied it around her with just her shoe tips showing beneath it.

"How would you like to be Mama today and stay in the house and take care of Lester and Grandpa while Arthur, Letha and I go do the outside work?"

At this, Arthur tensed and flicked a glance toward Letha. But they said nothing.

May was delighted to stay in the house. "What about Baby Victor?"

"You will have to take care of Victor too," Mama said. "That is part of a mama's job."

May was even more delighted. She giggled and twisted her fat little self all about the kitchen.

Victor was on Grandpa's knee pretending Grandpa was a horse.

"Here Victor, you can play you are a horse in the pasture," Mama said knowing Grandpa could not stand too much rowdiness today. Mama tied a cornered diaper about his waist and tied another like it to the one about his waist. This became the horse tether rope she tied to the arm of Grandpa's rocker.

"Now you are the horse on a rope in the pasture where you can graze and then lie down and roll over and rest," Mama told him.

To Grandpa she said, "If anything goes wrong and you need me, take off the tie cloth and wave it to me from the front porch."

"I can do that," Lester volunteered.

Mama gave him a smile and a nod, then turned to Arthur and Letha, who were refraining from their usual fussing while they washed the breakfast dishes.

"You two get a couple of gallon pails. Go to the haymow, look over the vines tied to the rafters and find the driest peanuts, not the green—that means raw—ones. We will roast them in the oven sometime today so they will be safe and good to eat tonight at lesson time."

Arthur and Letha got the pails. As they passed Mama on the way out the door she gave a hug to each. No words were said, but now Arthur knew it was a closed issue. He smiled at Letha in

128

relief.

"When they come back in, tell them they may help me in the garden," she said over her shoulder to Grandpa as she left the house. "I'll be digging sweet potatoes."

As Grace dug the moist earth in the garden, her mind was split three ways:

First, on the simple, healthy feeling of digging sweet potatoes.

Secondly, on keeping an eye on the house and hoping everything was all right there. No flag had appeared yet.

But mostly her mind was at work making plans for their future. She had given up hoping for John. John was dead. Her heart felt suspended in the vacuum.

As she dug deeper, she nicked her shoe toe and bruised her foot with a glancing blade of the shovel.

"Damn!" It felt glorious to curse out loud with no children around. "If only my body was as numb as my heart," she added with a moan.

Her precious minutes of freedom were soon over. As she leaned on the shovel and rubbed the top of her injured foot against the back of her other leg, Letha and Arthur were racing to the garden spot.

"Grandpa said to tell you everything is fine in the house, " breathless Letha said as she outran Arthur.

Then as Grace dug up the sweet potatoes they popped them into their gallon pails, arguing over who had the most. Back to normal so soon, thought Grace.

"Keep the cut ones and we will eat them first before they rot," Mama instructed. "The others we will put in the haymow before the chickens get to them. Spread them out when you get them up there so they don't touch each other or they will rot before we get them cured."

She put down the shovel and started for the house. "Take only a few potatoes in a bucket up the ladder at one time. And be careful not to fall."

When Grace entered the kitchen, she found Grandpa rocking quietly back and forth. Lester and May were playing on their stomachs on the floor near him, Victor still tethered to Grandpa's chair.

May was holding a black cricket in her cupped hands. Lester was using dominoes to build a house for the cricket modeled like the brick kilns he had seen Papa build.

Victor waited each time until the house was built, and then he punched one domino near the bottom and the whole house fell. He laughed in glee each time. Lester only smiled each time he rebuilt the structure.

May jumped up when she saw Grace standing by Grandpa's chair watching them.

"You can quit now Lester," she said. "All I wanted was a house to keep the cricket in 'til I could ask Mama something."

She turned to Grace and held out her hand. The cricket jumped out of her hand. But instead of jumping straight ahead, it jumped slightly to the left.

"Why did he do that?" May asked.

Mama stooped to look at the floundering cricket.

"One of his hind legs is gone. He can't push hard enough on that side and so he turns in that direction when he tries to hop," she explained.

"Oh," said May. "Like a loco cow. Poor little cricket."

Lester lay quietly on the floor, glad to be released from house building activity.

Victor, who was untied now, chased the poor cricket about the kitchen trying to catch it. He gave up quickly and turned to May. "Get me him," he said. May obliged, but not too willingly. She twisted her plump little figure about as if hoping the cricket would somehow find a way out. But it didn't. With a sigh she handed the "poor cricket" over to Victor.

Grace sat down on the arm of Grandpa's chair. "Pa," she said, "I have decided that I am going to file on a quarter section of land."

Grace took him by surprise. "A married woman can't do that, daughter."

"Yes, she can if she is not living with her husband." That was the law and he knew it—he had just hoped his daughter

130

didn't. He had no answer.

"And another thing, Pa. You filed on only 80 acres. Could you file on another 80?"

"I don't know for sure—think so, but Ekans can tell me," he said.

They sat quietly without speaking for a minute or two. Grandpa asked, "What's your plan, daughter?"

"I want you to file on the 80 that joins on the north of your west 40 acres. I will file on the other 80 in that quarter section as well as the 80 in the quarter section joining that to the east. That will give us 320 acres right together."

"But daughter, you'd have to live on your land and I have to live here another year before I can prove up." [1]

She had thought of that too. "We can get the neighbors to help us move this house where it will rest on the corner of this 80, the corner of the other 80 I want you to file on, and the place where my 160 acres join them."

He puzzled over that a minute. "I don't think that arrangement will satisfy the law."

"It satisfies the law for those no-good land ticks who ride herd for some ranchers. They file on several quarter sections of land and then build a house just like I have mentioned, with a door opening on each quarter section. When they prove up, they sell the land to the rancher. That is the way they do it all the time," she said.

Grandpa knew that, too. Again his daughter took him by surprise. He sat and rocked. He wanted to help her out. But for one thing, she was working too hard as it was. For another, he just couldn't help her with something that smacked so plainly of crookedness.

"That is crooked no matter what the cattlemen and land ticks do," he said. "I can't let you do it."

"It is crooked the way they do it," she said. "But I don't plan to sell you my land, so don't get your greedy hands out so soon," she teased with a quick brush of her cheek to his, and then pleaded, "Please Pa."

"I won't promise anything except that I'll think it over. We'll see . . ."

131

He sat in thought a few minutes.

"But all that land is worthless," he continued. "Just rolling sandhills and sagebrush. If it were good for anything it would have been filed on long ago. What can you possibly want with it?"

"It's being pretty well used for cow pasture by people who don't own it," she said. "And that is just what I want it for. I want a pasture big enough to pasture every cow in Waynoka during her dry period if her owner has no farm of his own to put her on.

"And I want to get a good bull to service those cows."

With this bold statement she blushed, even though Grandpa's eyes could not see her.

Grandpa let out a big laugh, slapped the arm of his chair and said, "What a financier my little girl has turned into."

"I'm going to need to be," she said. "I need to buy clothes for three children—two at least right away—so they can get into school. They need to learn things I can't teach them."

Grandpa couldn't argue with that, so he started rocking again. He didn't say yes, and he didn't say no.

Grace was hopeful again. She had a plan. A focus. Her spirits returned. Just in time to join the neighbors in the community effort of the harvest. Their sidewise glances didn't bother her anymore. She knew that in just a matter of time her children would return to school and she could hold her head up high again.

Then, just as she was beginning to relish being in control of her life again, the event she'd longed for, given up on, and vowed to live without—happened.

Above the clamor of clearing the supper table one evening, she heard hoof beats. She froze in her tracks, then managed to put down the plate she was holding.

Arthur and May heard it too. They dashed to the door and Grace filled in behind them. There in the road leading to the house came a prancing, shiny black horse. The horse arched its neck, arched its tail, and took dainty mincing steps as it danced in the same spot at the bidding of its rider. The man commanding the horse rode as if he were part of it. Their prancing brought the dust of the road up in a cloud to settle on the rider's neat blue serge suit. He took off his big white felt hat with the furrow down the middle of it and used it to beat the dust off his well-tailored suit.

With his hat off, Letha and Arthur recognized him. "Papa, Papa," they screamed as they ran toward him. "Mama, Papa is here," they yelled back over their shoulders as they ran.

Lester, May, and Victor pushed each other out the door and ran to him as he slid from his finely tooled saddle to the dusty road.

Grace stood leaning against the doorjamb. She made no sound. It was hard to believe the man she saw was the same man who had stood watching them leave for the west. The image she had carried with her from that day was of a man whose clothes were stained, torn almost to tatters, whose arms were bandaged to cover the burns made by the hot falling bricks. A bandage was about his head, bruises on his face. One eye was almost swollen shut.

He had been handsome even in his bandages, but look at him now. She loved him then—and she loved him now. A tornadic wind was sucked into her heart filling the vacuum created by his long absence. The wind swept away all the doubts, the hopes, the plans. Her every thought was replaced by the face of this "dashing stranger."

The children grabbed and hugged him, but their eyes were on the beautiful horse, the beautiful saddle. Their feet were on his polished shoes.

"Here, here. You're all acting like a bunch of cattle on a stampede."

They pulled back, obviously confused.

John looked up and saw Grace at the door. "I meant no offense. I was only trying to talk cowboy talk with them," he called to her.

"It's not a language they have learned," she called back.

He got back on the thoroughbred horse and began to make it prance about before the eyes of the wondering children. He was still the same old show-off.

133

"Papa, Papa," they kept screaming as they too pranced about.

"Is it John, daughter?" Grandpa was now beside her.

"Yes," she whispered, but she made no move to go to him.

"What's the matter, daughter? Is your heart dead?"

"No, Pa. It's my feet," and she giggled weakly. He gave her a swat to propel her forward.

Suddenly she felt her legs running and heard her voice screaming, "Oh John, John. Why have you been so long?"

He slid from his horse and caught her in his arms. She began to beat on his back with her fists.

"I told you I would not come until I had enough money to bring with me so that all of you would be proud of me," he said holding her tightly to him. "You'll never find me coming to you like a whipped pup with its tail between its legs," he chuckled as he tried to hold her still so he could kiss her.

"You are the best-looking Papa in the whole world," Letha said.

Treating him as if he were a knight in shining armor caused him to preen all the more.

Then Arthur ran to the faltering, staggering old man coming out the doorway and began to guide him toward Papa.

"Your father—"

"He is almost blind."

"Blind," John said in mock outrage. "You mean all this," motioning to his new suit, the horse and saddle, "for nothing?"

Though he had tried to make a joke of it, a grip like a vice clenched Grace's heart. The show was meant for her father, not for her. Her eyes swiftly took inventory. What he had spent for his outfit—the best and the latest in fashion—and for the thoroughbred horse and hand-tooled saddle, would have clothed all of them well and left some to spare.

Her eyes turned to survey his face. Spider-web tracings were at the corners of his eyes. Mill wheel lines spread out from around his thin-lipped, set mouth. Disappointment was in his eyes. But his strong arms were about her.

As always with his touch, her heart became like mush. The hard burning kiss was John's, too.

134

"Oh, John, John," she wailed. "I am so glad you are here at last." And she sobbed uncontrollably on the front of his brand new suit.

By this time Arthur had brought Grandpa to the group in the dusty road.

"What do you mean living in this God-forsaken part of the country?" Papa greeted Grandpa as he continued to flick the dust from his clothes and shake the sand from the cuffs of his trousers.

"God never made anything for nothing," he said to John, shaking his hand warmly. "He made the top of this land so worthless, I'm sure he put something worthwhile under it. You're just the one I've been looking for to come along and discover the oil I know must be here the same as they found up in the edge of Kansas. Welcome to our home."

Oil. She should have known. That's why Grandpa was holding out on her.

"Yes, I know about that Kansan oil field," she heard John say. "That's where I've been working. But this land doesn't look like oil land to me. It's as near nothing as I ever laid eyes on."

So they each had their own plan. But she was damned if after all she'd been through she was going to let them settle it without her.

That evening Grandpa insisted that she and John take his bed while he and Arthur moved to the floor of the sitting room. May was graduated from the foot of Arthur and Letha's bed to the head of Mama's bed to sleep with Victor.

Grace waited until all were settled and the house was quiet before going in to John. All those months of her longing ended in disappointment. There were no words of endearment. His need was too urgent. It felt briefly uncomfortable, briefly pleasant, and over in a flash. Lying there with her returned husband snoring beside her, she felt just as angry and lonely, if not more so, as when he was absent. The only thing she gained from the encounter was the possibility that she could be pregnant again.

Chapter 13

Clipped Wings

Five days of tramping about the farm with Grandpa and the children did nothing to enhance the land in John's estimation.

"The monotony of this kind of existence would drive me mad," he declared over and over.

He often turned to look back at where they had been. Not a trace of a track was ever in sight. The sand slithered into each footprint as soon as the foot was lifted. He only knew he had been anywhere because his feet hurt and the shine on his shoes was completely sanded away.

The kind of soil he liked stayed put when you shaped it —good red clay a man could hold in his hand and mold into something.

But now the children were clamoring to show him just one more thing—the loft in the haymow—which he had looked at three times already in as many days.

"My feet just can't stand another step in this sand," he told them. "I'm going in the house and talk to Mama."

He found Grace bustling about getting dinner ready. She smiled at him. Just seeing her made him feel better. He bent down to take off his shoes.

Grace smiled because she was happy that John was with the family at last, and happy because the children had taken to him so readily. It was as if he had not been gone at all.

But she was happy in an annoyed sort of way.

Mostly she was annoyed because of John's comment last night when she suggested to him that he file on the 160 acres near Grandpa's place—the ones she had planned on filing on herself when John's arrival was taking so long.

His derisive laugh alone was a trifle too much for her, but what had really stiffened her backbone was his reply.

"The one sliver of edible vegetation on that land is only fit

137

for goats and jack rabbits. Our kids seem to have learned to get about like jack rabbits, but plague-taked[1] if I'm ready to become some sort of goat."

His chuckle accorded these words a semblance of a joke, but his final words belied any joke. "You can forget about filing a claim. I will hear no more about it."

And though Grace relied on her Mama-has-spoken technique, she resented his coming in at the eleventh hour with his "Papa-has-spoken."

And just to rub things in, he was no sooner here than he began noisily pounding the ashes from his corncob pipe on the corner of the cookstove—when he knew how much that annoyed her.

Right now she was annoyed because the moment he entered the kitchen he shook the sand out of his shoes into a small mound in front of the stove where he had dragged Grandpa's chair. After putting the scuffed footwear back on his feet, he placed them on the reservoir of the stove, tilted back in Grandpa's chair, and started grumbling about the condition the sand had made of his shoes.

He got no sort of rise out of her, because she was determined to control her annoyance. There he sat like a king on his throne, puffing his pipe while sand continued to trickle from the cuffs of his trousers adding more mounds on the floor and more to her annoyance. Worse, she had to walk around him, tilted there in the chair, every time she wanted anything from the cupboard, and when she walked around him he blew a smoke ring toward her face. This last act of insolence annoyed her almost to the point of explosion, and the more annoyed her expression became, the more she could tell he enjoyed his little act.

"I'm only being playful."

"Well I'm busy and in no playful mood." Indeed, she was in a mood to get to the point and get something settled about their plans for the future.

Grace was about to speak when Letha bounded into the kitchen and skipped her way over to where Mama was cooking.

"Oh, goodie," she said, "We are going to have two kinds of meat today! We didn't yesterday, Papa, when you were gone."

138

It was true. Yesterday when Papa had saddled his horse and gone off to town alone, they had eaten their usual simple meal at noon. In fact, they had hardly noticed what they were eating because they were too busy pouting that Papa hadn't wanted to take them. He had returned with a stick of peppermint candy for each of them, but with no explanation of why he was gone.

"Run along, Letha, and set the table," Grace said. She turned to Papa and remarked pointedly, "She knows we only have two meats when we have company."

"COMPANY?" Papa barked, banging the front legs of the chair down on the floor. Letha jumped and Mama cringed. "You're referring to me as company?"

Grace mumbled an apology, but in truth that is exactly how she thought of him—company. In agitation she dashed to the cupboard, to the stove, and to the table several times before she finally settled down to finishing the meal.

As she stirred the gravy, the nagging question returned. Just what had John gone to town for? She had the biggest notion in the world to ask him. Yet she held back as she would with a stranger, afraid of seeming to pry into his business even if it did concern all of them.

Without another word, John sat down. And while Grace was occupied with gravy, she could feel him making a silent appraisal of her—something else that had annoyed her since his arrival. His eyes always seemed to follow her about the room. Yes, she knew she had put on weight, but how did she know he was going to turn up?

The children, having heard the outburst, filed in and quietly took their places around the table. A dreadful silence filled the kitchen.

John turned his attention to his children, sizing them up. Good-looking little rascals, he thought, if only they had decent clothes to wear.

Letha slipped a piece of bread to Victor, and Papa smiled around his pipe stem at his youngest. He was no longer a baby. The boy was certainly sure of himself. He would no doubt be a leader. Yes, he would get along fine, while the others, just as

139

bright, would more likely be your typical common laborers. Definitely his own blood coursed in Victor's veins.

John didn't plan on being any common laborer either—not for long anyway. He'd spend his efforts getting the laborers organized so they would be worthy of their hire. He thought that the real money and excitement would be in the organizing, and that was where he planned to be.

Though he felt a special bond with Victor, he felt more distanced from the other children than when he was away. He didn't even know how to talk to them. Even though they all openly expressed adoration for their father, which pleased him, he simply couldn't share their happiness in this place they had learned to call home.

Now the truth was out. Grace was right—he was like company. He felt like a rank stranger in this house, among his own family.

He resolved to settle their future that very night, if only someone would give him a cue to say what he needed to say.

He could hear Grandpa rocking in the sitting room.

"Joining us, Grandpa?" he asked loudly.

"Yes, Pa," Grace said. "Dinner's ready. Come and get it."

John's eyes followed the children as they swarmed to help Grandpa get an extra seat to the table. He felt a sharp stab. The children adored their father, yes. But they doted on their Grandpa. The loving hands of Lester and May carried his seat, only pretending to let Grandpa do it.

Suddenly, Arthur seized the chair on which John was tilting, all but jerking it out from under him. "This is Grandpa's chair," he said. "He only lets company have it."

It was, in fact, the only chair in the kitchen that had a back on it. All the others were store boxes or stools made from half barrels.

Grandpa, innocent of the earlier conflict, replied, "Oh no. Let your Papa have that chair. He's good company."

"No, Grandpa," Arthur said stubbornly. "He has been here all week, and he just got done saying he isn't company. It's your chair, Grandpa," and he stood belligerently beside it.

John stayed in the chair. But it was plain that no one liked

140

him the better for it. He decided that before nightfall he would say what he had come to say. Certainly if his father-in-law thought him company, he would stay no longer than necessary. Grandpa be damned, a man's family belonged with their father, and this family was leaving with him.

They ate in strained silence until Grandpa cleared his throat to broach a new subject.

"John, I'm not sure how to say this, but I want you to know how much regard I have for the thoughtfulness you showed in taking your father back to Missouri to bury him beside your mother. I had thought for many years that I wanted to be buried beside Grace's Ma in the Kentucky hills. But now I think I'd rather be buried here in the Oklahoma hills that have been made so dear to me by Grace and the children."

There's my cue, John thought, and he tilted back his chair to speak. But Mama beat him to the punch.

"PA!" she scolded her father. Then in a softer tone, "Please, don't be so morbid at the dinner table. That is something we can discuss when the time comes."

John postponed his speech for later.

Victor held up his arms to his papa. Much pleased at having one loyal little member in his family, John swooped him up. Victor put his soft arms around Papa's neck and flicked his cheek with his long eyelashes. John let him sit astride his knee. But when Victor wanted Papa to feed him, things had gone far enough.

"You feed yourself, son. Papa is hungry too." Suiting action to the word, John put a bite of boiled meat into his mouth. It was awful. He pulled the meat from his mouth and dropped it back on his plate.

"This beef is salty, Grace," he said. "And it tastes of cabbage. I don't like cabbage, remember?"

"A year and a half is a long time to remember a little thing like that," Grace said in a pointedly even voice. "But I stewed this chicken, too," she added with a weary smile.

She passed him the chicken and dumplings. He took some of the stewed chicken, but none of the dumplings. "I'll leave the biscuits—boiled or otherwise—to the rebels," John jibbed at

141

Grandpa.

Letha saw Mama brace herself. This was just the brand of humor Papa got working on rough jobs with rough men. The nearer it took the hide off, the funnier he thought the joke was.

And it got pretty close. Grandpa's body stiffened. He put his hand on his barrel chair as if to raise himself from the seat, but thankfully thought better of it.

Mama sighed, saying nothing. The strange silence settled over the table again where family plans, friendly banter, and bickering usually took place.

Letha looked quickly about to see why no one had anything to say. She prided herself in the fact that she was the one member of the family who could usually read Mama, but this time she could not figure out what was behind the smile Mama kept trying to keep on her face. It reminded her of the look their old cat Tabby had when she was sitting quietly by a hole in the haymow waiting for a mouse to come through.

Letha's gaze followed Mama's eyes. She was watching Papa as he toyed with his food and Victor. Letha sat staring boldly, not eating at all. She began to feel very odd inside.

Lester, still weak from his peanut-eating ordeal, sat leaning against Grandpa while Arthur on the other side of Grandpa was seeing to it that Grandpa had plenty of food on his plate.

Papa sat picking at the boiled chicken, the fried potatoes, and the uneaten boiled cabbage with his fork, eating little. It was plain to them that he was not only toying with his food, but with ideas as well.

May was accustomed to seeing people at the table get right to the business of eating.

"Why you eat that way, Papa?" her tiny voice breaking the silence.

"I'm not hungry," Papa said—with more irritation than he probably meant.

This was just the straw that broke Mama's back.

"You could have brought us something better to eat when you returned from town yesterday," she said flatly.

When Letha heard Mama's words, she pictured Old Tabby

142

pouncing on the mouse that had been foolish enough to come through the hole. She always felt sorry for the poor mouse Old Tabby caught. She didn't understand what was going on, but she knew it was making her queasy inside. She knew how to keep peace between Lester and Arthur, but between Mama and Papa was a challenge she wasn't sure how to meet.

"I don't like my chicken either," she said uneasily.

Mama ignored the whole thing. "We'd better all get busy," she said, briskly. "There's plenty of chores to do before bed-time."

Letha and the rest jumped from the table unusually grateful for their kitchen chores.

John leaned on the table and lit his pipe. He wished he could think of some way to begin what it was he wanted to say.

Grandpa sat quietly, holding his empty fork in his hand.

Grace began to restore the usual sense of family order. "Letha, you and Arthur clear off the cook vessels so there will be room for things from the table. Lester, you may get all the meat scraps off the plates and feed them to No-No. May, you take Victor outside to the wash pan and help him to wash his hands and face."

"Ride me, ride me," Victor cried as he held up his hands to May. John chuckled, got up and carried Victor outside for May.

When he returned to the kitchen Grace began an effort to make peace. "I'm sorry about the dinner and my unkind remark. For supper I'll fix your favorite meal—hot bread rolls with plenty of butter and jelly, sausage and fried eggs."

"No eggs," he said. "I've eaten so many eggs the past two years I can't look a hen in the face." He laughed heartily at his joke, hoping to clear some of the electricity still in the air.

Letha and Arthur joined in the laugh, obviously glad to have anything to laugh at.

Grandpa clucked his tongue. "That must be a joke on the hen," he said. But he didn't laugh.

Nor did Grace. "Why, did you eat ham and eggs at the hotel yesterday? What else did you get your fill of there?" she asked. But for the rattling of the kettles, the awful silence returned.

Grace sat down again with a sigh, leaned her elbows on the table and looked at some invisible spot near the center of it.

John cleared his throat. He decided to get on with it. "I've been thinking of your statement just before dinner, Mr. Yourt."

"Yes? Which one?" Grandpa asked.

"That you wanted to be buried here," Papa said.

The children's activity ceased. A pall settled over the whole room.

"I thought we'd talk about that when the time came." Grace looked directly at John as she said this, giving him fair warning.

Letha saw Old Tabby's back arched ready for a powerful spring.

"The time has come," John said, "but for a different reason." He looked into Grace's fiery eyes. Then he turned and addressed himself to Grandpa.

"I looked at these traveling acres of yours again this morning and decided to take my family away from here." Lightning flashed from his eyes as he turned to look into Grace's. He could see thunder coming, so he beat her to it. He struck the table with the palm of his hand. The dishes bounced, rattling as they came back down.

"Everything connected with this farm—if you can call it that—just leaves me cold."

Grandpa stroked his long beard with trembling fingers. "It's the true life for me. And I think a farm is the best place for children to grow up."

John kept his eyes fixed on Grace. He said, "When I was in town yesterday, I had Mrs. Swan at the hotel help me pick out and order some decent clothing for all of you from Sears & Roebuck. When the order arrives, I'm taking you away from here to some town where our children can get into school and be brought up like something other than jack rabbits."

"MRS. SWAN!" Grace closed her eyes tight, then said under her breath, "That woman who sits so brazenly on the hotel veranda, gold teeth protruding from between the sections of her flashing fake smile." Grace opened her eyes, and shook her head

144

as if trying to shake the image from her brain.

"Yes, Mrs. Swan at the hotel."

"Charming! And since when has some shopworn creature chosen clothing for me and my children?"

Grandpa tried to stand. His fork dropped, clattering to his plate.

"Will Grandpa go, too?" Arthur inquired.

"I stay here," Grandpa answered resolutely, now standing beside the table grasping it with unsteady hands.

"I will stay with Grandpa," Arthur announced in a tone of finality as he went to Grandpa's side.

"Me, too." Letha said coming to the table.

"You will all go with me," Papa stated significantly. "No child of mine shall slave as I know all of you have done since you've been in this God-forsaken place." He flicked his hand to encompass the sandy farm, the region in general and Grandpa's four walls in particular.

"This place," Grace retorted, mimicking his hand movement, "is but a little short of heaven compared to what your gallant efforts have provided for your children and me the past two years. This place has been our home for well over a year, while you were gallivanting all over God's creation, and it shall remain home for us until such time as you shall provide more suitable quarters—and in advance!"

John stood up so quickly that he pushed the table back. It would have pushed Grandpa over where he stood beside it had Mama and Arthur not caught him.

John ignored it and hit the table another resounding blow with his fist.

"You will do as I say. You seem to forget that I am the head of this family!"

Grace matched his anger.

"I will not drag our children about to live in shacks and shanties like your roving oil field workers do."

"Why don't you save your self-righteous act until I tell you what I'm planning to do?" asked Papa.

"Well, if you have something to tell us, what are you saving it for?" Grace demanded.

145

John saw it was time to play his ace. He calmed himself and sat back down in Grandpa's chair leaning back in grandiose manner.

"This is a new era for the working man," he calmly said. "It is my plan to follow the leadership of our great champion, Eugene V. Debs, and organize the working man so that each man will not be dependent upon his own single effort to get a fair wage and working conditions from an employer who looks upon himself as the master."

"YOU?" screamed Grace. "When you had the brickyard, you got laborers for as little as you could get them for!"

John ignored the insult. "Now that I'm on the other side of the fence, and I see what it is like, I plan to do something about it."

"We will stay with Grandpa," Grace announced as she resolutely placed her hands palms down on the table where she stood.

That was too much to ignore! "You will do nothing of the kind," he shouted, striking the table again as he got up.

Grace's hands bounced like the plates, but she didn't flinch.

They glared at one another across the table.

"We will stay here," she said in quiet firm voice. "Some may consider you the head of the household, but I am the neck, and the neck turns the head! Had it not been for my very stiff neck and Grandpa's generosity, the so-called head of this household would have no family at this minute."

"I am leaving, with or without you!!" John pronounced with finality. He would have stormed from the roomful of screaming, crying children, but at that moment Grandpa fell to the floor with a soft thud. There was a moment of stunned silence, followed by Grace's strained voice.

"John, help me get him up and into his bed."

He obeyed.

After they had got him into bed in his old bedroom, Grace completed her instructions. "Now get on your fancy horse and go to town for Dr. McGinnis."

John fled away at top speed.

Dr. McGinnis took a deep breath and knocked on the door.

146

A distraught Grace opened the door to him. He quickly examined her father and walked her from the room. "Your father has suffered another stroke."

"Another st-stroke?"

"The first one was slight. It only partially blinded him. I cannot say what this one will do. Only time will tell."

Grace was sobbing quietly now. "We shouldn't have fought in front of him."

"I heard. Your husband told me about it."

"Where IS my husband?" she cried angrily. "He's NEVER here when I need him!"

"He stayed in town—at the hotel. He is pretty upset at the turn of events. He said for me to tell you he would return only at your direct request."

Grace groaned. "There isn't anything that man couldn't do if he would just straighten his way of thinking. Unfortunately, now he thinks he can make a living for his family trying to organize people—workers—to follow that madman Debs."

That was a surprise to the doctor, but before he could say anything, Arthur yelled from the bedroom door, "Papa is just a plain stubborn mule!"

"ARTHUR!" Mama reprimanded.

"He is too. I've heard you tell him so lots of times," Arthur defended his statement.

She had said it, so she couldn't deny it.

"Go back and stay by Grandpa's bed," Mama said.

When Arthur had gone back into the bedroom, Dr. McGinnis said, "We all have our own viewpoints." He patted her shoulder.

"If John would only see and admit that a rolling stone gathers no moss," she said with a sigh. "But he just laughs at that old cliche and makes himself a new one: 'A rolling stone gets its rough corners rubbed off and acquires a wonderful polish at the same time.'"

The doctor chuckled. "Well, he may be right at that," he said. "Just remember you can't polish a soft stone. It merely keeps wearing away. I suspect you fell in love with that man because of his agate-like qualities."

"Indeed. John *is* a piece of polished agate. And I still love

147

him, if only— "

"Why don't you leave off the 'if only'," he advised. "Let me take word to him that you want him to return."

"I know I can't live without him. I just can't," Grace choked out the admission, adding coyly, "Besides he will have to help me to pay my doctor bill."

"Making peace with your husband is receipt in full for anything you may have owed me," he said. "I'll tell him to come, but don't be too hard on him. Things have been taken care of for the time being anyway."

"But at what a price?" she agonized. "Why, oh why do we have to have such differences?" She sat staring moodily into that ever-fascinating spot in the center of the dining table. Then she looked up at the doctor.

"Funny. My mother's favorite verse has just come to me."

"May I hear it? Never can tell, it might help both of us."

She began haltingly:

> "The day is woven from minute's yarns
> Of many different hues.
> Each strand is different
> From people's varied views.
> The threads from skeins of joy,
> Of laughter, and of tears—
> For the sorrows and the hopes of days
> Make the cloth of years.
> That garment, seamed, askew and bright,
> When worn gives undeniable proof,
> And shows invariably the price
> Of broken warp, uneven woof.
> So may I when my fabric's done
> Show by the pattern on my face
> A design of all my acts
> A life of firm but gentle grace."

She was like a schoolgirl, reciting before her teacher. She even gave a little curtsy afterwards.

He clapped. "Gracefully said, gentle Grace."

"I'm not graceful, nor am I gentle," she protested, then

148

moaned. "Why did my mother ever give me that name?"

"I think Grace a perfect name for you. Okay—maybe not gentle Grace, but certainly amazing."

She smiled wryly. "That's what John called me once—Amazing Grace."

"I'll be back tomorrow." He slowly shut the door behind him. As he drove his horse down the hill, he thought about Grace—so stern one moment, and yet so childlike the next. He'd seen it before in women who had many children. What is maturity but the ability to reflect and learn from past events? But a woman like Grace had little time to reflect. Her mode of operation was simply to keep doing what she had always done.

Chapter 14

And It Came To Pass

Grandpa's eyes followed their movements as they came into his bedroom where he had been reinstated since his fall.

"Can you see me, Pa?" Grace asked, as she had many times before when this phenomenon occurred. She peered into the clear blue depths of his eyes. His stilled lips did not answer.

"I don't think he can possibly be seeing you," the doctor said, and he waved his hand back and forth over Grandpa's face to prove his point. Whether Grandpa blinked more rapidly at that time or whether they only imagined he did, they were never sure. But his moving eyes did haunt them—especially John who couldn't stand it for long. He usually fled outdoors.

"I think he is only following the sounds you make," Dr. McGinnis contended. "His hearing seems as good as ever."

Even after a month had passed, and she and John had made their peace as the doctor advised, Grace felt compelled to continually return to father's bedside and keep an eye on him, refusing to leave the house. She would not go to church or even step outside for a breath of air.

"You love the outdoors so," John said. "Why don't you leave your father with me or with Arthur for a few minutes each day, tramp about and get some fresh air."

They were seated on the kitchen doorstep together. It was a terrible instrument of peace, but since Grandpa's collapse they had felt a closeness they hadn't had since the early years of their marriage in spite of the fact that John was now sleeping on the floor of the sitting room. In fact, his sleeping on the floor somehow ennobled and endeared him to Grace.

She put her hand on John's knee and gave it a squeeze. "That's a funny suggestion, coming from you," she countered. "You're always saying there isn't enough soil in the sand to soil the clothes we wear. It only sands them down, remember?"

John reached down and picked up a handful of sand and

151

watched it closely to the last grain as he let it trickle through his fingers. Then he repeated the process, saying nothing at all.

Grace refused to waver. It was true that Grandpa took food from any person who brought it to his bedside, and it was plain he preferred Arthur to look after him. Still, she would not be coaxed beyond her post near his bedside.

Arthur had resumed sharing the bedroom at night with Grandpa, and an even closer bond grew between them. Seldom did an hour pass without Arthur panting up to the house to ask, "Is Grandpa up yet?" It seemed her eldest just couldn't give up the idea that Grandpa at any moment might be up and ready to go into the wonderful outdoors that he loved so well—especially now with a lovely Indian summer.

John continued to nag at Grace about staying in the house so much. "I don't like what it is doing to you," he complained. "You are starting to lose weight, and you know I don't like my women thin."

Lately she had a resigned attitude about everything. That wasn't like Grace at all. He had never known her to be like this, and his remark was meant to taunt her into barking back at him. It found its mark. She barked!

"Perhaps if I get thin enough, I can dress up for you in that outfit the lovely Mrs. Swan picked out for me!"

John shot up from the doorstep like she'd stuck a hat-pin in his backside. He danced for glee like a boy who had swiped a cookie from the jar.

"Hey, there's life in the old girl yet!" He jerked his pipe from his mouth, grabbed Grace and gave her a resounding kiss.

"You're jealous!" he said with a gleeful chuckle. "Just plain jealous. Why it's just like the good old days when that school-teacher came back to Blackwell with a brand new husband. When I kissed her I only meant to pull his leg, but instead it was yours I pulled. Remember?"

He sat down and would have taken her in his embrace, but she gave him a hard push that sent him sprawling off the door-step where he sat.

"That'll give you some more sand to sit on and run through your fingers." He looked up in surprise.

"Damned odd way to respond to my amorous advances."

"If that's amorous, you can keep it!"

She got up and would have flounced back into the house, but he caught her apron strings.

"Aw, come on and sit down," he begged. "I was only ribbing you to see if you were still you."

She sat. But by the way she sat, he knew there was still work to be done.

"Don't worry about my being confined to the house," she said. "I have been spreading my efforts too thin for too long. As for your worrying about my not being me, maybe this will relieve your mind: I've made an equitable division of the work on this farm mentally, and now I'm ready to assign part of it to the 'head of the household,' as you so grandly call yourself."

He had no idea of what might be coming, but he was ready to accept it. Anything would beat the skepticism of these past weeks. He desperately needed a defined role to play. "All right, woman, lay it on me."

"You will manage the farming activity—the planting of crops, managing the pasture, the horses, cows, chickens, and the gardening. From the farming activity you will make a living for your family." She looked steadily into his eyes as she delivered this ultimatum. Her jaw was set. She did not smile. Then she continued.

"I will take care of the household. You will eat whatever I provide and there will be no complaints. I will get the children ready for school in clothes that I will make if necessary. There will be no fancy 'Little-Boy-Blue' outfits such as those favored by you and the charming Mrs. Swan."

To show that her words were final, she punctuated them by getting up, going into the house, and slamming the door behind her.

John sat in stunned silence on the doorstep. Me? Farm this place! Take care of the stock! Even the chickens!

Damn, he muttered. How I love that woman. I don't know why I do, I just do. And I love her best when she's sassy!

Oddly enough, though he loved to mold clay, any person he

could mold he soon despised. He only vaguely knew what was behind the reason for his deep love for her: her spirit, the individualism he could not break, or master. He just knew he felt complete oneness, completely whole only when with his spirited Grace. What was a man to do?

"So help me, I'll do it! Look out hens, here I come!"

He bounced up from the doorstep and clicked his teeth against the stem of his pipe as he thrust it into his mouth.

But he didn't go to the barn lot. He went into the house.

Grace was resolutely washing the dishes, her back to him.

He nuzzled her neck affectionately with his bristled chin—a gesture that never failed to get her dander up.

"So you have given me complete management of this farm, right?"

She pulled away from him and shot him a look that said: now what are you up to? But trapped by her own words, she could only reply weakly, "Right."

"Well, I don't want to hear a peep out of you when I start to make a few changes around here." Of course, he would have been as disappointed as all get out if she didn't scream bloody-murder over every change he tried to make.

"Changes like what?" she asked, pushing him away completely and staring at him coldly. She was all but holding her breath, so still she stood.

"For one thing I'm going to get rid of those white leghorn chickens," he said.

"Ye gods and little fishes!" she exploded. "What are you going to do? Stock the place with gamecocks?"

John chuckled. "A white chicken can't possibly hide itself from the coyotes. I find their bones behind every bush. I'll replace them with some buff colored chickens to match the color of this sand."

"Don't be ridiculous. Coyotes hunt by scent—"

He ignored this shot and went on. "A breed with enough meat on it to make it fit to eat and will lay eggs we can sell too."

"I will make no objection to that—seems sensible. The only stipulation I make is that you buy the buff chickens first. Then we will sell the ones we have. The income from the sale of eggs is the surest part of our livelihood now."

That took the wind out of his sails, and since he had no money to buy anything, he could think of no response.

She has no faith in me, none at all, he thought. Well, I'll show her.

But he didn't push it. "Since you are the general here in the house, do you mind if this backwoods private does one tiny thing about the house?" he asked nuzzling her neck again.

"And what is that one tiny thing you want so badly to do?" she said holding her breath again.

"I want to build a day bed on wheels for your Pa so we can wheel him outdoors or into whatever room we are in."

That completely undid her. "Oh, John." She fell sobbing on his chest with her arms about his neck. One thing he couldn't stand was a sobbing woman.

"Save it," he said as he pushed her from him and dashed for the door. "Save that brine to cure the next butchering of beef in." And he fled to the barn with his idea and a lump in his throat.

Mustering the best of his inventive skill, he was able to fashion a bed that could be trundled from room to room like a wheelbarrow. Its construction occupied his free time for several days, and his pride in the contraption occupied many more. Every day they placed Grandpa on the bed, and on all nice days they wheeled him out into the dooryard and even to the barn lot. Things were less gloomy and sad about the place after that.

In other things, however, his pride took a terrible beating. He tried with all his ability to keep things going on the farm. Luckily it was fall when farming activity was at a minimum. He would not accept help from the men of the community who flocked to the house when the news of Grandpa's illness spread.

In the end, he found himself turning to his son, Arthur, who was more than happy to teach him what he had learned from Grandpa on how to plow a furrow. Together they planted a small acreage of wheat for winter pasture. Once he got the hang of it, he decided there could be something in it after all and that he should try some acres of wheat for a money crop too, and began to make plans.

- - -

Letha was sweeping the front porch and enjoying the crisp autumn air when two of the well-meaning neighbors, who had been there before came calling again. This time Papa put the front door in their face. Letha heard their conversation as they walked toward their horses.

"That guy is an odd piece of human flesh. He talks to all who will listen—and to those who won't—when we gather on street corners in town, about how all of us ought to pool our talents and our resources and work together for the common good. He quotes and re-quotes that brotherhood of man stuff he got from that fellow Debs. Yet you just try to offer to help him and his family with anything—and goodness knows the darned greenhorn needs help now—why you might as well attack the honor of his wife. He's on the verge of hitting you."

"Yes, I've noticed that. Now I'm no brotherhood-of-man guy, but I'd sure like to find some way to lend them a hand on account of the old man and the family."

"You know what? I like Barnet himself better than I like his talk. I think the guy has had a pretty rough time since he lost his business and he's just got all mixed up wanting to help other fellows who are having a hard time too."

"We'd better let the horses cool off a bit more," and they came back to the porch and sat on the front steps, while Letha swept around them.

"To me he's an American at the crossroads," the bigger man said.

"How so?"

"He's got one foot firmly planted in the America we've always known, where a man only wants for himself and his family what he can earn by the sweat of his brow and his own brawn. And then what he earns is his to do with as he pleases. But his other foot is stretched a mile long into the America that Debs promises for the future: that one-for-all and all-for-one stuff that comes out in that new-fangled paper he sells."

"What? The Appeal to Reason? Have you read it?"

"I just subscribed because I thought maybe he made a bit on

156

the price of it, and it would help him out. But if you read it, you begin to see what's the matter with the fellow, and maybe with a lot more like him."

Letha was practically sweeping the tops off their shoes now. She just wanted them to go away and stop talking about Papa.

"Hey, Miss Barnet, watch where you're sweeping."

"Why don't you go fetch our horses some water?"

Gladly she went, so that she wouldn't have to listen to them. She took her time, but when she returned with a pail of water they were still in the thick of it.

"I agree, there's no place for farmers in that kind of shindig. Not one of us would have the gall to hold back a sack of potatoes when people were going hungry just to get a better price."

She handed them the water.

"Thank you, little lady." The big man tipped his hat.

"Of course I'm for fair living wages for everybody, but I just can't stomach this idea of collective ownership. And I don't think Barnet does either in his heart. I've noticed he likes to say 'me and mine' as well as anyone else. He's only giving lip service to it because he is hard up now and under the spell of that Debs fellow."

They gave each horse a few laps from the pail, then handed it back to Letha.

"We'll stop by from time to time," they told her, "to keep an eye on how things are going here."

"Somehow I have a feeling your father is going to do the job here about as well as the rest of us once he gets the hang of it," the bigger man said, as if to make amends to her. And then added, "Of course that's nothing to brag about."

"If he doesn't make a go of it, I bet your mama does. I never saw such an iron whiplash in my life," the smaller man piped in.

"Make no mistake, there's a rugged individualist from the old school, yes sir!" His companion agreed. "She'll see it done no matter how much it takes out of her—or anybody else!"

Chuckling between them, they were off.

Letha wanted to tell them that they need not worry about the Barnet family. They were doing fine.

157

- - -

As it turned out, the next time the two men came, Letha was pleased to see that they were surprised and somewhat amused at what they saw.

There was Papa in the middle of the field.

"Well, if that isn't the damndest plow I've ever laid eyes on."

And they waited until he came down the row towards them.

"Looks like your typical eight-disc affair, only it's got several spring-controlled arms that raise whichever disc strikes a sagebrush root, then drops it back down again when he crosses over the clump."

Papa grinned broadly and pulled the team to a halt when he saw them standing there.

"The gosh-darned thing looks like merry-go-round horses to me," the big one yelled as Papa approached them breathlessly.

"Looks more to me like a batch of bucking broncos hitched together," the other one offered.

"Where'd you get it?" Ekans asked.

"Get it, thunder!" Papa roared. "You don't get something like this. You make it!"

The men ignored his strutting and crowing because they were too busy crawling over the odd contraption to see if they could figure out how it worked. Finally they climbed down and looked back over the field.

"But look, Barnet, this thing leaves the sage roots in the ground. You have to grub those things out or they grow right back bigger and more stubborn than ever."

"Just you give me time," Papa retorted. "There's only one of me, so I can do only one thing at a time. I'll do the grubbing after I get the wheat planted."

The men scratched their heads, stood around and looked the thing over again. Finally the little one said, "But gosh, man, what good is it going to do you to plant? You can't harvest it with these sage roots in the field."

"Unless, of course, you're going to get out here with a scythe

158

and harvest it by hand," grinned the other. "And I wouldn't put it past you."

Papa took no offense at this backhanded compliment. "I plan to let the cows harvest this patch and I'll grub roots as I can this winter," he told them. "Machinery can harvest the money crop on the other patch down there." And he waved his hand toward the plot usually planted to wheat.

The two men exchanged glances, nodding at each other.

"Shake, farmer," the big one said extending his hand.

John was pleased to see he had finally won the respect of his neighbors and trusted they would spread the word this strange new man in Waynoka might have some useful ideas after all.

His newfound farming prowess, however, was confined to the field. He had no intention of taking on Grace's dairy business. He had little use for the cows, and the feeling was mutual. Every time he approached one of them in the haymow with a milk pail and stool, the cow swished her tail and lifted a hind foot to give him a rough push. He was willing to do anything else there was to do on the place, slop the pigs, even condescending to carry the wash water to the house. But he flatly refused to milk the cows.

"I don't mind a female sitting on my knee," he joked with her, "but I'm darned if I'm going to let one kick me there."

So Arthur and Letha kept the milking chores. And Lester, apparently remembering that he said he couldn't look a hen in the face, gathered the eggs.

Unfortunately, Grace still refused to leave Grandpa long enough to take the milk, butter and eggs to town to sell. So once a day he had to swallow his lump of pride and drive the deliveries to town, with Arthur and Letha along to carry them into the houses. With the money they collected, he bought whatever necessary supplies the few coins would buy.

But there was an errand in town he simply would not do. He would not stop by Dr. McGinnis's office to pick up the doctor's office laundry that Grace had been doing for him.

"I don't mind work," he told Grace. "But I will not be seen doing menial tasks."

"It is an honest way to earn money to pay the doctor bill we have no other way of paying," she retorted.

John shuddered, but he would not budge. So while he did the buying at the store, Arthur drove the wagon by the doctor's office and got the laundry.

When John took over the reins, refusing to acknowledge the bundle in the back of the cart, he dropped Arthur and Letha off at school. They either walked home or rode with some farmer who picked them up on his own way home.

On one of his trips to Waynoka, John found an old train bell at the roundhouse yards where it had been abandoned. He plopped it in the back of the cart on top of the laundry, and took it home. He installed it in the yard so that Grace could ring him if needed, or call the family to supper. That pleased her.

In spite of his efforts, John knew that farming wasn't his calling. So as his innovations on the farm began to free up some time, he gravitated back to town. Invariably, he headed to the Mexican quarter near the railway. He observed the impoverished state of the railroad hands there, and became determined to improve their lot. He had noticed, while making milk deliveries to them, that during the first few days after payday they seemed happy. But during the remaining days of the week their eyes held an element of discontent—as well they might. He decided to try organizing them as the admirable Debs was organizing other railroad men in Ohio and Kansas. But try as he would, he could make no headway with them.

"You men need a balanced life," he told a gang of them one day as he tilted on a chair on the veranda of the hotel.

The Mexicans nodded and smiled, but did not seem to understand a word he had said.

"Your lives are made up of hard work with little pay, mighty little to eat and no fun at all."

"That what you think," one of them grinned, and he pointed toward the swarm of Mexican children coming down the railroad track. He laughed uproariously and slapped his thighs. To the last man the Mexicans joined him in the joke.

That gave John his cue on how to handle the situation. They needed more money to support all those children.

If he were honest he'd have to say the workers repulsed him—they sweated too much. So on his visits to town, he made it a point to get on friendly terms with the man who seemed to be their leader—the section hand foreman, Ernest Gilliza.

When John first broached the subject of organizing the section hands, Gilliza was strictly against it.

"I want you to understand that I'm not opposed to them having their jobs," John explained. "What I am interested in is that they get more—and you too—for the work they do. A dollar a day is no money at all for the work they do on the railroad. I'm for all working men being paid a decent wage."

"But dollar is all railroad will pay," Gilliza said. "And if they don't work for that, the bosses bring in some more Mexicans who do."

"That is just what I am talking to you about," John said. "You need to be organized. Did you ever hear of this man Debs?"

Gilliza had. He threw up his hands and backed away. "I don't wanna go jail. That Debs is a socialist. Are you socialist?" he asked and he looked around to see if anyone might have heard them even mention socialism. He shook his head and tried to leave.

"I never said a word about making a socialist out of you, or them, or about me being one either. The only reason Debs is a socialist is because he is convinced that is the only way to get better living conditions for the mass of working humanity."

To Gilliza's unease, a few people had gathered around them. But John was just getting started. He had an audience to whom he could expound the virtues of the new plans for the working man. He continued.

"I'm not talking to you about politics. I'm talking economics—more money for you, more money for your workers."

Gilliza didn't see the difference between politics and economics, but he obviously liked the sound of more money.

That evening he told Grace about the conversation over the supper table.

"But you are contradictory in what you preach and what you do," Grace pointed out.

161

"What do you mean, contradictory?"

"Why, you are encouraging downright economic dependency of one man on another. Yet for yourself you demand utter self-sufficiency."

John rubbed his chin as he appraised his wife. He had no idea she would have given this topic a thought—much less such a pointed analysis.

"How'd you get so all-fired smart on the subject of economics?" he asked with a grin.

"Well, I've been reading your copies of <u>The Appeal to Reason</u>."

"The devil you have!" he said as he banged down his chair legs. But since there was nothing really wrong about her reading it, he could think of nothing else to say except, "First thing I know, you will be wanting the right to vote!"

"You are so right," she said. "And even if I don't vote, I know enough about democracy to know that you vote on what is to be done and then conform to what the majority say."

He began to feel he was losing at the ballot box. He squirmed in his chair and twisted his pipe about in his mouth, resolving to hide his copies of the paper.

"Speaking of papers . . ." he said and started to get up.

But Grace wasn't through yet.

"So what you are suggesting to Gilliza—that his workers conform to your ideas—is that the idea and spirit of either democracy or socialism?"

"Damn," John exploded. "I should have known better than to have opened my mouth on the subject. Every time I say anything, we get into an argument."

"I'm not arguing," Grace said. "I just asked you a question."

"Democracy is not for the ignorant," was his retort.

"Ignorant like whom?" she shot at him heatedly. She got no answer. He thought himself deeply enough in hot water that he needed to tread carefully.

They sat in silence while he mused on the idea that it seemed they were good companions only in such silence. When they talked, they argued—neither able to sway the opinion of the other. And he always ended cornered with some unanswerable

162

question or some irrefutable quotation from the Bible, which only addled his thinking.

Since he never won in an argument, he decided they would hereafter enjoy silent companionship. He got up and left without a word, leaving Grace baffled.

By Thanksgiving there was an air of mystery hovering over the place. Grace could put up with the silent treatment only so far. Plus she had noticed that John was spending less time in town during the day, but less time around the house, and sometimes he went outside for an hour or so after dark when supper was over. To top it off, when on some pretext she rang the bell in the yard, he came with a "cat-that-swallowed-the-canary" look.

Finally she could stand it no longer, so she asked him point blank what he was doing that kept him out in the new field so much.

"Well, after all it takes some time and a lot of work to grub out all those sage roots," he said evasively.

"Oh, so that's what that smoke is I've been seeing over the hill there. But you silly, why don't you bring those roots up to the house? They're good at holding a fire in the firebox, which we'll need each night now with winter coming on."

He managed to fill the woodbox at least once each day with green sage roots.

In the end, it was left to the children to spill the beans.

"Papa what are you going to do with the kiln of brick you are firing down in the new wheat field?" Arthur asked innocently one evening.

John jumped as if he had been shot at. He stood up looking as mad as the dickens, then his eyes darted to Grace.

But then he chuckled and sat down again. "Well, I'm going to build another room onto the house," he said to Arthur. "I'm making brick." Then looking her straight in the eye he said, "I think we need some more room, don't you?"

Grace's hands flew to her waist. "How did you know?" she asked. "Do I show that much? I hadn't planned to tell you for a while yet."

The pipe fell from John's mouth and clattered to the floor.

163

He slumped his head down into his arms on the table. "Oh my God, my God," he moaned as he rocked his head back and forth.

Grace felt an instant stab of pain.

"I can find that in the Bible," chirped Letha, ever helpful in the awkward silence that ensued. She ran into the next room to get the Bible, no doubt anxious to demonstrate how, after only two months of lessons, she could read some of it.

When she came back lugging the big book, she caught Grace holding her confounded husband to her bosom.

Letha stopped, somewhat embarrassed, but was doggedly determined to help ease the situation. "What verse, Mama?"

"Matthew 27: 46," came the automatic reply.

Letha turned to the New Testament. She flipped the pages. "Here it is: My God; my God, why hast thou forsaken me?"

Mama, ever the teacher, found herself saying, "It's also in Psalm 22."

Letha hesitated and Papa said, "That's enough, Letha. Go to bed now."

With Letha gone, John held out his arms to her.

They clung to each other in silence for a while.

"When do you think it will be?" he finally asked.

"Sometime in June."

"Grace, I've tried. But one more? We can't afford it. We've got to have more than the peanuts that are trickling in now."

"Things will work out some way."

He gave her a fierce hug and dashed out the door. She heard his horse pacing rapidly out of the farmyard and down the road toward town.

Grace spent the evening in a prayerful vigil by Grandpa's bed. Surely John would not desert them now, but she knew his shock had been great.

He did not come home.

The next morning Dr. McGinnis came calling.

"John told me you are pregnant."

"True . . . " was all she could say.

"He left to find work."

She collapsed in a chair.

164

"He came to see me before he left. I'm sorry. There was no stopping him. But we agreed that he would send you a letter by registered mail every week. The letter will be addressed to you in care of my office, and I personally will see that you get it. There will be no way for it to get lost on the rural route that way." He paused. "He said he's not much of a writer."

"True . . ." she laughed.

"I told him: If you can't think of anything to write, just write your address on the sheet of paper and fold the money into that—every week. Be very sure about the weekly address so we can get in touch with you if need be." He put his hand on her shoulder. "I'm sorry. It was the best I could do."

Christmas came without John. Since he was not there to lift Grandpa into his traveling trundle bed, the family celebrated Christmas Eve in Grandpa's bedroom. They gave each other homemade Christmas presents. They sang a few carols. Letha read the Christmas story from Luke.

"And it came to pass in those days that there went out a decree . . . Joseph also went up from Galilee . . . to be taxed with Mary his espoused wife . . . "

Grace hoped to find comfort in the familiar story, but she only heard fragments, each one piercing her like a fragment of glass. The holy family, and then hers—broken.

When Letha got to the multitude of the heavenly host, May cried out, "Let's go out into the fields and see if we can see the angels!" She rushed to the front door, and the others followed.

"Shut the door," Grace called after them.

They obliged and stepped out into a clear, cold starry night.

Grace picked up the Bible and finished reading the story for Grandpa, ending with: "But Mary kept all these things and pondered them in her heart."

She put her hand in his and felt a squeeze.

165

Chapter 15

Three Sheep in the Cow Pasture

Letha tried not to be angry with Papa for leaving. He was doing what he thought was best for the family and would be back soon, surely. Even Dr. McGinnis said so when he came out each week to deliver the promised letters—a few dollar bills carefully tucked inside each time.

So they didn't starve that winter. And at last they were attending school in a real schoolhouse. Each morning when they finished their milk deliveries, she and Arthur tied up the horses and wagon to the post behind Dr. McGinnis' office, gave him the collected money, and went off to their lessons.

But they had trouble with their schoolmates. Not only were they outsiders, strangers, but they were country folk instead of townies. They got taunted in the schoolyard at lunchtime. "Barnets are varmints" went the refrain. Finally Arthur couldn't take it any more and all but got into a fistfight, until Letha managed to pull him away.

After that, they took their lunches over to Mrs. Swan's hotel and ate there. Mama didn't seem to mind. It looked as if she had changed her opinion about Mrs. Swan and decided Papa might be right. Mrs. Swan was a nice woman, certainly no threat when Papa was away. Besides, Mama needed all the help she could get.

What Letha loved about the arrangement was that Mrs. Swan combed and braided Letha's hair every day after lunch. She had taken to combing just her bangs before she left for school in the morning, saying the braids held the rest of her hair in place. She loved the way it felt when Mrs. Swan took down her hair, combed it in long tender strokes, and talked to her while she braided it.

"Where'd you get such beautiful, long, black hair?" Mrs. Swan once asked. "You got some Injun blood?"

"My great-grandmother was a Sac maiden." Letha replied proudly. "Papa told me that my great-great grandparents took her into their family after us white folks massacred her people, and she later married one of their sons."

"You miss your Papa?"

"I do."

"He's a charmer, that one."

One week in mid-March no letter arrived. Dr. McGinnis came out on Saturday anyway to examine Grandpa. Mama put on her tight-lipped, set expression, so Letha could tell she thought the letters were ended.

"Relax a little, can't you? You've got a letter every week so far," the doctor told her. "You'll hear by the first of next week I feel sure. You're pulling yourself up so tight you won't even give your little tyke room and you'll deliver before June." His tone was teasing, but then he scowled at her.

"I know you are worrying about getting spring farm work started. But under no circumstances are you to touch one hand to the plow or above all the spade. Let that garden spot strictly alone."

"But I've got to get things started, and I don't want to take Arthur out of school, especially since he hates it," she said. "Letha is outdistancing him now, and I'd never get him back in school if she gets too far ahead."

"Seems you're the one getting ahead with your ifs—have a little faith, woman!" And he went in to take a look at Grandpa.

"No change, is there," Mama said despondently as he came out of the bedroom.

"I'm afraid not." He straightened out his hat and put it on. "Well, I'll be on my way." He walked to the door and turned. "By the way, you don't need to worry about Arthur. The way he sets about with those deliveries and collections—he's becoming a first-rate businessman. While Letha here," nodding towards her, "sits on the bench with her nose in a book, he goes in the store and gets more for his money than anybody I ever saw."

168

The doctor gone, Grace went alone into the kitchen and set about preparing supper for five hungry mouths. She began wondering what she would have ever done without the good doctor McGinnis. He had become like a second father to her. She chuckled as she remembered their first encounter when Lester had eaten the raw peanuts. He had set her to reading the Bible in an entirely new light. Without him she knew she would have struggled greatly.

And as it turned out, he was right about John. On Sunday afternoon, a strange sight arrived in the farmyard, a two-seated spring carriage with a fringe on top—albeit a bit frayed—drawn by two high stepping bays and a strange driver. John was riding out in front on his own pacer. Bringing up the rear was Dr. McGinnis in his two-wheeled cart grinning broadly as if to say, "Here's your delayed special delivery."

John slid off his horse and started running, pushing the children from his path as he raced toward Grace. He embraced her while everyone waited.

The man on the front seat of the carriage slid to the ground and stood beside them grinning sheepishly. Finally he advanced a step or two toward them and said loudly, "Hey Grace, remember me?"

It was John's younger brother.

"Clifford!" She looked past him. "But where's Clara?"

Clifford lowered his head.

John, never one to soften a blow replied, "She had smallpox. We buried her the first of the week up at Independence where we've been working. I've brought their three children for you to . . . sort of mother . . . until Cliff gets hold of himself and can decide what to do."

Smallpox! She felt a knot in her stomach as she surveyed the children. She did not need more children around the place even if they were healthy. And what if Clifford should run off like John and leave the whole family there?

"But isn't small pox contagious?"

Dr. McGinnis stepped forward. "You needn't worry. When I left your house yesterday, I met them coming this way. I took them back to my house, had all their clothes fumigated and had the family scrub in a hot bath. They won't be infectious now."

"We're clean as a whistle," Clifford said.

"Oh, Clifford," Grace replied warmly to make up for her misgivings. "I'm so sorry this has happened to you. And I'm glad John brought you and your children here."

She tried to hug the three children, but they stood as stiff as bricks against the legs of their father.

Poor little things, she thought.

No amount of coaxing could get them to smile. It appeared they wanted nothing from anybody—at least not now.

When Clifford and John went to the barn to put up the horses, the three of them tagged along so close to Clifford he had difficulty in walking. Their five cousins followed along as well in silent curiosity at the children who would have nothing to do with them. Grace and the doctor watched them go.

"They may be your brother-in-law's children, Mrs. Barnet, but they are certainly a different breed altogether—and they've got their claws out," the Doctor said. "I came out with them to suggest you go easy with them. I don't think they will go much for the direct way you have of managing your own family. Leave most of their bringing up to their father, if you possibly can. It isn't like they will be your responsibility forever."

He smiled, shook his head and said, "The two boys fought just about every kid in town the few minutes they were on the street this morning. I'm telling you this so you will have some idea of what may be in store."

"I can't have children fighting among themselves around here."

"I'm not asking you to turn a blind eye, but don't get yourself mixed up between fighting kids. You are in no condition for that. Remember that Arthur and Lester are no longer babies. Let them settle a few of their own disputes with the other boys. They need the practice. They can't sit on Mrs. Swan's porch forever."

That evening at supper, Grace learned that John's difficulty was not in getting a bricklaying job but in keeping it.

"The trouble with John, here," said Clifford, "is that he's too damn good."

"Any job worth doing is worth doing well," John said

170

grandly.

"Well?" Clifford rolled his eyes. "Your problem is you've got to excel. You've got to lay more brick in a day's work than anyone else on the job!"

Addressing Grace, he continued, "At first everyone was ready to admit that he was the fastest worker and could lay the straightest, neatest wall of them all. They might not have held it against him if he'd kept his mouth shut and not ribbed them about their work in comparison. Worse, he couldn't keep his talk of labor organization to himself, but was constantly preaching about it."

"And where else were they ever going to hear about it? It seemed to me that on the job is the best place to get the ear of those who labor."

"Yes, but within earshot of the foremen?" His brother burst out in both admiration and exasperation. He groaned an aside to Grace. "It was the same wherever we went."

Then back to John. "If you'd only be quiet on the job, get the job done and do your talking at the rooming house or on the street corners, you'd be better off and so would I!"

"Well, you can thank me now for having a roof over your head—and a good one at that," John retorted in good humor.

Grace bowed her head to keep a smile from showing. At least John was beginning to see this house as a pretty good place to be. And it felt so good to have adult conversation at the table again!

However, to ease what might become a wedge between the brothers, she said, "You know, Cliff, I am sorry Pa is not able to say this himself, but I know he would want me to make you and your children welcome here."

That settled the men down, but not the children. Six-year old Tillie who had refused to sit on a box to eat was whining. She stood complaining to her father while he ate. Fortunately Sammie, Arthur's age, only pouted over his plate of food and four-year old Dickie was far too sleepy to be bothered about anything.

Auntie Grace could turn her back on the pouting, but could not shut out the piercing wail that followed Tillie's whines. Maybe it was a temporary condition. She hoped so.

The big problem now was how to bed down so many. At best the house could hold only one more—or two if one of them slept on Grandpa's wheeled bed that was seldom used these days.

Tillie refused all the beds in the house, but John paid no attention to her whines.

"The men will sleep in the haymow and Tillie can sleep in the bed with May and Letha. Maybe keep Victor in the house too. I don't want him stumbling around and falling from the haymow to a manger and scaring one of the horses to death." He tickled him in the ribs to keep him from starting to fuss.

But he could not direct his eldest.

"I will stay with Grandpa," Arthur announced and he stalked into Grandpa's room. Grandpa was a delicate subject, so John dared not challenge it.

Tillie simply brushed by him and went to the barn to sleep.

John said he had no recourse but to go to the barn himself, saying you couldn't very well shove just your guests in the barn with the stock.

Grace had a sleepless night. At least she was spared the disappointment she had experienced the last time John returned home. She went over and over all the old thoughts. She and John seemed damned if they did, and damned if they didn't. Would they ever find a way to be together?

The conversation the next morning at the breakfast table revealed more information. On his way home John had stopped at the land office in Alva where he had discovered that by placing some improvements on a piece of land, the right to occupancy could be established prior to filing on it. Better still, six months could elapse after filing before residence need be established for the "proving up."

John took a bite of toast and turned to Grace. "If you still insist on staying here—and I can't find steady work some place—Clifford and I have decided to file on some of that no account land up in the hills."

Grace narrowed her eyes. "And do what with it?"

"Build us a house! The first thing to do is to begin making some brick up there. In the meantime, down here we can use the brick, still standing in the kiln, and go ahead and build an extra room onto this house so we won't be so crowded."

"What I'd like," Clifford said, "if it's not too much to ask, is a large room built a little way from the main house for me and my family."

For someone who preached common property, John was oddly in accord with Clifford's idea. "That will give each family a place of its own."

Grace could scarcely contain her joy, but she said nothing because she did not want to push her luck too far. However, she did have a suggestion about filing on the new land.

"Instead of making improvements first and then filing, why don't we file right away anyhow? That would make the proving up time nearer. If we decide to abandon the place it would only be a few dollars lost."

By the end of the week the new one-room house on Grandpa's place was completed, and on Sunday John and Clifford saddled their horses and started for Alva to see about filing.

When they returned on Wednesday John was so pleased with what they had done that anyone would have thought the idea was his in the first place.

"I filed on 160 acres and Clifford filed on another 160," he said as he slid off his horse at the doorstep. "That will give the Barnets altogether 400 acres—to starve on or get rich on, whichever way the dice rolls."

So Grace got to choose a spot on the new land for the house and John got busy drilling a well. Grace had to admit, to John's obvious delight, that his knowledge of oil-well drilling came in mighty handy. They had to drill a hole seventy-five feet deep before they found enough water to supply the brick making.

"The brick we make here will not be as good as what we made at Blackwell because there is no clay here to mix with the sand. These brick will be little better than adobe except that they will be fired and that will give them more resistance to the weather," John said. "But we certainly could use a little cash. We need a windmill and stock tank to keep up the water supply."

Grace didn't say a word. She boldly reached in her bosom and pulled out a roll of bills that would have choked the greedy.

She handed it to John.

"I sent that to you to live on!" he said indignantly.

"But Papa," piped in Arthur. "You didn't need to. I made the living while you were gone."

"What a man," John crowed proudly, clapping Arthur on the back. "Stay in there boy and get some schooling and you won't have to be living on this sandhill all your life!"

Arthur frowned. It was just like Papa to turn praise into a lecture. He liked life on the farm. But he didn't like school. He had secret ambitions that Papa would one day take him into his brick making business.

With the expanded family, every meal became a lively event. His cousins were basically a pain in the rear. There was tattling and complaining about what the other kids had done every night at the supper table. Tattling was something Mama never tolerated from her own children, but she seemed to put up with it from Uncle Clifford's, which really annoyed Arthur. Why didn't she stop it? And if it wasn't tattling, it was whining, or bickering and kicking feet under the table. Of course, he did his fair share of the kicking.

Although Mama never said anything, you could tell she was fed up with it. The baby inside her was making her even heavier than she normally was and she always looked tired.

Finally, Mama suggested that they take their lunches to the new brick-making site, which was great, and they didn't come home until nearly dark. Anything outside was better than inside.

Planting time had arrived and the added farm chores took many days of their time away from building the new house, but Arthur could tell that things were progressing even better than Papa had planned.

Grandpa could be out in the yard much of the time now, which would have been wonderful, but Arthur had to stand guard beside him considering all the little Indians racing about.

Sammie was the worst. No regard for Grandpa at all. Finally, when Sammie annoyed Grandpa once too often, Arthur took a swing at him, and they had their first, long-delayed fight. The rest joined in a regular free for all, ending with the whole

174

gang being lined up in the Barnet tradition for a good paddling—Mama spanking her children, and Uncle Clifford his.

June finally came, and with kindly aid from many of the
neighbor women, Mama had a baby girl. Letha and May hovered
over her constantly. May insisted on naming her Poppy. "'Cause
she opens up so pretty and sweet in the morning like the white
poppies in the hills, and she closes up when she sleeps just like
they close their petals at night."

So Poppy it was, and the name really did fit her. Even Arthur had to admit that if the baby had to be a girl, she was a very
cute one.

When Dr. McGinnis came for his first post-birth visit, Mama
was already out of bed. But when he went to see Grandpa, he
had more serious concerns. Arthur stood outside the door listening. "Your father is becoming weak and wan. I do not believe he
can possibly survive the heat of another summer."

Arthur's heart sank.

"If only the children would not quarrel so," Mama said.
Their voices are always so shrill and high. I can hardly stand it
myself, and I know it annoys him terribly."

Mama was right, but Arthur squirmed at this because when
he tried to protect Grandpa, he knew he only made matters
worse.

"Yes, I have noticed a difference in him since Clifford's
children came," the doctor said. "They are like sheep in the cow
pasture. What sheep don't use themselves, they somehow stink
up until no self-respecting cow will use it either."

Arthur stifled a snicker while his mother continued.

"If Clifford and John were not getting along so well with the
brick making, I'd suggest to Clifford that he take his children
someplace else—though I don't know where. It's just that John
seems more like himself than he's been since he lost the brickyard in Blackwell. I'll put up with a lot to keep him that way."

So his Uncle and the pesty cousins stayed on, and on. . .

Then one glorious day Uncle Cliff took his children to town
for the Fourth of July celebration, and Arthur got to stay at home
with his own family—the first time they had been alone for

nearly four months. It felt so peaceful, but then something strange and terrible happened.

It seemed that Grandpa chose the quiet of that day to go. He simply did not awake from his afternoon nap. Arthur went in to check on him. He looked like he was sleeping, but his skin had turned grayish. Arthur touched his face. It was cold.

Sobbing, choking, Arthur yelled for the family. They came into the bedroom one by one and simply stood around the bed looking at Grandpa. Not one of them shed a tear.

"Why aren't you crying?" he yelled at them. "Mama? He was your father."

Mama looked startled.

"Nobody must have loved Grandpa like I did!" he blurted out.

"That's true. No one loved him as you did." She tried to put her arm around him but he slapped it away and ran off. He went into the pasture, fell face down and sobbed his bitter, angry tears.

When he finally went back inside, the doctor was there, which was stupid because there was nothing he could do about it now. To make matters worse, he was full of his usual advice.

"Since he had not proved up on his claim I would advise strongly against burying him here as he wished," he counseled. "Better to bury him in the town cemetery."

This time he missed the mark, and for once, Mama said the right thing.

"I want him near me."

They chose a spot where the wild poppies grew in great numbers near the site where they were constructing the new house.

Arthur helped Papa build a crypt made of sandroll brick, brick made from Grandpa's land.

"You know, son, I fear that now your mama will be tied to this land forever."

Arthur nodded in agreement as he wiped more tears from his eyes.

Chapter 16

ABC Equals XYZ

Once his course was set, no force could distract John from his purpose. After the death of Grandpa, he and Clifford dove into their brickmaking for the new house with a frenzy.

Dr. McGinnis advised them not to mention to anyone—not even Clifford—that Grandpa had not proved up on his eighty acres.

"He as well as you, Mrs. Barnet, earned this place," he declared. "I don't know the law on the matter and I'm afraid if we try to find out what it is, some prairie louse might get wise to the fact and take the land away from you before you have time to get established on your new place."

"Damn," John said to Grace. "If you hadn't been in such an all-fire hurry to file, I could have filed on this place myself and been sure of it."

Grace admitted that things had taken a turn she hadn't foreseen. But they decided to play the cat-and-mouse game the doctor had suggested. Doubts about possession of the land on which they now lived only added impetus to John's urgency in the hills.

Save for a few jarring incidents, the next three months became a series of neighborhood picnics at the Barnet work site. True, he had refused their help in the farming, but this was different. Boys from miles around, often accompanied by their fathers and sometimes the whole family, spent their every spare moment with them. Some came out of curiosity at what manner of thing was being done. But soon they found themselves working joyfully with the others.

Each family brought the usual well-filled basket, as they did to the day dinners after the community church service at the school. When the food was cleared up after their feasts, no one of them would take any of the "leavings" home.

177

"Maybe the Lord blessed this like he did the loaves and fishes," Grace would say. So the strain on the food budget of the four added mouths of Clifford's family was miraculously eased.

John was in his element. He could lead out, show everyone how to do something, organize, and in the process, get free help. You might think him a laborer rather than the boss since he had lost the brick-making business, but when it came down to it, he was still a master-hand at organization on the work site. Counting out the number of workers, he assigned tasks to each—a certain number to the sand-sifting crew, so many to the water bucket brigade, so many to dig skunkbrush and sage to keep the kilns burning—until the brick-making job became a veritable assembly process with each worker depending on the skill and speed of the others. This method increased both since no one wanted to be found lacking.

He and Clifford personally did the mixing of the slop for pouring into the molds the women called "loaf" pans. In them they could make sixteen brick at a time and on good days were able to turn out more than a thousand bricks.

To the girls and small boys he allotted the chore of turning the brick in the sun to dry before being put in the kilns. Once school was out, this became a major help.

While he was a farmer, and the neighbors were trying to help him in farming operations, he spurned their help. But the offers of help bore a different face now he was doing the showing-how. He knew from A to Z how to make brick and he showed this in detail with complete gusto.

He used the building's progress to illustrate his latest doctrine—now taking the country by a storm. "See what we could really do in this country if all of us would just work together," he said over and over again at the close of a successful day's work.

"We just need to organize and labor together for the common good, then divide the spoils of labor according to need."

Only Grace seemed to notice, though she never pointed it out, that John and his family were the only ones getting the profits in the venture. If any of the others noted it, they said nothing. Everyone who came to work and put in a good day's labor seemed happy because that was what they had always done among themselves when a neighbor needed help. This was not some new doctrine to them. It was the American way.

Grace would have worried about John's twisted rhetoric if she had the time. Instead, she tried to put out of her mind the inconsistencies of the Socialist cause. She, in fact, became employed in supervising the child labor gang, stopping squabbles before they began. With Poppy tied upon her back she kept an eye on things. The trickiest part in turning the bricks was standing them on end. Once Victor couldn't resist knocking his over, knocking down a whole row like dominoes. Both he and May got a paddling for that—he for doing it, May who was working beside him, for not preventing it. She was always harder on her own children than the rest.

There were diversions. Once Lester spied a burrowing owl perched low on a gnarled tree limb. One of his cousins went around behind the owl in order to sneak up on it from its blind side. The owl twisted its head following his maneuvers. Noticing this, the boy continued on around the tree three times and told Lester that the owl followed him around with his head all three times.

"Did not," laughed Lester. "Why if he had turned his head all the way around three times, it would have dropped off at your feet!"

"Oh, yeah!" and his cousin proceeded to twist Lester's head to prove it could be done.

Grace didn't know whether to burst out laughing, or run to Lester's rescue, but remembering the doctor's advice she held her breath. Much to her pride, Lester wriggled out of the head-lock and ran back to join Arthur at the brick turning line.

Grace got to the point where she listened like a sieve, with practically every sound they made passing straight through her consciousness and only the most terrible sounds arresting her attention.

For May especially, who needed answers to her questions, being shut out by Mama was difficult. One day Grace realized she was missing from the group of children on the hill. She told Letha to watch Poppy on the pallet, hopped in the wagon, and

179

drove down the hill. She searched and called for her all over Grandpa's place where she finally found May in the granary feed bin where she was letting baby mice run all about and over her. First Grace grabbed the child and gave her a sound spanking. Then she inquired of her what on earth she thought she might be doing.

"When I asked you why mice are so scared of us you wouldn't answer me. Lester said they were born that way, but didn't you see Mama, they are not!" she said through her sniffles. "Not any of them are afraid of me if I just sit still and let them run on me."

When her sniffles stopped she looked at Grace and asked, "Why did you spank me?"

"Oh, I give up!" Grace laughed and in a rare moment of affection, put her arm around her and walked her to Grandpa's grave, the spot she invariably gravitated to when doubts overcame her. There they found No-No stretched out among the wild flowers with his muzzle on the brick top of the narrow crypt. They joined him for a moment of peace before driving back up to the hill.

One fiercely windy morning when the dust was blinding their work, Lester overheard her muttering, "Every time we take a step up hill, we slip back two."

"Best way to do it then is to turn around and go up backwards like the tumble bugs do with their load," he suggested.

Again a good laugh and a hug. "But would you really want to be a tumble bug in this wind?" she asked.

The wind never stopped from early spring until late fall, particularly nerve-wracking when accompanied by rumors and stories of tornadoes that the neighbors brought in.

Each day kicked up its own wind—the one of the day before having died a wheezing, moaning silt-laden death soon after the setting of the sun or, if it chose to blow through the night, at least an hour before daybreak the next morning. This allowed a few hours for the dust to drop back to earth someplace so as to leave space in the sky for the next day's onslaught.

Dust in the house, a layer of sandy silt, was a never-ending battle. Grace was hoping against hope for glass windows in the new house, rather than the oiled muslin of her father's house.

Lately there'd been more to listen to at night than the wind. Activity up in the hills seemed to have made the coyotes and wolves uneasy, their nightly serenade occasionally joined by the eerie tenor of a bobcat.

"It's enough to make the white leghorn chickens on their roosts glad they are destined to become mincemeat in Christmas pies rather than face a worse fate at the jaws of such yowling beasts," Grace told the children to calm their worries.

But since these wild creatures seldom showed face, they posed no real danger to the busy family.

It took a daytime encounter with a voiceless creature to put a nagging fear into Grace's heart as the children roamed about the new home site valley.

It also gave her a new appreciation for her brother-in-law, who had been increasingly irritating her. There were two things Clifford did she found the most annoying. One was finding Clifford's soiled clothes each week in a bundle on her doorstep. The other was when he walked over to her Majestic stove before dinner, lifted its lid and spit a load of tobacco juice into the fire.

It was during a lunchtime break when the children were off playing while the men were having a smoke, and she was cleaning up, that Letha suddenly came running up to them screaming.

"A snake is on Poppy's pallet!"

John snatched his mud-mixing hoe and ran, Clifford following with the pitchfork and Grace, for want of anything else to grab, took off running with the stub of a broom.

The snake was so close to Poppy that John dare not strike at it with the hoe. He dashed the hoe between Poppy and the snake and gave a quick pull. This rolled Poppy a short distance away as if she were brick mud in the mixing box. She now joined the chorus of howling children.

Clifford deftly shoved the tines of the fork under the now coiled snake and pitched it over his shoulder with all his might.

The thoroughly rattled rattlesnake landed squarely in front of Grace's running feet. She pinioned it to the earth with one swift jab of the broom stub.

Clifford, apparently now fearing he might now impale

Grace, dropped the fork and pounced upon the snake with his bare hands. One hand caught it firmly just behind the head and in front of her broom.

Signaling to John, standing with his upraised hoe, Clifford yelled, "Hold its tail down so he can't lash about with it and let me show these kids something they won't soon forget."

Before the wondering eyes of all, Clifford spat squirt after squirt of tobacco juice into the wide-open mouth of the big snake. In a few minutes a quiver sped from its head to its yet rattling tail. Another convulsion followed and the tail dropped to the sand. The flicking tongue ceased to flick and the great body lay quivering. In a few minutes the once fearful monster was as helpless as the fishworms the children used to play with on the riverbank at Blackwell.

Mama gathered the screaming Poppy into her arms.

"Gee, I'll never chew tobacco," Lester said.

"Why did it kill the snake, but it doesn't kill you?" This, of course, from May.

"Well, he doesn't swallow the stuff, May. Haven't you seen him spitting it in the cookstove fire?" Lester pointed out.

Grace could not hold back an appreciative look to Lester for his innocent, yet deft reproof of Clifford.

Despite such dramatic interruptions, work on the house continued at a good clip. By late August it could no longer be kept from Arthur that No-No was definitely ailing. Clifford proposed shooting him unbeknownst to the children and disposing of the dog's body in some far-flung part of the farm.

But Grace would hear to no such thing. "No-No is the children's last link with Grandpa," she insisted. "We will just have to let him die a natural death and then ease their grief as best we can by saying he has gone to be with Grandpa."

And so it was. The feeble dog was carried to and from the wagon each morning and night to go with them up the hill to work and back.

His quiet death during the night on the last day of summer was, after a few hours of terrible grief, accepted philosophically by all except Arthur.

Arthur was inconsolable. He demanded that a crypt be made

182

for No-No beside that of Grandpa's. When he started to build it himself, Papa relented and came to his aid.

Arthur handed Papa every brick that went into its building and Lester carried the hods of mortar for him to use.

"There," Papa said when they completed it. "A noble job for a noble dog."

For days after, Arthur boycotted the building process. He took up a solemn, lonely vigil at the expanding gravesite, eating little, speaking only when spoken to and then briefly. The tearful outburst he had when Grandpa died had been his last. After all, he was eleven now. He rebuffed all kindly solicitation from Mama, nor could Papa goad him out of it.

"School begins in a couple of weeks," he heard Papa say. "He'll snap out of it then."

"But how is that going to help?" Mama asked. "He hates school."

"That may be just what he needs, a good big hate to fill the void."

To be sure, Arthur hated going back to school, but Letha was in her glory, a feeling she shared with Lester, who was making his debut, joined by their cousins Tillie and Sammie.

Arthur still had trouble in the schoolyard, and with his new anger he was ready to fight. He challenged one of the new boys at school who claimed he was from a far-away place called Iowa.

"There's no such place," Arthur said. "I've lived here all my life, and I know there is no place but Oklahoma and the Indian Territory."

"You callin' me a liar?" and a fight ensued.

Letha stood by helplessly, holding her breath.

But not Sammie. Though they fought each other at home, when Sammie saw his cousin being attacked, the law of the pack prevailed and he too plunged into the fray. Their teacher warned that if it happened again, they'd both get expelled.

Tillie, little miss priss, did nothing but whine.

Lester caused problems, too. When the teacher gave him a primer, he immediately turned it upside down. When she tried to turn it around for him, he slanted his head around to one side, then slanted the book the other way before he would begin to read. When she asked him to read out loud he did fine, but the book was upside down.

All the children in the class thought it was hilarious, and turned their books around to see if they could do the same.

Letha was mortified that Lester was being laughed at, so at recess time she stayed behind and told the teacher about the home teaching sessions and how it was that Lester had learned to read upside down.

The teacher sighed and sat down at her desk. She absent-mindedly shuffled a few papers then stopped.

"Your family poses quite a problem for me. Not only do I have the challenge of teaching Lester to read right-side-up, I have to tolerate the whines of your cousin Tillie, plus keep Arthur and Sammie from fighting with the other boys. In fact, I've been advised to expel the both of them ..."

"Oh, please don't. I'm afraid if you do that my father might make the rest of us drop out too. Arthur will soon settle down, I think." And she explained to her about Grandpa and the death of his dog.

The teacher thanked her and sent her back to recess. As she was leaving, Letha passed by the doorway of the upper class room where lessons were in session. She paused there, watching the teacher write equations on the blackboard, and became enthralled with the magic of algebra.

That night at the supper table she told the family how he had filled the whole blackboard with formulas to prove that ABC equals XYZ.

"I will never quit school until I learn how to do that too," she announced.

"And what good would that do you?" challenged Arthur.

"I could teach others how to do it," Letha retorted.

And she went on to tell them about the Thanksgiving program. She and Tillie were going to sing one of the new hit songs that Clifford had taught them, and Lester was going to give a demonstration on reading and writing upside down.

Mama was not happy. She did not like the idea of Lester being shown like a circus freak, and she wasn't at all happy about the new fan-dangled song. She insisted that they should stick to the singing of some good religious song.

"That stuff is old-hat," Clifford retorted to which Mama replied that if religion was going out of style, she thought they should all go with it.

Ignoring the difference of opinion about their song, Letha and Tillie practiced out in the farmyard whenever they got a chance, and Mama finally relented, glad to see them happily occupied.

The night of the school program arrived and every Barnet, spick and span and sworn to their best behavior, piled into either Clifford's surrey or Papa's spring wagon and they set out for the school house with plenty of time to spare.

John had his mind set on dropping a few telling words to the townfolk on proposed additions to the recently organized Farmer's Union. He was going to personally see to it that the farmers not only organize to market their surplus products in town, but to withhold them if a good price was not forthcoming.

"To the producers belong the surplus and the profits made from its sale," he declared practicing his speech on Grace as they drove along toward the schoolhouse, still crossing his wires between capitalism and socialism.

Grace was only half listening. She was more worried about the children's performance than his. The girls were in Clifford's surrey practicing their song, entertaining all within earshot for the whole two miles to the schoolhouse. They scarcely needed to sing the song at the program, for everyone passing them or meeting them on the way got a complete preview of it. Grace cringed when she heard the words:

> In school I have an awful time
> To learn arithmetic.
> I cannot learn my go-zin-tos;
> The teacher says I'm thick.
> One go-zin-to two;
> two go-zin-to four,

185

Ma go-zin-to Pa's pants
When he go-zin-to snore . . .

Such a sassy, horrible song praising a woman for sneaking money from her husband! But the surrey was ahead of them and there was no stopping it now.

When they got to the school, she left John to his soapbox, and tried to catch up with the girls, but it was too late. Lester seemed happy and confident, so she let him go too.

But he never got to perform. The girls brought the house down, almost literally. Although their duet got off to a wheezing start, by the time they had arrived at the chorus, they came into full voice that carried to the rafters.

"One go-zin-to two,
Two go-zin-to four.
Pa go-zin-to Ma's pant;
When she go-zin-to snore."

They realized their mistake immediately and stopped, but did not know how to go on, and had no notion of the meaning of the jumbled words.

Grace braced herself in dread.

Silence reigned for a split second while the full impact of the girls' error filled the minds of the audience. Snickers came first from the teenage boys and girls. The women hid blushing faces behind their shawls and tittered. The men stomped their feet and beat each other on the back.

A chant arose from the young ones: "Barnets are varmints." One of the men rose and added: "And their father's a scheming socialist!"

John sprang like a Bengal tiger, and another man jumped to block him. As more joined the fight, Peck and Eakins tried to maintain order, but they were soon overcome. The Barnet boys, including young Victor, joined in the fight for honor of their name.

Grace stepped in to stop the boys, while Clifford pulled his brother out of the scrape. The boys in tow, she quickly rounded up the rest of the children, and the crowd escorted them all to the wagons. Tillie and Letha jumped in with her and hid under the wagon seat. Clifford loaded John into the back of the wagon and she took the reins. As she drove off, she heard Clifford behind her in the surrey.

"Me and mine will never set foot inside that town again."

"If you'd only let them sing the gospel songs like they've always done," Grace yelled back at him, "this would never have happened. But no, you had to fill their mouths with those racy words which will plague us for the rest of our days!"

"I'm not talking about the song, it's the Barnet name that's the problem!" he shouted. Fortunately, John, cursing and moaning in the back of the wagon didn't hear this. With the mood he was in, he would no doubt have jumped out and finished off with Clifford.

After that night, silence took over and remained with the two families for the next few days. Only Letha was brave enough to swallow her pride and return to the school.

That silent week the family got established in their new house up on the hill, with Clifford and his children remaining down at Grandpa's house. The plan had been to move the frame house up to Clifford's claim on the hill.

But when John drove back from taking Letha to school on the Monday morning after the move, he found a note signed by Clifford tacked to the door of the house, brought it up the hill to Grace, and handed it to her without a word.

Grace took the note from him and read. "I have decided you are right when you say that every tub should sit on its own bottom. Furthermore I do not plan that my children shall become objects of ridicule. Things have gone from bad to worse the past few weeks, and I have stuck it out only to help you get your house finished. Tell Grace thanks for doing her best to help me out with the children. I'm going to where no one has heard the Barnet name. Clifford."

There was no indication of where that might be. He was just gone.

John dropped down on the doorstep like a deflated balloon. Grace knew that his plan for developing the farm had included the cooperation of Clifford. Now Cliff was gone.

187

Chapter 17

Up on the Sandhill

In the aftermath of Clifford's departure, John's feet began to itch to be doing just what Clifford had the courage to do—leave this ignorant neck of the woods and get back to civilization where he could make good the Barnet name.

The new house was posing a problem of serious proportions. It was a two and half story structure with no stairway whatever. Its absence was not intended, but was the result of one of his practical jokes that backfired.

Although he and Clifford were excellent bricklayers, neither of them could pound in a nail straight. Mr. Green, the carpenter whom he had hired to do the framing and nailing, was a man whose religious faith forbade the eating of pork. At every meal with the family, he dutifully refused such meat, but he ate lavishly of fried chicken, and fairly soaked his bread in gravy.

"Mrs. Barnet you make the best gravy I ever sopped my bread in," he said one day after eating a hearty dinner.

For over a month, John had hidden a wicked smile behind his own slice of bread as he watched Mr. Green's gravy eating. Suddenly he could keep the secret of the good gravy no longer.

"Well, Mr. Green," he said with a chuckle, "You're a condemned man by now."

"How so?"

"You know you may as well eat the devil as drink his broth, or sop your bread in it either. You've been feasting for the past month on gravy made from the fryings of fat pig meat!"

Mr. Green looked wild-eyed. He put his hand on the pit of his stomach, pushed back from the table with the other hand, and left the house without a word or backward glance.

The "stair-less" house became a constant reminder of the ill-conceived joke. No one else in the neighborhood knew how to build a staircase, so the house had to get along with only a ladder braced against the back of the kitchen stove and poked through a hole cut in the floor above.

There was only one ladder, so when something was needed from the storage place in the attic above the second floor, the ladder had to be pulled through the opening and used to climb there. This proved to be a rather convenient arrangement for the children, who shared the bedroom space on the second floor. When they wanted no interference from adults, they drew up the ladder on the pretext of needing something from the attic.

They were further aided by the fact that the trapdoor opening into the second floor had been made, quite innocently, so small that Grace was unable to squeeze her hefty hips through it. This left the housekeeping chores upstairs—or more strictly upladder—defined by the children's ideas of what constituted good housekeeping. True, Papa occasionally made an unexpected foray there, but what he knew about housekeeping would have made almost as thin a book as what the children knew. Grace periodically went up the ladder as far as her hips would allow so she could make a sergeant's survey of the room above. In this way, the children's quarters maintained some semblance of order, at least some of the time.

The big room downstairs, about twenty-five feet wide and seventy feet long, was divided by a huge fireplace whose chimney also split the children's dormitory above. The girls slept on one side and the boys the other.

The fireplace opened to the sitting portion of the downstairs room, and against its backside the big Majestic range was placed facing into the kitchen end of the room. The sitting room doubled as a bedroom for John and Grace and baby Poppy.

In the winter no heat, other than that radiated by the brick chimney, was available for the rooms above. Once the pots and pans had been cleared from the cookstove at night, the children tossed down their clothes to land on top of it. They shivered as they climbed down the ladder to put on their warm clothes, set aside by Grace before she stoked up the fire for breakfast.

When Saturday washday came, the family supply of clothing was accounted for either at the washtub or on their backs. It was on one of these accounting days that his eldest daughter found herself in a jam—or, more strictly speaking, in the ketchup—when she could not account for her second pair of panties. In pitching the dirty clothes downstairs the panties had, unbeknownst to her, fallen into a large kettle of ketchup being simmered to thicken on the cookstove. There they had simmered with the ketchup for quite some time before Grace permitted Letha to give up her search for them in the upstairs room.

Letha found them later when she was sent to stir the ketchup for Grace who was busy outdoors over the washtub. Letha's dislike of her erstwhile favorite condiment was sudden and insistent—at least until that year's canning supply had disappeared from the shelves. Luckily, the panties, being made of khaki colored denim, could be rinsed out and returned to the fold.

To John's wife, the house was a haven of sorts in which to bring up her increasing brood, in some want of course, but not in as much as there would have been had they been wandering about with him trying to follow his bricklaying.

To the children it was a never-ending source of something new to wonder about. Compared to where they had lived before, the house seemed a mansion. They could easily see that they were luckier than the Mexican children. So if they thought about it at this early stage in their lives they surely thought themselves well off.

But to John, the house was strictly a trap in which it would soon stifle him if he did not find some way to escape.

For the most part during their first winter at the sandhill house, he was the most unhappy. Winter was no time to get out and try to find a job to bring in ready cash. In spite of his Socialist speech at the school, it hurt his pride no end to make any kind of deliveries of surplus products in town. He was not born to be a peddler. But he had no choice under the current situation. It was peddle, plow, or watch his family starve. He plowed the hateful acres, which returned hate for hate by leveling the plowed ridges to flatness within an hour of their being turned.

"Lift up thine eyes unto the hills," Grace quoted one day after hearing his complaints for the umpteenth time.

"I can get 'em no farther than the dusty window sills," he

191

ribbed her.

"Well, if we had glass windows I might manage to keep them clean."

"Women. Never satisfied," he retorted. But then come to think of it, neither was he.

To his credit, his scheme to change the color of the chickens to buff to match the monotone of the sand had worked. The coyotes stopped coming around, and coyote pelts were no longer added as throw rugs on the wide planks of the floor through which the winter winds found their way.

After the Thanksgiving humiliation, to Letha's shame and disappointment, her brothers did not return to school. Admittedly, Arthur was not made for school. He loved the freedom of the coyote chase or rabbit hunt from which he seldom came back empty-handed. Whereas from school he had often come back empty-handed, tossing any homework into the brush on his way home. If he had learned anything at all from his formal education, he kept it strictly to himself, thereby convincing Mama and Papa of the futility of sending him to school in the first place.

But Lester, wise Lester. With so much potential, he surely needed to be in school. Letha tried with all the reasoning she could muster to persuade Lester, but he said he preferred the solitude of the hills and the company of the quiet cows. He strictly disliked being crowded into a room with forty or more rowdy children. He said their noise and constant escapades made his brain so befuddled it simply refused to think. Not to mention the difficulty of being forced to read with his book right side up.

All this resistance worked to strengthen Letha's determination to go to school. Although she gave up singing forever, school was to her a daily song.

"If I'm going to learn all there is to know," was her new refrain, "I can't miss a single day of school."

No assignment was too difficult or tiresome if it would eventually lead to more knowledge and her goal of becoming a teacher.

So that winter she formed a partnership with Mama, and brought lessons home from school for evening sessions with

192

Arthur and Lester. While Letha watched the little ones, Mama had a chance to rectify the problem she had created. She taught reading and writing with Arthur fidgeting on one side of her and Lester sitting beside her on the other—his lesson at last facing him right side up.

After reading and writing, Letha swapped places with Mama and taught them arithmetic, while Mama stood on the ladder and saw that the little ones got to bed, and May washed the dishes. If Letha didn't give the lessons for love of teaching, she would have done it for hate of washing dishes, which had been her chore for as long as she could remember.

"After you learn your sums, your take-aways, your multiplication tables," she told her brothers, and in low voice added, "and your go-zin-tos," then brightened, "I'll teach you fractions and decimals. And then someday we can take on the letters and equations I saw on the blackboard. We'll swap arithmetic for mathematics!"

She made it sound like such an adventure, that Lester and Arthur went along with it and learned their numbers. With his business head, Arthur especially responded when she gave him reading problems involving making money.

While school was going on, John sat smoking his pipe thinking about things. One night he silently studied Grace's backside as she stood on the ladder cajoling their brood to bed, musing on the indomitable spirit of his woman which kept him trapped here.

Trapped in this God-forsaken land, though Grace didn't see it that way. In every argument she acted as if God was definitely there and even more definitely on her side. She always silenced him with some irrefutable quotation from the Bible. His only recourse was to retaliate with some mean word or deed.

A lump came into his throat and mist blurred his eyes. He loved her—if only she would lean on him just a little, perhaps he could be more content. But as this thought came into his mind, he knew it could not be so—he would then feel only contempt for her.

An uncomfortable feeling brought him out of his reverie.

193

Was he trying to break Grace's spirit so he could leave her and be free? He wanted to tell himself that wasn't it, but in truth he couldn't because he was not sure. Was this drive to hurt her, this inability to truly love the woman he thought he loved, the real reason for his devotion to the "brotherhood of man?"

To dispel the discomfort of his thoughts, John stood and tapped his pipe loudly on the cookstove, emptying its contents down the hole. The same hole Clifford had spat in. He smiled, remembering how much it irritated Grace. He also realized then how much he missed the man-talk.

As he packed his pipe with fresh tobacco, he decided he needed a new project. In the last days of digging for brick, he and Cliff had hit upon a lode of unusually fine clay, which they had set aside. Now he hit upon a plan for using it, and he would keep it secret from Grace.

John remained in this relatively happy frame of mind during the next morning's breakfast. He chomped his food noisily, glad for the chance to have something on which he could expend his built-up energy.

Grace watched her husband from the corner of her eyes. I wonder what he is up to now, she mused. Off on another tangent, I'd bet my last good eyetooth! Well, whatever keeps him happy.

She caught herself sighing deeply, and to cover up the sound of it she called for a second helping of the simple food she had prepared. Such second helpings may have done something to lighten her flagging spirits through the years, but certainly nothing to lighten her bodily heft. But if she had thought about that at all, she would have defended herself with the idea that a hard-working woman needs to keep up her strength both physically and mentally. Especially now—for she had her own secret.

For lack of a mirror Grace could not take a look at herself, but she wondered if John suspected there was another child on the way. She was afraid to mention it for fear he would be off again in search of cash.

She hoped that perhaps he was intending to sell the brick he was making and get some cash that way. So, when she wasn't busy about household chores or in town with deliveries, she pitched into the brickmaking. Time would disclose the source of his zeal, and for this she waited, as she waited for the day he would notice her condition.

Every moment he could spare, and some that he couldn't, John used to further the new venture. He began working as furiously at making the new brick as if the devil's horns and pitchfork were prodding him along. He recruited Lester and Arthur into the labor force. Even Victor found his legs at last and tagged along.

In truth, there was hardly a lazy bone in John's body. He worked like a fiend. When not grubbing sage and skunkbrush roots for the firing of the kilns, he sorted the already fired brick into racks of equal quality and color. Grace could not see how he could honestly preach the sanctity of an eight-hour day to the railroad men in town. Why, he always worked at least eighteen out of every twenty-four!

Throughout the winter, John seemed too tired to notice that she came late to bed and slept quietly on her own side. He was also too weary to notice that she was always up before he could drag his body out of bed in the morning.

A tumbleweed served as their Christmas tree that winter and with no money or time for gifts to put on it, its whitewashed beauty was able to stand the strain of the few ornaments they managed to hang.

Soon after the first of the year, a catalog came in the mail from a fruit tree nursery in Missouri, filling John with nostalgia.

"In Missouri everybody who was anybody had an orchard," he said while studying the beautiful specimens of fruits as he eagerly turned the pages. "And I'm going to have one here."

Inspired again to be a farmer, he sent away for two each of apple, peach and cherry trees.

They came in late February along with planting instructions.

"Leave the gunnysack wrappings on the young trees to prevent rabbits from gnawing the bark from their trunks," he read.

John followed the instructions, and every few days the children carried gallons of water to them. But somehow this did not

195

guarantee an orchard. Unfortunately the rabbits couldn't read. They tore off the wrappings, and within a fortnight had eaten not only the bark from the tree trunks but from the limbs as far up as their thieving mouths could reach.

When John surveyed the damage, he stretched out face downward on the ground and squeezed great handfuls of it. Had he been a small boy he would have cried, but after a time he stood up and pawed the earth with his feet like a bull in a frustrated rage.

"I will not stay here," he yelled at Grace. "And if you do, you can do it alone."

When he looked over at Grace to see how she was responding to this outburst, he at last saw her in all her glory —as swollen with life as the buds he had envisioned on his fruit trees.

He slumped again at her feet, and this time great sobs shook his body.

"You're going to have another baby," he moaned. "Why did you do this to me?"

Grace's backbone stiffened.

"I had your very willing help," she said, and she gave each word proper emphasis as she spat it out.

Then she sat calmly down beside him.

"I only have to hang my pants on the foot of your bed, and you get pregnant. There are ways. You could do something. It's your usual trap," he shouted. "Every time I decide to leave, you become bigger than life and twice as natural."

She sat there saying not a word.

"We have so many children, I can't even remember their names! We'll stay here until this baby is born and then we're getting out. Getting out! Do you hear me? And we'll not come back to be sandhill ticks ever again!"

She still said nothing. Her gaze shifted from him to Grandpa's and No-No's grave at the edge of the yard clearing.

"You may be married to this place, but I'm not. I'm leaving as soon as the baby is born." He turned away from her, and then back. "When will that be?"

"In early summer. Look, you may not be married to this place, but you are married to me in case you'd forgotten. The

196

child is ours—not mine alone—and I want your help to take care of it and provide for it—for me and the other children." She got up without another word and went quietly into the house.

After that John was far too perturbed to do farm work and worked in a doubled frenzy of effort at the brick-making site.

"Sure miss the help of the people of the community," John said innocently one day in his first effort at companionship for many a day.

Grace had to admit, she missed the neighbors too, the crowd of women at the church and the dinner and gabfest that followed.

They hadn't been to church since the fracas at the school, but they agreed to go back to church on Sunday.

Grace began to prepare the food, and John prepared the boys. "We are bound to be in for a great deal of ribbing even after these months of absence. But surely we can put up with it to put a smile back on Mama's face."

"Promise <u>you</u> won't fight?" Letha asked, looking her father right in the eye.

"I won't fight," he promised.

She turned her accusing eyes to the next victim.

"Arthur?"

Arthur grunted a reply.

Sunday morning found the Barnets dressed in their best bib-and-tucker, clothes they wore every day, but washed and ironed to a fare-you-well.

They held their heads high in spite of the whispers as they took their seats. When the sermon was over and the audience was getting ready to sing, John stood up.

"Hold your song a minute," John said. "I plan to preach a sermon, too."

A groan ensued and Grace held her breath.

"Oh, it's very short," he insisted. He went to the small platform.

"My text is: Do unto others as you would be done by."

He paused.

They stirred and shifted in their seats.

"My sermon," he said, "is equally short and to the point. It is: Rib me and even my wife, if it will add to your pleasure, but leave our children out of it or I'm going to raise cane."

His meaningful gaze swept the crowd.

Then he tossed in a bit of wit as a clincher.

"And no telling which one of you may turn out to be Abel if I raise Cain."

A short silence was broken by a single "Amen."

Arthur didn't know what to make of Papa's sermon except that he felt it was unnecessary. They didn't need Papa's proclamation, they could take care of themselves. He was just glad when the church service was over and he could enjoy the outside church, where he often learned more than came from the pulpit. The town children, of all ages and sizes, played all kinds of games by rules different from the ones Arthur and his siblings were used to.

Fortunately, by this time, they had reinforcements in the presence of young Victor, who was becoming a force to be reckoned with—he had found his legs and they were almost as long as Arthur's and just as fast at running. So with this added confidence and their father's sermon ringing in their ears, they joined the gang of children gathering in the churchyard. It was an unseasonably warm day for March, so the group decided to play "work up" baseball. The game started with a race, organized by one of the older children who had agreed to be the umpire. From a starting line, the kids raced to the different positions of play. Where they landed was where they started the game, and when the umpire called "batter out" the positions were rotated.

Victor got to the prized first base at the start of the game, clearly ahead of all, but closely followed by a bigger boy named Matthew. Matthew kept pushing Victor off the base, refusing to let him play, but Victor got in the way so the play could not start.

"Cheater! Cheater! Cheater!" he chanted up to his face.

Matthew hit Victor a good solid shot in the nose.

Because he'd promised not to fight, Arthur fought his natural instinct to jump in and defend his little brother. Besides, Victor hadn't made the promise, and it was time to see what he could do on his own. Victor did the Barnet name proud. He stood his ground, punching back until the blood from the original blow

198

started getting into his eyes, forcing him to an ignoble retreat.

Arthur ran and got some cool water on his handkerchief and gave it to Victor to put over his eye. When the food was served he got Victor a plate with lots of deviled eggs, which he knew were his favorite church food. They sat a good distance from their parents because they didn't want Papa causing another scene.

When they approached the family wagon to go home, Mama spotted Victor's swollen eye and laid into him.

"Victor? Great Heavenly Days! What happened?"

Arthur explained what happened ending with "Victor needs to learn to punch back."

To their relief, Papa chuckled.

"So, Victor, you led with your nose, eh? I think your brother's right. Arthur needs to teach you how to lead with your fist."

Mama started to object, but Papa stopped her.

"I'm not encouraging you to be a bully, Vic, but when the words of reason will not avoid a battle, then I think you are justified to get in the first blow, especially if the other guy is bigger than you. You will be amazed how a bloody nose will reduce a bigger boy to your own size."

"Vic's a lefty," Arthur said. "It won't be easy."

"All the better. A good left hook can take the other fella by surprise."

Little Poppy sat and rode beside her hero big brother Victor in the back of the wagon. Arthur saw her slip her little hand into Victor's and squeeze it tightly, giving him the consolation he didn't get from Mama.

After that Sunday, the March winds howled and ranted full-tilt for two weeks without a lull.

"It takes grit to live in this place," Papa told Arthur after they finished putting the third kiln of brick to fire. "And I'd say the wind is cooperating by furnishing plenty of it."

Arthur told him that the rains usually came by mid-April, so that meant several weeks of putting up with the avalanche of dust.

199

Chapter 18

Papa is An Organizer

"We will make no more brick until the rains come and go," John announced at the supper table. Grace was standing at the cookstove, stirring the cream gravy. When the bubbles formed, she poured it into a pitcher and took it to the table. Then she brought in a steaming platter of chicken.

Nobody asked John why he had made such a proclamation, but he answered anyway.

"For one reason I can't stand working out in this dust, and for another we'd just about get a big bunch of brick on end to dry in the sun and a big rain would ruin them all. I'm going to sort what brick are ready and then spend a few days in town hobnobbing with the men. I'm getting sick of being a hermit."

John had yet to reveal his plans for the brick he had sorted into the "good" piles. The half-brick and odd shaped ones he cast into a heap beside the brick site. Grace had decided she wanted those discards. She missed the brick patio they had at Blackwell made from just such discards as these. But when she suggested another porch, John discarded it as easily as the brick.

"A porch is a place to sit in leisure to stare at passers-by and be stared at and envied by them," he said. "There are neither passers-by nor leisure time here, so why a porch?"

So when John was in town, Grace started the patio herself at the south door of the house with the help of the children.

John screamed like murder when he saw the result of their first day's efforts. "Gosh all hemlock," he yelled, "if I've got to look at that thing every time I come or go I want it done right."

He began furiously throwing the brick right and left so he could start over.

"Why are luxuries more important to you than the necessities?" he growled.

"Well, if I knew what the necessities you are talking about

201

were, maybe I could make a wiser choice," Grace said.

But John didn't bite. He still refused to tell her his plans.

"I'm willing for you to use the good brick for anything you have in mind, but the culls are for us. And when you finish the patio, I want a smokehouse beside it."

"A smoke house!" In a rage he threw his trowel. "We're leaving here as soon as the baby is born—remember?"

"But in the meantime we need to eat, and we can't face another summer without meat. It needs to be built right away so we can get a small hog butchered, hung, and cured before the hot weather sets in. And we could use a vegetable bin or two dug into the hill and lined with brick—"

"Stop, woman, stop. One thing at a time," and he began to work with a fury.

Within the week she found out what John was doing with the good brick. When she went to town on Saturday to make deliveries and get groceries, she saw a big pile of the brick on a lot adjoining the hotel.

When she went to the Mexican quarter to make deliveries, she saw another big pile of the "seconds" on the vacant strip of land west of the railroad.

Pinned down with this evidence, John admitted that he was going to build a room onto the hotel for Mrs. Swan to put in a restaurant.

"The reason I didn't tell you, was that I was afraid you'd be jealous."

Suddenly Grace felt too weary to summon up any jealousy or indeed any kind of response at all.

"And what about the seconds in the Mexican quarter?"

"As soon as I get the restaurant building done I'm going to build some row-houses up there for the Mexicans to move into so they can get out of the miserable tin shacks they live in now." He started to say more, but stopped.

He turned instead to Arthur. "I want you to start taking management of this place so I can get out and make a living laying brick. In time your Mama can go with me."

This pronouncement managed to startle her, but she held her tongue. Arthur was delighted.

202

Thinking it over in bed that night she was glad John had given up the idea of dragging the family around with them. She was pleased he wanted her with him, but she was staying put. Most likely she could talk him out of it, for surely they could not leave the young girls there to shift without their mother.

She managed to stick to her guns, and within a week a working truce was achieved. The family re-organized the farm duties and plodded on through the summer while John was spending more and more time in town.

One Saturday in town Grace spotted him on the veranda of the hotel giving a speech, a small crowd gathered around. He looked grand, and his voice rang with fire and conviction, but when you listened to the words, it was the usual gobbledygook about the cause, organizing the Socialist party, and subscribing to the paper "The Appeal to Reason." She shook her head and returned to the farm. At least he wasn't cockfighting or drinking or spending time with another woman. At least the family was still together for the time being—on Sundays anyway.

Yes, on Sundays John was at her side keeping up appearances at church, and she was meant to be at his side to make him look good during his speeches after church. But she usually busied herself spreading the food for the dinner and cleaning up afterwards to avoid the embarrassment of his ill-conceived speeches.

As she got nearer the end of her pregnancy it got harder to make the trip to town. One Sunday as they left the church she said, "I'm sick, John. You've got to get me home and go for the doctor." She climbed in the back and lay down beside Letha.

John looked upon her with fright in his eyes.

"Arthur, take all the children to the hotel," he commanded. "Except Letha—she's staying with us. When you get there, phone Dr. McGinnis and tell him I am taking Mama on home but he must come right away."

Arthur started down the street, but John called after him.

"Wait a minute. He won't be able to get up the sandhill in his new Ford. Tell him I will come back down to Grandpa's house in the wagon and meet him there."

Grace felt frightened too, and in pain. Something was wrong

and she knew it. She had not felt the baby move for days. She had been telling herself that it was just in position waiting for nature to take its course. Perhaps she and the doctor had miscalculated the delivery date, because she was very large.

Each jolt of the wagon sent the pain from womb up her backbone into her head so that she could hardly think. "Slow down—no hurry," she heard herself moan incoherently.

Letha gripped the wagon with one arm and tried to brace Mama with the other. Mama had never been in trouble like this before. Papa was at his wit's end trying to comply with her erratic orders.

As they passed Grandpa's house, to Letha's horror, water began streaming from between Mama's legs.

"Hurry, Papa, hurry!" she screamed.

John drove the team up the hill as fast as he could no matter how much Mama moaned.

When they got to the house, he drove right onto the patio and up to the doorstep, jumped down and managed to pull Mama out of the wagon by reaching under her arms and pulling her back against his chest. Letha carried her feet.

When they got her to the bed Mama was delirious. "Go for the doctor and tell Letha to wait outside," she murmured to Papa.

Letha backed away in a daze, turned and went out onto the patio.

"Stay near the kitchen door," Papa told her when he came out. "Mama doesn't want you in the room, but stay near in case she needs you. Stay here until she calls for you."

Letha felt herself trembling and she couldn't look Papa in the eye. He took hold of her shoulders and shook them. "There is nothing to be so frightened about. Cows have calves every year and get along fine. Your Mama has had six babies and she will be all right!"

Before Letha could reply that this time was different, Papa was in the wagon and driving down the hill.

She stood there frozen, watching him go. She strained to hear Mama's groans, but she didn't call her. It was even more terrifying when she didn't hear anything. With every moan she

204

felt both relief and agony. [1]

She waited and waited. She was dying to pee, but didn't dare go to the privy. So she stepped off the patio, squatted, and pushed it out as fast as she could.

Coming back to the doorway, she could still hear Mama's groans. Then after what seemed an eternity she heard a piercing cry. Still her mother did not call. She could stand it no longer.

She burst into the open room. Mama seemed far away at the other end. She was sitting up in bed, holding high above the covers, in each hand, a slimy blob of human flesh.

"Get me that ball of string and scissors in the drawer of the kitchen table," Mama yelled at her.

Letha's shaking legs somehow got her there, and her trembling hands fulfilled the command, but as she brought them to her mother, even she could see it was of no use. The cords were a tangled mess around the lifeless bodies.

"Mama, Mama. They're all blue." Tears gratefully blurred her view of them. "Mama. They're not breathing."

When Papa finally arrived with the doctor they stumbled through the open doorway. There in the twilight they stood looking at them—Mama lying listlessly staring into space with the bodies of twin boys near her side, Letha still sobbing across the bottom of the bed.

Dr. McGinnis quietly cut the two twisted cords while Papa found some cloths. As the doctor wrapped one, then the other, Mama whispered, "Bury them beside Grandpa." John covered them with a blanket, went to the barn to get a shovel.

"The children?" Mama asked the doctor.

"They're at my house. We'll keep them there for a few days."

She gave him a grateful look, moved to the bottom of the bed beside Letha and began stroking her hair. Letha wept because Mama had never caressed her in such a comforting way, and wept because she felt she should be the one comforting Mama.

- - -

John turned from the scene between his wife and daughter

205

with overwhelming bitterness. The doctor gathered up the bundles and followed him to the gravesite.

As he dug, each spadeful brought up another thought. True, he had not wanted another baby, but an awful thing like this was not to be borne. First he blamed the doctor and his damn Ford. He blamed his rickety wagon. As he dug deeper in the hateful soil, he blamed the land. Then he blamed the government for even opening up the land to the homesteaders in the first place. Finally he got around to blaming himself for not taking his family away and God for making such land and expecting people to live in it.

After they covered the two parcels of unfulfilled life, the doctor went back in to Grace, then came back out and said, "Make sure she drinks lots of fluids. I gave her some water, and put it beside the bed." He said he would walk back down the hill.

When John went back in the house, he stood looking at Grace. She had fallen into a deep sleep, Letha whimpering beside her. He climbed up the ladder, tossed down some bedding and lay on the floor beside them. Grace slept through the night. Letha awoke from time to time, only to cry herself to sleep again.

But John could not sleep. He began to realize the real reason he was angry: How could they leave now as he had planned when she was in such a devastated state? He would have to wait awhile until she got her strength and spirit back.

Chapter 19

Bronzed Stoics

Several days passed during which Grace made no effort to exert herself—hadn't the will or the strength to do so. She couldn't get the horror of the miscarriage out of her mind. She could only arouse herself when the pain in her engorged breasts was so intense she had to sit up and use the breast pump Dr. McGinnis had given her to use.

Each time the doctor came to see her, he tried to coax or goad her into action without success. On his third trip to see her, he brought a crying baby in his arms. He put the infant down beside her.

"The mother of this baby is so weak," he said, "she cannot nurse him. If you don't do it for me, I shall lose both patients."

Grace gave him back the breast pump, took the baby in her arms, and nursed it, tears streaming down her cheeks. Letha sat beside her stroking the baby's head.

"I want to leave the child with you for a few days until his mother is able to take care of him herself." Without waiting for an answer, the doctor was gone.

At first Letha helped with the baby's care, and by the end of the week when the doctor returned, Grace was beginning to totter about the house. He left the baby another week, and by that time said he knew the baby had saved both his patients, and took him back.

With the baby gone, Grace turned her attention back to her husband, and whether or not he would be staying. He had already gone back to work in town, and when the restaurant building was completed, he received enough money to buy three things—two hounds with which to hunt during the winter and a registered Jersey bull to breed better dairy stock than they had on the place now. She then realized that John would stay on the

207

farm with them at least until the next winter. He was apparently still obsessed with the idea of building a decent place for the Mexicans to live in. Grace didn't object, for she recognized that such a project provided him companionship with people other than the family—a need that seemed to be essential to him. She was even glad that he wanted to help them.

When the building was finished, she went herself to help with the process of moving. Each family was assigned, free, one big room—a sort of oversized stall in the long building. True, the doors did not fit the openings, but how could they? They had been salvaged from the corrugated tin shacks where the Mexicans had previously lived. There the doors had been hanging often by one hinge for many a year, so they could not help being bent and warped.

While helping with the move, she learned that John and their foreman, Gilliza, had been organizing a union. If the railroad company didn't grant their request for higher wages and shorter hours, they were planning a strike as well

She feuded with John about his involvement all the way home.

That evening, while they were at supper, Dr. McGinnis arrived hurriedly without having been called. "You're going to have to leave here immediately, Barnet," he stated without any preliminaries or maneuvering to pull John away from the family.

"What's up—what's the matter?" John asked.

"This afternoon a whole new crew of Mexican section hands were brought in without notice by the railroad. They were given the jobs of the ones who were here—the ones you helped Gilliza to organize."

"Our men? But where are they now?"

"They were herded, along with their families, into the same box cars the new ones came in and were shipped back to Mexico—Gilliza included." Dr. McGinnis said. "Your nice apartment building was emptied even faster than it was filled up yesterday. Even the tin doors have gone back to where they came from, and the railroad officials who came in with the new crew are out hunting for you. You've got to leave with me right now. If they catch you, it will mean jail for you, the same as it did for that

Debs fellow in Chicago."

Grace looked around the room. Her whole family was aghast.

"I'm sorry, Grace, but they would have heard about it sooner or later, and better that they got it straight from me." Then he turned to John. "You'd better hurry. I left my car at home. If they find out I'm here tipping you off, I'll be in this up to my neck too. If we get back to my car before the railroad officials find it, I can take you to Alva tonight to catch a train. You wouldn't dare to try to catch a train in Waynoka." With that, the doctor went out to the team he had hitched in the yard.

John repeated his desire to have Grace to go with him, but she refused. "When you get settled in a steady job and have a place for us to live, we will come to you," she said, knowing the odds were that would never happen. "Until then we stay here."

John went out to gather up his bricklaying tools, then came back in to her. He put his hands on her shoulders, but before he could speak she began the obligatory lecture, "You are not to do any more union or socialist organizing— " but her voice broke, and she bowed her head to keep him from seeing her smarting eyes.

He lifted her head gently. "Don't let those tears rust your iron nature," he said smiling down at her. He pulled her to him and they walked to the wagon together.

His climb into the seat beside the doctor was accompanied by a warning. "Just as before, Barnet, you must send money every week by way of my office. If you don't, as much as I like you, I'll see to it that the railroad officials find out where to locate you." He shook the reins and they were off.

"Of course I'll send you money," John called back to where she stood in the road. She watched as they disappeared down the sandhill.

This time when Papa left, Letha found she could hold her head up high. In the small community where he had made his mark, her father had become a martyr. As the local men, both rural and urban, gathered in knots on street corners or on the hotel veranda for the next several weeks, they hashed and rehashed his words and relived his deeds.

"Your Papa has given us a new awareness," one of his most ardent followers told Letha. "What he told us is a finger pointing to the underlying truth about the flaws in the American way of life."

The Mexican housing, with its many unframed doors, situated as it was where farmers passed it coming into town, and railroad men passed it going to and from their work in the railroad yards, was dubbed "Barnet's Folly" by his critics. Yet it was pointed to with pride by many as the result of the sincere effort of a farseeing man who sought to better the lot of the lowliest working men among them.

Letha soon found being the daughter of a living legend granted more dignity than having Papa with them. She returned to school, spent most of her time studying, and passed the eighth grade county examinations with an outstanding record.

Arthur happily took over as the man of the family. He also stepped up to the management of the farm and their growing dairy business.

Lester could at last read right side up and was persuaded to return to school. But he chose to go to the smaller and quieter rural school for which they qualified. May went along with him, delighted to take his hand in their walks through the pastures, exploring the countryside along the way. In the mornings and evenings, Lester herded the cattle and sheep, each to their own pasture.

Gregarious Victor preferred the town school and went along with Letha, making the morning deliveries as usual. From time to time, he felt called upon to defend the Barnet name with his newly discovered and surprisingly effective left hook. In the evenings, he did his assigned chores, but somewhat haphazardly and at his leisure.

Only Poppy remained at home. An unusually silent child, she sat watching Mama sew, wide-eyed with her thumb in her mouth. Mama had used some of the money John sent to buy a sewing machine and made new clothes for everyone so that they could be presentable for school. That done, she began to take in sewing for some of the working women in town. Mrs. Swan became her main customer.

In short, they managed fine without Papa. The first winter he was gone was filled to the brim with people, work, and school activities. Mama seemed to be everywhere, urging them on in their efforts. In time it seemed the rest of the family had all but forgotten that Papa was or ever had been.

But not so for Letha. She missed him terribly. Without Papa there, Mama became harder to get along with. The closeness she felt toward her for a while after the twins had died had become replaced with resentment toward her, for she felt in some deep, inexplicable way that Mama was to blame for Papa's absence.

The fights Mama used to have with Papa now seemed to be focused on her. Mama was constantly finding fault with her. She criticized her posture. She didn't like the way she was fixing her hair. It seemed she was always harping on one thing or another.

In order to find a little space to herself, Letha often retreated after supper to her corner of the room upstairs.

One evening she was deeply involved in a book when Mama yelled up the stairs.

"Letha Faye, what are you doing up there?"

"Reading."

"Reading what?"

"A book."

"What book?"

Letha came to the ladder and showed it to her. "A book on the reading list at school."

Mama reached up for it.

Letha made the mistake of handing it down to her. Mama opened it and read a page here and there.

"And this Rochester and Jane live in the same house together unmarried?"

"Mama, she was his governess, and the book is considered a classic!"

She handed it back to her. "It's trash."

"Mama, I've gotta read something besides the Bible and the Sears catalogue! It's a big world out there!"

"Well, right now, you need to take care of the dishes right

211

here, so get yourself down here immediately!"

Mama couldn't stop her from reading novels for school assignments, but she flew into a rage one day when a fashion magazine Letha got from one of her girlfriends slipped out from among her books.

Without a word, Mama picked it up, flipped through it and then tossed it in the cookstove.

But the worst incident of all was when Mama silently climbed the ladder and caught her trying on the corset Letha had borrowed in the interest of a fashion experiment from Mama's closet. It was so big she had to wrap it around her twice, and was busy binding it in place with the lace strings.

To her humiliation, she was ordered downstairs on the spot where all could see her, and to add injury to insult, Mama slapped her across the face.

May was sympathetic to her, helping her hide behind the cookstove and unlace the corset.

Fortunately, Arthur was outside at the time, busier than ever with the management of the farm.

With so much friction in the family, it was small wonder that they turned more and more to their chief bronzed stoic, Lester, to settle disputes. They would find him in the pasture at the end of the day and lay their cases before him. He would quietly listen to all sides of an argument, weighing them in silent Indian-like fashion while he chewed on a blade of grass. Finally he would suggest a practical conclusion, typically a compromise acceptable to all.

They reached one very important decision in such a manner. In a powwow in the pasture just before wheat planting time, they decided to rent Grandpa's place to a young couple who would take on managing and increasing the dairy herd in the pastures.

The extra hands on the farm proved useful as a new challenge arose now that Oklahoma had became a state.[1] In order to combat typhoid, the Federal Government pressed for the state's compliance with the Pure Food and Drug Act.[2] That meant milk had to be sold in sterilized bottles, and meat could not be sold in the open. All meat was to be dispensed from stores with glass cases to display and store the meat. Dr. McGinnis had been commissioned to inspect and enforce the Act's regulations.

Letha overheard discussion of the new food adulteration and sanitary codes during lunch at Mrs. Swan's hotel restaurant. In her very knowing manner, she informed all within hearing that adulteration had been against the law ever since the days of Moses, and that she doubted that the government was going to be able enforce it. She just about brought down the rafters with that one, and felt even more humiliated than when she sang the song at the school.

Occasionally a letter from Papa came along with the weekly check. Once he announced a new scheme to get his family to join him in the cause.

> *My dear family,*
>
> *The United States is on the verge of siding with our old enemy, England, and declaring war on Germany. Arthur and others like him will be called to fight that war for the damned capitalists who will line their pockets at the expense of his blood.*
>
> *Two members of our brotherhood, Laudermilk and Varden, have come to the conclusion that this country's interest in the cause of the working man is hitting one of the lowest ebbs in years, mostly because of this war talk. They are organizing a band of workers, including farmers, to go with them to New Zealand where there is a well-organized colony of cooperative workers on one of the islands. I would like us all to go there.*
>
> *Your devoted husband and*
> *loving father, John*

The family held a meeting, Lester presiding, and decided unanimously against this proposal. Mama wrote John the answer, and they didn't hear from him again for a long time.

But eventually another letter came from Papa exploring a new possibility:

"There is a new school over in the foothills of the Ozarks. It is called a self-help school, following in the true spirit of the brotherhood of man. All the pupils in grades one and two work on the farms, in the shops, in the restaurant, in the housekeeping chores, the bakery—do everything and anything—for their keep and the privilege of attending the school.

"A man and his wife operate the school and are teachers for the advanced courses while the pupils in the higher grades teach the classes below them."

Letha, ready to escape the town and become a teacher at last, thought the idea was wonderful! But Mama and the rest of the tribe would have none of it and wrote him so.

Letha thought long and hard about it, and in time, proved herself her father's daughter by coming up with a scheme of her own and writing to him:

> Dear Papa,
>
> Remember the brick row-house with its many stall-like rooms that you built for the Mexicans? A bunch of the young farm men, including all of us young Barnets, plan to establish a cooperative market there where all can bring their produce and sell it. Storeowners can come out too and buy if they want to have a better choice of things than relying on just one -broker at a time to come to their stores.
>
> Dr. McGinnis has assured us that no law will be broken as long as we keep meat under glass. We will all have a way of getting cash every week, or those who wish can take due bills from the stores and go to town to trade them for groceries if they want to deal in that way.
>
> So you see, your guiding spirit is here and we have found a way to bring co-operation and private enterprise together. Barnet's Folly will now be known as Barnet's Market.
>
> Who knows? Maybe next time you come back to see us, you will find a bronze statue or at least a plaque in front of the market dedicated to the inspiration of John Barnet.
>
> Love, Your daughter Letha

She knew that he would know she was only teasing him, not making a promise, for where had she learned such tactics?

But she never got a reply.

Like her father, Letha could only continue to hope and dream of an escape from the sandhill house.

214

Mama Grace
Part Three
1918-1920

Chapter 20

A New Proposition

After a long absence with no word, John suddenly reappeared one day while Grace was busy baking. He rode up to the porch, got off his horse, burst in the house, announcing that he had traded their property for a new farm in the Ozarks of Arkansas.

Grace was stunned. Arthur was outraged!

"You had no right!"

"I had no choice. I had to offer this place as collateral on the new place."

"You should have consulted us," Lester said.

"There wasn't time. It is such a nice parcel of land it couldn't wait—it would have been gone. Other people were looking at it when I was making the deal. I had to sign papers. But, believe me, it's a thousand times better than this place. Rich, fertile soil, forests, green pastures— and a nice, clean log cabin. Grace, you won't have to fight the dirt anymore."

"I don't have dirt inside the house anymore. Arthur put glass windows in. Didn't you notice?"

"And Papa, we have a telephone!" piped in May.

"Is there a telephone in the log cabin?" asked Victor.

"Not yet. But let me tell you about the place."

Arthur turned on his heels and walked away as Papa continued his sales description.

"There is a three-acre patch of dewberries with fruit the width of my thumb and half as long. There is a ten-acre apple orchard with Arkansas Blacks, Winesaps, and Ben Davises, a golden colored apple they called a Washington something, several Bartlett pear trees—all well cared for and offering good crops. The house is a two-story log cabin and the barn has a large loft and is in good shape. Water, cold and crystal clear, is drawn from a deep well. No one knows how deep that water is. It must be an underground lake or large stream. The forest is of oaks,

217

walnut, hickory, pecan, chinquapin, paw-paw, and persimmon with the fruit the size of a hen's egg and sweet as honey."

Here John paused to take a breath and looked around the circle of expectant faces.

"What is a Paw-Paw?" May asked.

"A Paw-Paw is a tall slender tree growing in moist river-bottom land. Its fruit, I was told, is shaped like a pear but not quite so large at the blossom end. It is sweet when ripe. There are acres of wild blackberry thickets scattered throughout the forest in the clearings. And there are Bobwhite quail, partridge *and* mountain lions they call panthers, don't ask me why. There are coons, 'possums, skunk—they call them 'civet cats'—great barn owls, bats, squirrels, both gray and red fox, hawks, and buzzards.

"What have I left out—oh yes, people live there too! Did I say streams? Well, a half-mile from the house, on a neighbor's land, is the prettiest little stream of sparkling clear water fed by springs here and there along the bank. There are trout, rainbow and spotted brook, perch, and crawdads up to a foot long.

"What's a crawdad?" Victor asked.

"A crawdad is like a tiny lobster, only it swims backwards. He doesn't care where he is going, just wants to see where he has been." He kept a straight face, but Grace saw Victor had his doubts.

"He has two legs on each side of the front part of his body that he crawls around with until he gets scared or in a hurry. Then his tail flips under him several times and he darts backwards. On the front end, his eyes stick out on both sides on small stems. A long feeler is beside each eye, and they help to alert him to danger. Last, but most important, he has a large, dangerous looking pincher on each side in front of his smaller legs."

He was looking at Victor as he talked. "Victor, why do I have the feeling you don't believe a word I'm saying? Well, young man, let me tell you something more so you will know about this kind of thing. These big boogers are bullies. They fight with each other and sometimes one pinches a pincher off the other one. The loser gets away with only one pincher. Before long he begins to grow a new pincher.

218

"Now, I know you think I am a bald-faced liar. You just remember about the crawdads, Victor. When we get there we'll catch some. Their tails are good to eat. You peel them off their shell-like plates, dip them in egg batter and fry them in deep hot fat in a skillet. You wait. Don't let me forget."

Grace wasn't won over with the pretty words and the promise of catching crawdads. But it had given her time to think. She knew how much John had hated the sandhill. It had driven him away. Maybe it was only fair to give the marriage another chance in a place that he loved. Most of all, hearing his fresh enthusiasm, she realized how very tired she was. She was tired of being the one in charge, tired of the responsibility of running the farm, even with her grown children to help. The Pure Food and Drug Act compliance, to which she agreed in principle, had become the near ruin of their business. It was all becoming too much.

"All right, John Barnet, it seems I have no other choice, since you've sold this place out from under us. But you must stay and help us close down and make the move."

John said, "Of course I will." He gave her a hug, then rushed out to put his horse in the barn. But his horse was gone. And so was Arthur.

John returned as quickly as he had gone.

"The damned thief has stolen my horse," he yelled. "Where's that telephone?"

May showed him.

"I'll have him arrested for this," he shouted as he rang a general ring. He paused to listen until he heard several phones had been taken up.

"Anybody who sees a half-grown boy riding John Barnet's pacing horse, report it to the sheriff's office. The horse has been stolen."

He hung up the receiver and faced the quieted group.

Grace bounded to the telephone and rang another general ring.

"Our son, Arthur, is riding that horse. The horse is OURS—Arthur's as well as Mr. Barnet's. Arthur cannot steal from himself. If you see them, report to me, Mrs. Barnet."

She hung up, but continued to stay near the telephone.

Within a few minutes the sound of the Barnet's ring came. She grabbed the phone.

"Hello" she called.

"This is Dr. McGinnis," came the voice from the other end. "On his way past here just a few minutes ago, Arthur told me he was fed up, and was running away to join the army. Said he'd rather die than have anything to do with moving to hillbilly land. He should be in town by now."

"He's joining the army," she announced to the family.

"He's too young!" Letha wailed.

"Boys lie about their age all the time to join," Lester said.

"Want me to do anything?" the doctor on the phone was asking.

"No," she said finally. "Under the circumstances, I think that would be the best thing for him to do."

John grabbed the phone. "He can join the army if he wants, but I want that horse back. Do you hear me? I want that horse back!"

"I'll see if I can catch him in town."

Dr. McGinnis brought the horse back the next morning. John was relieved, but it was small consolation for the rest of the family.

In the months that followed, John asserted his place as head of household. He had a goal to work towards and he was in good form. With Lester and Victor beside him, he harvested the end of the crops. They sold the cows and made preparations for the move. The family was pulling together again.

Then Grace discovered that she was pregnant yet again. She knew John was itching to get his feet on the good soil of Arkansas, but preparations would have to be curtailed until after the arrival of the new baby.

"Dammit, you've gone and done it again! By God, this will be the absolute last one."

It was a long wait.

Chapter 21

Reverse Pioneering

"Pay no attention to meandering roads or trails. Stay on the straight road and head due east by the sun," Grace said, mocking the words he had said to her ten years before, "and you're bound to get in the vicinity of Siloam Springs sooner or later." She gave him a peck on the cheek and took one last teasing shot. "Do you need the face of a clock?"

"Ah, but I have a real compass for this trip, and a map," John grinned. "Two advantages you didn't have. Good thing, too. I need all the advantages I can get. I don't think I could match your determination . . ."

"Well, I think you're just as determined to get to your dream farm in the Ozarks as I was to my Pa's—"

"Besides, I only have to ask people along the way. Everybody knows where Tulsa is. And after Tulsa, everybody knows Arkansas."

"Well, stick to the asking, John Barnet, and don't start any organizing along the way or you'll never get there."

"Don't worry." He shook the reins and the horses pulled ahead. "My organizing days are over." He turned briefly to wave and saw Grace lifting baby Zelda's hand to wave good bye. The two of them would join the family later.

The rest of the children yelled and waved out the peephole in back of the wagon as long as they could. Little Poppy was crying, but Victor took her in his arms and comforted her.

Driving the team, John comforted himself with his own thoughts. Yes, by golly, he'd give up organizing, for a while anyway. The socialist party would have to get along without him for the time being. The Barnet name was well-known for organizing in Missouri, Kansas, and Oklahoma, but not in Arkansas, unless word had drifted across the border.

Arkansas would give him and his family a fresh start. They

could leave their complicated history behind. He'd thought he'd never be able to talk her into it, but his stories of the land he purchased in the beautiful Ozarks had won over all the children except Arthur, so Grace had caved in.

He'd left his spring wagon and his prized pacer with Grace on the farm. She'd use them after he'd sent her word of their arrival in Siloam Springs. There simply wasn't enough room for Grace and the baby in the wagon box, even in Arthur's absence.

He couldn't believe Arthur was in the Army! But in a way, it made things easier. Try as he could, there was no making peace with the boy. Too many years of resentment built up. Not that he blamed the boy what with his own comings and goings. But Arthur had no idea of how hard he'd tried to stay with the family. God only knew how many pressures were beyond his control.

Still, he had his second son Lester riding the new filly behind the wagon and his favorite son Victor, so like himself, sitting proudly on the bench beside him. And the girls seemed to adore him as always. Things would be all right.

Letha bounced in the back of the wagon between May and Poppy, bracing herself against Mama's Majestic oven. Mama had stuffed the oven with their belongings, so there was no chance Poppy would get trapped inside it as May had done when they came west.

If Mama had been willing to give up her Majestic, there might have been room for her. But then, baby Zelda was too young to travel, even younger than Victor had been on the trip west.

Secretly, Letha was glad Mama hadn't come along. Their relationship had not improved, it had just been put on hold, which felt even worse. At least Mama didn't slap her in Papa's presence.

Dear Papa, on the other hand, had never struck her, or any of the children. He didn't need to. If he was annoyed, all he need do was give them a look and raise his sleek eyebrows.

It was wonderful having him all to themselves for the first time ever. She'd go anywhere with him. But she was especially excited about moving to Siloam Springs.

"Forty of the prettiest acres this side of paradise," Papa had claimed.

And he'd promised Letha she could attend the new school in the foothills, a cooperative school where the students learned not only the academics but earned their keep working together to run a dairy farm, a cannery, and even a print shop. It would be a perfect school for Lester, Victor, and May.

"In fact," he said, "I reckon my number one daughter will have no trouble at all getting a job as a teacher there."

Imagine! Her dream of becoming a teacher actually happening in one of the most progressive schools in the country.

"Victor," Letha shouted to the front of the wagon box. "When we start going to the new school, promise you won't fight?"

"Er-r-r-r," he stammered.

"Promise!"

"Okay," he replied half-heartedly.

"Son," Papa said in a low even voice, "you do whatever you need to do. Don't be tied to petticoats. Your big sister and your big mama are two of a kind."

Letha only half-hearing busied herself brushing the accumulating dust off her dress. This trip back East was definitely dustier than the one coming out. She was glad she had packed away her best dress to save for when they went through Tulsa.

Imagine! Seeing the city she'd always dreamed of! Maybe she could even buy her own corset in a shop there.

She looked out the peephole to see if she could spot Lester on the filly and saw a sprawling city of prairie dogs. A stab of pain hit her when she realized how much she missed her big brother and how she wished he were there to retrace their journey back with her. She had written him and told him about the move, but she had no way of knowing whether he would get the letter, or if she would ever see him again.

"Hey, Lester," she shouted out the peephole. "Remember the time Arthur bowed to the prairie dogs?" He nodded and smiled back at her.

Lester, the bronzed stoic. As long as Lester was with them,

they'd be all right.

She settled back against the stove. This wagon was definitely harder riding than Papa's spring wagon. But they needed a bigger wagon, so Papa had restored the old wagon box that brought them west, replacing the side boards and canvas Mama had removed to make her bed when they first arrived at Grandpa's.

The more Letha jostled about the wagon the more it annoyed her. Nobody traveled in a covered wagon anymore. And they were going right through Tulsa! The thought of rolling through its busy streets in a prairie schooner mortified her. After all, this was 1918!

She moved forward in the wagon.

"Papa, could I see your map?" she asked. He reached into his pocket and handed it back to her without looking back.

She studied the map a while, which was difficult what with all the bouncing.

"Do you think we could take this road around Tulsa?" She stuck the shaking map in his face, trying to point.

"I can't look at it now! But you heard your mother's warning to us. Stay on the straight roads. We can't afford to get lost."

That night they found a place to camp by the road and build a fire. Letha cooked a fairly decent supper, and they sat around the fire singing Mama's old gospel songs, as well as some of the new popular songs Uncle Clifford had taught them, the ones that Mama forbade them to sing. It was glorious, tasty freedom.

The next morning Letha put on her best dress, made sure the rest of the tribe was clean and presentable, and they headed on towards Tulsa. The road soon turned into a paved highway.

As they approached Tulsa they couldn't believe their eyes. Great tall buildings, streets full of automobiles, people everywhere.

As the traffic increased Letha's excitement gave way to embarrassment at being in the wagon, but Papa refused to listen to any more suggestions of a detour.

Down the main street they went, a prairie schooner stuffed with a lone man, four children and their possessions, pulled by a

224

pair of skittish horses not used to city traffic, followed by a fifth child on a nervous bay filly.

At noonday, in the heart of the city, the front wheel of the wagon dropped between the split rail and the main rail of a streetcar switch and became firmly wedged. The horses couldn't budge it. They began to rear and plunge. Papa jumped down to the street and grabbed their bridles. But they tossed him about until finally, by voice command, he managed to quiet them.

But then, just as they had settled down, a streetcar came to a stop a short distance ahead and one came in from behind. The horses were trapped between them and panicked.

By now a crowd of city dwellers had gathered around, amused at a page from the very recent past unfolding before them. Thankfully, one conductor of the stalled streetcars came to their rescue with a steel crowbar. He pried the wagon wheel loose and helped Papa lead the horses to one side of the street to relieve the traffic jam. Then he drew a map on a piece of paper for Dad, showing him how to escape the heavy traffic area of Tulsa and come back to the highway on the other side.

Finally they cleared Tulsa, the images of the skyscrapers receding, replaced by the rolling prairie ahead. Lester was now riding close beside them since he could see no traffic coming and the roads were still wide.

Suddenly Letha burst out laughing.

"Won't that be a story to tell Mama?" she shouted with glee. "Our getting stuck on the streetcar tracks in Tulsa. It almost beats the time when she got stuck on the railroad tracks."

Lester laughed. "You mean the time she chopped off the end of the two railroad ties and wedged them under the wheels to get us loose?"

Papa roared. "She didn't! With an ax?"

"The same ax we've got now tied in the same place under the wagon," Lester replied.

"That's my Grace. Amazing Grace. She always did wield a mean ax." It was clear Papa still had a great admiration for Mama, perhaps fonder because of distance.

"And then she used it again to chop wood to earn our keep when we stayed that night with that family in the prairie," Lester continued.

"Two nights," Letha corrected.

Victor loved to hear the stories. He was proud to know that he was there on the first journey west in the wagon, even if he was too little to remember.

"Tell the one about the Indians," he begged.

"Well," Lester responded, "We were riding along minding our own business, when suddenly we were surrounded by five Indians."

"Where'd you get <u>five</u>?" Letha demanded.

"Arthur told me."

"Well, he's a liar."

"Careful, daughter, he's not here to defend himself," Papa said in mock warning.

"There was only one Indian," she countered. "The other was an outlaw: Three-fingered Dick."

Papa looked at Lester and they both burst out laughing.

"There were stories about a Three-fingered Dick back in Blackwell," Papa said, "but I doubt you came across him on the prairie."

Lester expanded on his version. "There were five Indians, and the chief Indian asked Mama to marry him."

Now Letha laughed outright.

Lester persisted. "He said 'You come be my squaw—I make you number one squaw. Have three other squaws to help. You no be alone again.' "

"Who made that up, you or Arthur?" hooted Letha.

"It's true," Lester insisted. "You didn't hear it because you were too busy nursing your bottom full of prickly cactus!"

That shut her up. She blushed in spite of her years.

"And what was Mama's reply to the Indian?" May asked.

"She said she already had a man, and she only wanted one. That he was coming behind them. And that he himself was part Indian," Lester said. "Then the Indian grunted, 'Hmph. Half-breed. No good.' and Arthur laughed."

Victor didn't care much about which account was true. The family folklore meant everything to him. He usually hung on to whichever made the best story. So far the only family stories about him were about his fights at school. But now that they were making a fresh start in Arkansas, he was determined that he was going to be a leading character in many a good story. Oh, the possibilities. And most of all, the thrill of not knowing how it would end.

"Papa, can I have a turn on the filly?" Victor asked.

"Sure, little man." He pulled on the reins. "Time to take a break now anyway."

By nightfall they were camped alongside the Spring River. It was their last campout. The next night was spent in the log cabin on the farm—their new home.

Chapter 22

Broken Promises, Broken Dreams

Victor remembered every word Papa had said back in Oklahoma when he described the new farm. It turned out to be all Papa had said it was, and more. The apple crop was ripe for the picking, blackberries hung heavy on the many thickets. Walnuts, hickory nuts, pecans and chinquapins were falling and it was a race to beat the squirrels to them. The opossum, coons and birds were after the berries and apples, so they had their work cut out for them. As for catching crawdads, that would have to wait. They gathered and picked bushels of apples, and baskets of berries. If Mama had been there she'd have set them to making jam. Instead they ate until they had the runs.

The next item of business was to build a shelter for the horses. There were no bricks to build with, but that didn't deter Papa.

"We'll have no Okie haymow here," he said. "We'll have a corral and a shed, with one corner of the corral built over the stream so that the horses can water themselves as needed, downstream from the well."

The whole family went into the "forest" at the edge of the farm to chop down logs. Never mind that there was only one ax and Papa did most of the chopping, he liked to have his children about. He liked having an audience for the excitement when he yelled, "Tim-m-m—ber-r-r!" And it was exciting, at first.

It took two weeks of working long hours to build the shed and corral. Victor was proud of the fact that this time he had more weight to pull on the project. Soon after they finished it, Mama and the baby joined them, and all the attention Papa had focused on his children became diverted to battles with Mama.

Papa had left her Majestic oven outside because there wasn't room for it in the cabin, and she was furious!

They had to build a room around it with a chimney con-

229

structed from old brick he managed to get from a neighbor. No spindly little logs like they had used for the stable. They had to match the logs on the cabin. So it was back into the forest, where Mama selected each tree to be chopped down. At least she helped with the chopping, and she was still good at it.

Neighbors came to visit and look, and saw how little the family had for the long winter ahead. Victor was amazed at their generosity.

One neighbor came back leading a young jersey cow, heavy with calf, which he claimed he didn't have the graze to feed over the winter. To Victor's joy, he'd always wanted a dog, a beautiful female collie came with the cow. She, also, would have pups soon, and he hoped they would get to keep one of them.

Another neighbor came back with three 55 gallon wooden barrels of salted hog meat, which he insisted was only a loan they could pay back later.

Next a neighbor came with a big duroc sow heavy with farrow. He would take his pay for the sow the next year in some of her porker pigs.

The miller came from the mill with enough corn for the hog, plus some meal for the pot for winter breakfasts, to be paid back from a future crop.

One of the women folk, with her children, came to show them some of the edible greens that the fields grew in abundance. These could be canned for winter use. They had packed their entire supply of glass canning jars, they only needed to buy some rubber sealing rings to be in business again. When they asked for permission to pick greens on their property, the women only laughed.

"God put them there and we can't use 'em all, hep yerselves!"

"We didn't have neighbors like this back in Oklahoma!" Victor declared.

"Yes, we did," Letha replied quietly. "You were just too little to remember. When we first arrived at Grandpa's lots of people were coming to see us, but then they stopped."

The most important visitor to call on them this time around was the chairman of the school board. He asked when the children would be coming to school.

"Soon, soon," Papa replied. "Right now my children are learning from the school of life. And I'm not sure a formal education is all that important. Look at me: I've got a B.S. in Liberal Arts, and although I sure spread a lot of B.S. around," he paused to collect the obligatory chuckles, "it sure doesn't qualify me for the work I do now! Oh, I tried teaching for a couple of years. But the children were such an unruly lot, that most of my efforts went into discipline. I quit and got a job as a tool dresser on an oil drilling rig—less hassle and more money."

"Well, I want to be a teacher! And I'm going to that new school in the foothills!" Letha blurted out.

The chairman of the local school board looked at her with surprise, took in the tense silence that followed, then shrugged and changed the subject. He needed a native stone fireplace built for which he would trade a span of Kansas mules and a riding plow. Papa really needed the team to plow the pasture in the spring, so he took time out to build the fireplace.

He took Victor and Lester along with him and carefully instructed them as they mixed the mortar in a big, flat box. They also helped by stacking the stone within reach of where he worked. After three long days, the fireplace was completed, ready to be seasoned for winter use.

Meanwhile, Mama and the girls completed the canning. All was in order at the Barnets' new farm before winter came, but by then the promised crawdads had long dug into the mud.

Then came the snow. There had been occasional blizzards of snow in wind-swept Oklahoma, yet nothing to compare with the enchanting world the snow created when it fell gently on the farm in the Ozarks. They had their first white Christmas, decorating one of the trees outside.

But inside, the log cabin became damp and chilly at night and in February baby Zelda broke out with St. Anthony's fire[1] and died within weeks. Mama was inconsolable and took to her bed.

"To lose the twins at birth was hard enough," she said, "but to lose one that you have held at your breast and cared for is unbearable."

231

While they were still mourning the loss of baby Zelda, Arthur suddenly turned up. He did not look good. He was pale and irritable. How he found them he never explained, but Letha smiled knowingly. She acted thrilled to have him around again, and began telling him all about the trip across the prairie and through Tulsa.

To Victor's delight, Arthur had some good stories of his own to tell about his adventures in the army while he was stationed at Galveston, Texas. His capper was a story of a hurricane.

He said he was lying in the barracks close to the sea wall when the great gulf storm hit. Mountainous waves came over the sea wall and slammed down on top of his barracks, crushing the roof. Many of the soldiers drowned or were washed away. Hoping to be counted among the drowned and lost, and taking advantage of the causeway that had been washed away, Arthur and a buddy deserted and swam to the mainland near Houston. Outside Houston, Arthur found a dead soldier about his size, put on his uniform, and parted company with his buddy. The ruse might have worked, but his buddy got caught and ratted on him. Arthur was on his way to Louisiana to cut telephone poles in the swamplands, when a U.S. Marshall caught up with him and he had to serve time in the Federal Penitentiary at Leavenwort!i, Kansas.

Grace sat grimly listening to a history she could never brag about. Was it all true? She certainly hoped not. She hoped it was just a case of the inevitable Barnet blarney. And her impression of him only got worse. While in prison, Arthur said he had discovered new talents and pleasures, such as dealing cards and rolling dice.

At this point, her feelings jumped from worry to alarm. She knew what cards and dice meant—gambling. But she kept quiet, hoping the children wouldn't realize it.

After supper, Arthur demonstrated dealing with a deck of poker cards. Victor was in awe. Arthur was so good, it was impossible to tell whether he dealt from the top of the deck, the second card down, or the bottom. His hands were so quick and deft that he could "cold-deck" the cards. He could deal around the five highest hands of draw poker with the royal flush falling in his place.

When Arthur asked Victor to cut the deck, he happily obliged. Arthur then picked up both halves in one hand, put them back together in their original order, and dealt the same five high hands. Since none of his younger siblings had the courage to play against one so obviously skilled, he went on to the next demonstration—dice.

He had several pair of dice, but his prize was a set of "tap" dice. The core of each die was moveable and heavy. By turning up the desired number, then tapping the dice sharply on the table with that number up, it would always point up whenever the dice were rolled.

When he had exhausted his dice tricks, he returned to cards and showed them how to mark the backs of the high cards with a clear or white crayola. The markings were then rubbed off carefully so they could not be seen with the naked eye. But by wearing a pair of dark glasses, the marked cards were easily identified.

"Don't ever play cards with a man who wears dark glasses," he counseled wisely.

"But you can mark a card another way," he continued. He made a dent with his thumbnail in the Ace of Spades. "Now, if your fingers are sensitive enough, you can feel the dent as the card is dealt."

After watching and listening carefully, Lester finally spoke up. "Now that we know all your tricks, we will mark all 52 cards and play you."

"Put your money on the table!" Arthur declared loudly.

"There will be no money," Mama declared. "You will play for matches only, as we've always done in this household."

"Fine," Arthur replied. "Matches will be our poker chips," and added in a low voice, chuckling, "we can settle up later." He began shuffling the cards.

"I'll do the dealing," said Lester, taking the deck from him and carefully marking each card with his thumbnail.

Arthur feigned patience as Lester slowly dealt the cards.

That was the beginning of many a card game after supper and at noontime as well when the weather was bad.

Even when he seemed to be playing fairly, Arthur showed great talent. He had a phenomenal memory and could guess closely the cards held by each player by remembering how each had bet, how many cards had been drawn, and calculating the mathematical odds.

While Arthur was around, however, Mama and Papa quickly found chores for all of them to do, whenever weather permitted.

The "forest" where they had chopped the trees had now become a sparsely wooded parcel of five acres on one corner of the farm. Papa announced that they were to go ahead and clear it for pasture. Victor and Lester had the task of clearing the brush, while Arthur and Papa chopped the standing timber. They dragged the logs to the woodyard area and cut them into firewood lengths. They had to pick up rocks from the cleared land and pile them along a line to make a fence from the corral to the pasture. Finally they hauled a mountainous pile of manure from the corral and spread it over the pastureland.

It was after spreading the manure that Arthur decided to leave.

"I've got more to do with my life than stay here and be Papa's slave," he told Victor. "By the way, how's that left hook?" he asked, throwing him a few jabs.

Victor automatically responded, landing a good punch before his brother could duck.

"Holy smoke, you are fast. Keep up the good work, buddy. It could be your ticket out of here. Boxing is taking the country like a storm, and there's money to be made. When I hear that you're in the ring, you can bet I'll be betting on you."

Sadly a boxing career seemed a long way off for Victor. His muscle-building program was of a more practical nature. That spring he steered the team while the animals pulled the plow across the new pasture, complicated one afternoon by the fact that he plowed right through a nest of honey bees.

Another chore was to draw water from their well that dropped down 208 feet to an underground lake. Victor performed this chore with the help of his older brother Lester. They drew the water up on a half-inch rope wrapped around a wooden drum and turned with a windlass, stationary handle. A hand brake on the axle of the drum controlled the descent of the empty bucket. The boys took turns pulling up the water.

One day as Victor was pulling up a bucket, Lester uncharacteristically took to teasing him, apparently thinking that he could get away with it and that Victor would have sense enough not to turn loose of the handle. But he failed to consider his younger brother's temper. When Victor could take it no more, he lost all semblance of reason and turned loose of the handle to lead with his left jab. As they fought beside the well, the bucket, rope and all fell down the long drop. Even Mama heard the echo out of the well and the long silence that followed.

She gave them a harsh licking. When she had finished the lashings with her hand, she continued with her tongue. "We'll have no more of you fooling around here. You will march into town and fetch some new rope and bucket, and if you're not back before dark, I'll give you another licking."

"Now, Grace, what did you prove by that?" Papa challenged. "You proved only that you are the stronger and can force them to do your will, but you didn't convince them of anything else. One day they will be stronger than you. What will you do then? Drive them out of your home?"

A flicker of confusion and panic crossed Mama's face, but she only acknowledged the original question.

"By the time they get back they will have learned how to work together."

That they did. It was five miles into town, and five miles back. The two boys discovered that two hundred feet of half-inch hemp rope is no small bundle no matter how you wrap it. Along with it was a four-foot long cylindrical bucket four inches in diameter. They tried many ways of packing the rope bucket. Finally, they tied the big hank of rope on the bucket, and shouldered it with the rope hanging between them. Fortunately they were about the same height. It was lock-step march all the way home.

With the prospect of a second licking, they didn't dally. No one could stand two of those in one day.

235

Thankfully spring could be counted on to deliver its promises. Green things began to appear. The cow delivered her calf. The collie had her puppies. And the sow was set to deliver her piglets. But here nature required some assistance.

While Lester and Victor were in the corral doing their morning chores before breakfast, they heard Papa's yelling from the stalls behind the stable.

"Lester, Victor! Come here!" There was extreme urgency in his voice. They got there in seconds.

Papa was knelt down, bending over the big sow. She was in labor, trying to deliver her litter, but something was wrong. The straw on which she lay was soaked with a watery, bloody discharge. She just lay there grunting, her head and neck extended forward, her eyes closed, in obvious pain.

"We've got to help her."

He sent Victor to the house for the big jar of Vaseline, and when he returned with Mama and girls following, Papa looked at him, sizing him up. Victor was now slightly taller than Lester, but still thin and wiry.

"Victor," Papa said, "your hands and arms are small and strong enough to get inside her through her passage. Strip your shirt and I'll help grease your hand and arm."

Victor took off his shirt and held out his left arm to Papa. That done, Papa knelt again, holding the sow steady and gave Victor further instructions.

"Close your hand and fingers to a point, son. That's it. Make it as small as possible and begin putting it inside her—right here." He pointed to her swollen vagina.

Victor's arm went in slowly at first as he pushed against the sow's resistance. Suddenly it went in quickly and he felt something.

"When you feel a little piglet, get it by the hind legs and pull."

Victor did as he was told and was rewarded for his efforts by three little wriggling pigs on the cloth Mama had spread beside the sow. After that nature took back its duties and when it was finished, there were thirteen squirming piglets looking for their breakfast—one too many. The sow only had her God-given twelve teats. The runt of the litter would have to be hand fed with cow's milk.

"Papa, can I be its substitute mama?" begged May.

"If you think you can handle the responsibility," Mama inserted.

"I do, I do." May insisted.

She got the job and did well. Soon the little pig was following her around just like a pup, even in the house. The pig thrived on love and scraps secretly passed under the table and grew to be the biggest in the litter, lording it over his brothers and sisters. At that point Mama banned the pig from the house to the pen.

By that time, Victor had plowed the manure into the pasture, and they had planted strawberry plants.

Once the rest of the spring crops were in, Papa got restless.

One night after they had been sent to bed, Mama and Papa had a huge row. Victor and his siblings couldn't help but hear it through their bedroom walls.

"I've got to go again, Grace," Papa was saying. "We need a cash income here to succeed, and we sure can't make enough from strawberries. Making bricks again is the only way. And there's no such work around here. I'll send you money to help you get along."

"I've heard that promise before," Mama replied tersely. "The last time you pulled this there were too many weeks when no money arrived. It won't be any different this time." She proceeded loud and long, unloading years of bitterness and past history.

"Grace," Papa countered, "What is past is gone, frozen in concrete. But, just for the record let me remind you. If you had listened to reason, as I tried to show you many times, there would not be so many children for us to raise. If I stay, there will be more. We cannot possibly give them what they all so rightly deserve to have, a decent education and a skill with which they can make a decent kind of life for themselves.

"Every time I hang my pants on the foot of your bed you get pregnant. I tried to educate you on the measures we could take to prevent so many pregnancies but you, because of your archaic religious beliefs, absolutely refused to listen. I honestly thank God that our last three babies were taken Home rather than being forced, by you, to lead lives of drudgery. Don't you think God is trying to tell you something by taking them?"

There was a long, painful silence, during which Victor realized he had actually broken out into a sweat.

"Why, in the name of God, can't you do something to stop the flow of children? The whores don't get pregnant. They use a vinegar and water douche when they get up. Why the hell can't you?"

"John," Mama replied evenly, "if you wanted a whore for a wife, why didn't you marry one? I am not a whore, nor do I think like one. I try very hard to live by the teachings of the Bible and it clearly says: Thou shalt not kill. If you leave me again, with all the responsibilities of raising our family, you need not ever come back."

Papa remained silent for a moment, but carried on relentlessly. "I am willing to do my best by the children we do have. But if you force me out of their lives, as you have said, then you are responsible for it. *You* can raise *your* children."

Those words were the last Victor ever heard from his father and they remained forever engraved in his mind.

The next morning, not a word was spoken. After breakfast, Papa left on the bay filly, riding stiff backed and staring straight ahead. He never looked back.

Was it because his eyes were full of tears?

Victor suppressed a pathetic urge to call out to him: But Papa. What about the crawdads you promised? We never caught the crawdads!

238

Chapter 23

Iron Filings

The family had done without Papa before, but always with the hope of his return. This time Victor knew he would not.

Each time he left, the family adjusted, readjusted, and some might say maladjusted, but they survived.

This time, it felt like it did after the babies died. Silence among the family. But it didn't last long.

Life became vigorous again once summer began. They picked enough strawberries to sell to the neighbors for cash to buy the few essentials: flour, salt, pepper, baking powder, soda; cloth for shirts, dresses and pants that Mama and Letha made on the sewing machine, with May doing the hand stitching.

In the afternoon while the women were sewing and they had finished their chores, Victor and Lester were allowed to wander off, little Poppy tagging along. Most often they went swimming in the beautiful swimming hole on the bend of Flint Creek. It was on a neighbor's property, but he had given them permission to swim whenever they wanted. They took the collie dogs and Welsh pony along with them, for they loved the water as much as the children and would swim along with them and take part in the fun on the hot summer afternoons. When they tired of the swimming, sometimes they would hunt for rabbit holes in the thickets alongside the creek.

But lately, their favorite haunt was the neighbor's oak grove surrounded by a ring of young saplings. An attraction since they no longer had a forest of their own, two recently added features now made it irresistible.

First, to Victor's fascination, early one moonlit night, they had discovered a group of flying squirrels passing through the woods. They were amazed as they watched the squirrels "fly" from one tree to the other across the wide expanses of open space between them. When the children squinted up at them they noticed a flap of skin between the front and hind legs on each side.

"You can see how they are cousins to bats," Lester observed.

By jumping from the top of one of the taller trees, spreading their legs out to each side, they could take on the shape of a flat kite, about ten inches long, and sail away. By properly moving their front feet, they could control the angle of the glide like a steering wheel.

The morning after the flying squirrels had so entertained them, lightning in a furious thunderstorm struck a giant hollow oak tree on the edge of the grove and split it from top to bottom. The torn tree fell among the saplings, making it a wonderful place to play in spite of Mama's warning to keep away from it.

The three children were playing follow-the-leader in the tangle of limbs and bent saplings when Victor suddenly remembered the flying squirrels. He'd show them a stunt no one could follow. He stood on the fallen tree, grabbed a high limb, and swung down to the next limb. But his hands slipped from it and he plunged downward. The snapping sound he heard was not the tree limbs, but his own left arm.

Mama came running when Letha went to get her.

"This is just what I feared would happen. Why don't you listen to me?" The pain was between the wrist and the elbow. She examined the bone between carefully.

"It looks like it is broken in two places," she announced in the same tone Dr. McGinnis would have used. "I have got to splint it."

She straightened out his arm the best she could with his hand flat open on a board that went from his fingertips to his elbow. With strips of cloth she tore from scrap clothes, she wrapped his arm to the board. Then fashioning a sling to support his arm, she hung it on his neck.

Having his left arm in a sling was quite an ordeal for Victor. The pain did not go away. Had it been a simple break, it might have been all right, but the bones didn't join properly, and when they did heal, Victor could not open or close his hand.

Grace finally had to swallow her nursing pride and take him to the doctor in town. The doctor told her he would have to operate and set the bones surgically. When he saw the look on her

240

face, he added. "I won't charge you this time. But next time there's an accident, come straight to me."

By the time it had healed again, Victor had learned to do all the necessary things with his right hand.

This included catching crawdads. Papa had not lied. The shallow part of the creek was full of them. Victor had been determined to catch them, and since swimming was out of the picture, now was the time. He remembered Papa's instructions to the letter. While Poppy held a bucket and cheered him on, he would sneak up behind a big one, or rather in front of it since it swam backwards, and use his own "pinchers"—the thumb and index finger of his right hand—to suddenly grasp the crawdad's body between its front pinchers and back claws.

As he collected them and plopped them into the bucket, Poppy would name them. The biggest crawdad would be "Granddad," and if a bigger one was caught, it would be "Great-Granddad"—babies, those under eight inches, were thrown back. They took them home for Mama to cook, despite Poppy's objections. They were hungry, and the batter-fried crawdad tails made a delicious appetizer to the string of perch and trout Lester would so patiently catch.

The crops were ready for harvesting, when two men, dressed in business suits, came to call on Grace. They were from the bank in Siloam Springs. The smaller one, who did the talking, introduced himself as Mr. Gill. He shifted nervously from foot to foot as he explained to her that unless the back payments were paid, the bank would be forced to foreclose on the mortgage.

"What mortgage?" Grace demanded.

"Mrs. Barnet, here is the promissory note your husband signed, promising to pay monthly payments. You have been delinquent for over a year. We were hoping he would send the payments from wherever he is, but he has not. We do not want the farm, but we must have the money he promised to pay."

"Mr. Gill, my husband did not say anything to me about this and, frankly, I don't know where he is. I haven't heard from him since he left, either."

"Mrs. Barnet, if you have doubts as to the veracity of our

claim, I would suggest you consult an attorney. However, I assure you, it would be a waste of your money. Your husband's signature is valid and so is the promissory note."

"No, Mr. Gill, I do not doubt your word. I am just shocked to think that my husband would leave us in this fix. When do you have to receive your money?"

"I can give you another three months. That will give you time to harvest your crops. Then I must have the money in arrears and reasonable assurance of future payments, when due."

"How much money is owed on past payments, and what is the balance due?"

"The total note is $2,000.00. The monthly payments are $50.00, and you are in arrears fourteen months. That is a total of $700.00. The balance due is $1300.00 with interest at 5% per year, until paid in full."

"Well, the information is appreciated, but there is just no way we could have paid, even if we had known what money was due. Neighbors loaned us food when we came here. If you will allow us to harvest our crops, we can at least pay them back."

"Certainly, Mrs. Barnet. It is not our intent to cause any more hardship than can be helped. I hope you are aware of my position. I must protect the interests of my depositors, at all costs. They have trusted me to handle their money wisely. We gave as much time as we dared, hoping to hear from your husband."

"I do not think any of us will hear from him again. I did not want him to leave and we argued. He will not be back."

Grace could see clearly, but too late, why John had been forced to leave. She was furious. Had he told her the facts, maybe, just maybe, there could have been a different ending. As her father used to point out to her, "change one element in a chemical composition and the end compound will be something entirely different." But now that the facts were in, she didn't have time to brood on them.

Victor heard everything the men said. Though the workings of this kind of finance were strange to him, he understood that life on the farm was at an end.

242

They harvested their crops and paid back what the neighbors had loaned them.

The man came after his duroc sow and her litter of porkers. He paid Mama for seven of the thirteen. She stashed the U.S. dollars away in the bottom of her dresser drawer.

The corn crop went to the miller who paid more big dollars for the overage beyond what he had loaned.

The man who owned the jersey cow came and collected her with her heifer calf, the collie dog and all five of her half-grown pups.

The chairman of the school board came to buy back his span of Kansas mules and the riding plow. He offered more help.

"Grace, we don't mean to pry, and if you have good plans then we'll shut up. If you ain't got plans maybe we can help." He was an unlettered man unable to even write his own name, but his native intelligence was respected by all who knew him and he had been elected to the school board by his friends and neighbors, and then elected chairman by the board.

"Thank you for your kind offer. I have been offered a job cooking at the Dripping Springs Inn. It pays ten dollars a week, but that will not take care of us all. What do you have to suggest?"

"We figured something 'bout like that. We can take your wagon and team, long with what you have to sell to Springville to the auction sale there. That'll get a few more dollars. Then you can get a room at the Graves Boarding House down on the southeast corner of the Park in Siloam for seven dollars a week. Getting your meals at the Inn, that'll take care of you and the littleuns. Then I know a feller name of Turner—his wife is childless—that has a dairy farm who can use the two boys if'n they can milk and help out 'bout the place. He'll give them board, room and clothes and ten dollar a month plus schooling during that term." He looked at Letha.

"I'm getting a job teaching at John Brown College,"[1] she said. "Poppy and Victor can stay near Mama, but I'm taking Lester and May with me. Les can work on the farm there, and May's a good worker when she wants to be, too. They'll get their room and board and a good education as well."

243

He looked back at Grace and around the room and said, "Now, how does that sound? Can y'all get by with that?"

Tears were rolling unashamedly down Mama's cheek. Hardship never made Mama cry, but kindness did. She began trying to find words to thank the man, but he held up a hand to stop her.

Letha, May, and Les packed what clothing they had in some wooden boxes and the chairman of the school board took them to John Brown College. Letha and May lived at one end of the long dormitory building, Les in the other. They helped prepare and serve the food in the dormitory downstairs. In another building, they studied their lessons. May finally got to try her hand at a sewing machine, and Letha excelled at a typewriter, a skill that served her penchant for writing. Les worked in the co-operative dairy where he learned the principles of pasteurization.

Letha taught reading and writing to the younger ones, and embarked at last upon the study of mathematics, deliriously happy to engage at last in the magic of algebra, and fascinated to learn that ABC did not necessarily equal XYZ.

And something else happened. She developed her first big crush on the college's twenty-four year old founder and preacher, John Brown. She went to church every Sunday he preached and was mesmerized by his sermons. He may not have been as fiery as his namesake, John Brown the abolitionist, but he was certainly persuasive. He had the same appeal her father had before an audience, and though not as good-looking, John Brown had the added advantage that his words made sense. His faith, vision, and commitment shone through and she admired him immensely. She devoted herself with total commitment to her studies at the college.

Grace had to part with her beloved Majestic oven and learn to cook on the gas range at the Dripping Springs Inn. She went to live with strangers at a local boarding house, with Poppy as her only companion. Victor was nearby at the dairy farm and came to eat with them after church on Sundays.

Grace simply could not picture life without children. She

244

was determined to keep her two youngest with her as long as possible by whatever means. She didn't know how long she could survive as a cook, and needed the extra income Victor could provide. He and Poppy would do fine at the local school. They were not particularly good students anyway.

As soon as she was settled, Grace sued John for divorce. The lawyer, who handled the case for free, wrote to John at an address he got from the banker. He also learned that after foreclosure, the bank had received money from John to try to make up the payment arrears. But it was already too late. The books were closed.

The lawyer received a prompt response from John. He did not contest, in any way, the suit for divorce.

The Barnets were like iron filings, scattered among the hills of the Ozarks.

FOOTNOTES

Chapter 1

[1] Biscuits dropped from a spoon onto a baking sheet instead of being rolled and cut.

[2] Greyhounds were imported in the mid-1800s from Ireland and England not to race, but to rid midwest farms of jackrabbits and coyotes. With their gentle and quiet dispositions, they made good pets and became a familiar sight on farms and ranches in Kansas, Missouri, Oklahoma, and Texas.

[3] The Chicago, Rock Island and Pacific line, built in 1890.

Chapter 2

[1] The original meaning of dashboard was a piece of wood or leather on a vehicle that protected the driver from water and mud, from an old meaning of the word dash which meant splash.

[2] My mother actually remembers her grandmother Grace doing this.

Chapter 3

[1] John is based on my grandmother's father who graduated from the University of Iowa at Ames with a major in Liberal Arts, then taught school for two years. He never again used his education vocationally, though in the 1920's he wrote editorials for the Daily Worker, and became known as a public speaker when he organized the American Federation of Labor's Bricklayers and Hod Carriers Union in the Southwest.

[2] Most people would say sandcastle, but not these land-locked people.

[3] The Cherokee Strip was a piece of land running along the Kansas border opened for homesteading in 1890.

[4] According to John Edward Hicks in his article Cherokee Strip Was Pandemonium, Blackwell was started by a company of town site boosters from Winfield, Kansas, headed by Col. Andrew Jackson Blackwell of Claremore, whose wife, a Cherokee, had an allotment adjoining the site. It got off to a good start but had a bad scare in the way of a rival across the river a mile away, promoted by Isaac Parker. The rival had brick buildings and a railway being built when something went awry. Blackwell got the railroad and Parker faded away. Could it

246

have been because of flooding? The flooding of the Chikaskia near Blackwell remains a problem causing a major evacuation as late as 1998 when it rose 34.40 feet. Flood forecasts are still issued routinely for the area year round.

[5] "Pride is for dessert" another old expression meaning pride is luxury we can't afford.

Chapter 9

[1] The general store near the hotel was Olmstead's. Waynoka historical society has a photo of its owner.

[2] The Mexican quarter in Waynoka was actually located northeast of town along the road to Alva.

Chapter 10

[1] Kaffir was a rough, tough corn brought to America by the African slaves.

[2] Haymow was colloquial for the barn.

Chapter 11

[1] Dr. McGinnis was based on Waynoka's beloved town doctor, Eben Paul (E.P.) Clapper, who set up a practice in 1901 and retired 38 years later. Clapper Memorial Hospital was opened in 1949, and now serves as a treatment center for alcoholic women.

Chapter 12

[1] "Proving up" was part of the legal process, demonstrating that you were actually living on the land you had claimed.

Chapter 13

[1] "I'll be plagued" was a derivative of "may the plague take me!" an expression that religious Americans substituted for the forbidden word: damned.

Chapter 16

[1] This actually happened to my grandmother Letha, with a different outcome: the successful birth of one of her sisters. Her mother deliv-

ered and washed the baby before the doctor arrived.

Chapter 19

[1] Oklahoma became a state in 1907, the year the family arrived in Waynoka.
[2] The Pure Food and Drug Act was passed in 1906.

Chapter 22

[1] Erysipelas, a skin disease due to streptococcal infection for which there was no known cure at the time, but later treated with the sulfa drugs.

Chapter 23

[1] John Brown College was founded in 1920 near Siloam Springs and is still active today.

Printed in the United States
83663LV00007B/40/A